FRACTURED LIES

BOOK 1 IN THE MAC SECURITY SERIES

ABIGAIL DAVIES

For my husband.

ACKNOWLEDGMENTS

Where to start?

I have so many people who helped me bring this story to life.

I want to thank my husband, Mike, for putting up with all my late nights (early mornings), and my constant chatter and ideas. For telling me to chase my dreams of writing, and for supporting me fully in everything that I do. You're amazing and I thank my lucky stars every day, that I found you.

To my two daughters who inspire me to chase my dreams every day, who are now writing their own stories after watching me type furiously on my laptop. I love you both to the moon and back.

To my amazing BETA readers. Steph, Sarah, and Danielle, for reading my book whilst it was still in the rough. Thank you so much for all of your feedback.

My beta reader Danielle, who has not only been a

beta reader but has become 'my person'. Thank you so much, for staying up with me until the sun came up for several nights in a row as I sent chapter after chapter to you. Thank you for all of your input, this book seriously wouldn't have been what it is without you!

And most importantly to my readers! Thank you so much for reading this book! I hope that you fall in love with these characters, and that you enjoy it as much as I enjoyed writing it.

For my husband.

Chapter One

"WHAT PAJAMAS DO you want to wear Eli?" I asked, waiting for his answer as I bent down and opened up the drawer.

"Spiderman, please, Mama," he replied in his small voice. I pulled out the red Spiderman pajamas then turned, and sat on the bed. It creaked as I sat down, a reminder that it wouldn't be long before it needed to be replaced.

The whole room was a mismatch of furniture. I'd done all that I could with what little money I was given and it didn't look too bad considering. The walls were painted in a variety of different blues, Spiderman stickers covering most of the paint and all the cracks that ran along the walls. Eli didn't care what it looked like, as long as it had his favorite superhero up there but I wanted to make it perfect for him.

I held the pajamas up and flicked my wrist for Eli to move forward. His eyes narrowed as he crossed his arms.

"Not those ones, Mama, the blue ones," he huffed.

I knew the look on his face, it could go one of two ways. I'd either be able to diffuse whatever situation was about to arise or he would have a meltdown. Everybody talks about the terrible twos but no one ever tells you about the frustrating fours. I'd learned to pick and choose my battles and when I won one of them, I always gave myself a mental high five.

"You said Spiderman, Eli." I held them up in the air. "And these are Spiderman."

Drops of water hit me in the face as he shook his head fiercely.

"I only wear the blue ones on Wednesday, and today is Wednesday, Mama." He rolled his eyes and puffed out a breath.

I opened my mouth and closed it. It was on the tip of my tongue to tell him that it was actually Friday and not Wednesday. Instead, I swapped the pajamas and he got dressed without any other complaints. Sometimes it was just better to give in.

Like I said: I pick my battles.

"Time for bed, sweetie." I told him, pulling back his covers and helped him up onto the bed.

"But I not tired, mama." Raising my brow, I tilted

my head to the side. He always did this, said that he wasn't tired, then he would be snoring his head off two seconds later.

"What book do you want tonight?" I asked.

"Hmm..." His little pointer finger tapped on his chin, head tilted back as he looked up at the ceiling. "Can we read two?" I settled down next to him and nodded.

"The dog one first." He shuffled down the bed, pulled the covers up to his chin and looked up at me. "Then the wolf one."

I pulled them both down from the shelf next to his bed, aware that he was watching me with those emerald green eyes. He had such stunning eyes, so bright that I swear they were otherworldly. An exact replica of his father's, the only difference between them was the way they looked at me. Eli looked at me with love, I always knew where I stood with Eli because he showed all of his emotions through his eyes.

His father was a different story. I never knew what he was going through his head, but he always knew what I was thinking: he saw right through me. I hadn't quite worked out yet whether that was a good thing or not.

I wore my emotions on my sleeve, much like Eli did, but I was getting better at putting my walls up.

I had to.

I planted a kiss on the top of his head, his curly brown hair soft against my face.

Eli may have had his father's eyes but the rest of him was all me. Sometimes I wish that he looked more like him instead of having *those* eyes.

"There was a dog, his name was spot..." I started, I hadn't even got halfway through before his soft snores sounded in the room. I closed the book and watched him for a minute.

How we had made something so perfect was beyond me.

I lifted off his bed as quietly as possible and placed the book back where I pulled it from then crossed the room. I tried my best to miss all the creaky floorboards; I never managed it always hitting one. I froze as one creaked, staying deathly still as I listened for a minute. Lifting my foot slowly, I stared at the offending floorboard: I really needed to do something about that.

I walked down the hallway, the old carpet scratching at the bottom of my feet. My eyes followed the framed photos that lined the walls. All but one were of Eli. The first was the day he was born and the last taken just a few weeks ago.

I stopped at the end of the hallway. Opposite the apartment door was the one and only picture of me and Max.

It was taken at my high school graduation: Max had come back from college for the day. That was the day I found out I was pregnant. We both had huge smiles on our faces: we looked so happy back then. We were staring at each other, Max's face was so open and

I knew that if I looked closely I could see the love that used to shine through his eyes.

I frowned at it and shook my head.

All that changed from the moment I told him I was pregnant.

I could understand the change that happened. I was due to go off to college and Max was halfway through his degree. At eighteen and twenty, we weren't ready to be parents.

Max had left college to get a job and I never went. I knew that he resented me for it but I wouldn't have changed a thing.

I heard a key turn in the lock and stared at it with wide eyes before rushing into the kitchen and starting to warm up Max's dinner. How had I lost track of time? I should have known better than to get stuck in my memories.

Max's boots thumped against the floor, and I knew that if I didn't have his dinner ready by the time he sat on the couch then I had a hell of a long night ahead of me.

Our apartment wasn't much but I tried to make it as much of a home as I could. The cream walls gave the small space a light and airy feel which made it easier to breath: easier to exist.

"Kaylee!" I grabbed the plate and a beer from the fridge, rushing forward and using my back to open the door that joined the living room to the kitchen.

"Bout fucking time," he grunted when I placed it

down on the coffee table. That was another second hand bit of furniture.

I handed him his beer and tried my hardest to keep the disgust off my face before I spun around and left him to it. There was nothing worse than hanging around him. That was another one of his pet hates.

I finished cleaning up the kitchen and collected the plate from Max when he was done. He didn't say anything else to me, but I preferred it that way. His eyes were glued to the TV so I made sure not to disturb him.

"I'm going to bed now, Max." I waited for a couple of seconds; silence greeted me but I knew better than to breathe easy yet.

I waited for his reply and when he still didn't acknowledge me, I walked out of the room and headed to the bathroom. After I brushed my teeth, I popped my head around Eli's door and smiled as his soft snores filled the room before I headed back to my room and changed into my pajamas, sliding into my own bed.

That's when I allowed myself to finally take a breath. Each day that didn't end with me doing something wrong was a day to be celebrated. My lips lifted at the corners as I closed my eyes. Today made it a week since Max had to correct me.

Once I had made it to two weeks: maybe this time I would go beyond that.

I WOKE WITH A START AND GRABBED MY CELL IN panic to check the time. It felt like I had slept the day away.

Six am.

Maybe not.

I rubbed my eyes and swiveled my head to the side. The cold sheets greeted me so I knew the other side of the bed hadn't been slept in.

I was not a morning person, I needed a shower and strong coffee before I felt any semblance of normal. I rushed through having a shower, brushed my teeth and dressed in a pair of leggings and t-shirt that covered my butt before tiptoeing down the hallway, careful not to wake Max. I could hear his loud snores which was probably the reason that I'd had a good night's sleep.

I started up the coffee pot and watched as it brewed, staring anxiously at it. Pouring myself a cup and taking a sip, I moaned as the coffee hit my tongue. The first taste was always the best.

Shuffling over to the small table that sat in the corner of the room, it wobbled as I put my cup down, a reminder that I needed to put something under one of the legs. All three chairs were different, but I loved the quirky look that I'd created.

I sat on the chair nearest the window: this one was Max's chair as it didn't wobble at all. Eli and I didn't get so lucky, ours were deathtraps to sit on.

I gazed out of the window, watching as the sky lightened and the streetlights flickered off. My breaths became heavier the lighter it became: Max still hadn't woken which meant I'd have to wake him.

I never knew what mood he'd be in when he woke up. I had to be gentle, the last thing I needed was to put him in a bad mood that he always seemed to be in no matter what I did.

I stood and rinsed my cup in the sink, took a deep breath and walked into the living room.

"Max?" I called out softly. He didn't stir so I moved closer, placing my hand on his shoulder and shaking it gently.

"Max? It's time to get up." I spoke a little louder this time and his snoring stopped but he still didn't move.

Chewing on my bottom lip, I scanned the wall above the TV. If he didn't wake up soon then he'd be late, there's nothing he hated more than being late. Then it would be my fault for not waking him up on time.

"Max." I grimaced as I shook him harder this time.

His eyes flew open and his arm shot out. I gasped as his hand wrapped around my wrist and squeezed painfully.

"Max," I croaked. "It's time for work." His emerald green eyes stared right through me. He was handsome; the all American boy: straight nose, full lips. He wore it like a mask, not letting the evil under the surface show to anyone but me.

"Max, you're hurting me." I fidgeted as he tightened his grip.

He sat up slowly, his eyes piercing mine with unspoken promises as the sun peeking through the blinds shined off his inky black hair.

"How many times do I have to tell you?" He stood, my arm burning as he twisted his hand. Although he was only a few inches taller than me, he still towered over me with his presence. *I hated being this close to him.*

"I-I-I'm sorry," I gasped. I willed the tears to stay away, to not break free because all it would do is make him angrier.

"Doesn't matter how many times I say something, it never gets through that thick skull of yours does it?"

I was almost panting now from the grip he had on my arm and the fear that was rolling through me

"Never touch me without permission!" he roared right in my face. I flinched as spit flew from the corner of his mouth and then berated myself for doing that: for showing him weakness.

He squeezed once more and let me go with a push. My arms flailed as I tried to steady myself; I pinched my lips together when the back of my legs caught the corner of the coffee table. I desperately wanted to squeal but I knew better than to show him how much I was really hurting.

He shoved his feet into his boots that sat next to

the couch and stomped around the apartment, completely ignored me.

The door slammed shut minutes later but I didn't have time to get my bearings as I could hear Eli coming down the hallway.

"Mama?" he called in a sleepy voice.

"In here, sweetie." I looked around for something to cover the angry red mark on my arm, but couldn't find anything in time, so instead I hid my arm behind my back. It throbbed so I tried to rub it but that somehow made it worse.

I didn't want Eli to see. I didn't want to explain to him that I had done something wrong, that I knew better than to touch Max without asking first.

I wanted to ask how was I meant to ask to touch him first when he was asleep? The old me would have. The new me? She knew better than to question him.

"Mama?" he asked, rubbing his eyes with his fists as he stumbled toward me.

"Morning, sweetie." I wrapped my arm around him, steering him to the kitchen and sat him in his chair while slipping my own mask in place.

"What would you like for breakfast?"

"Cereal," he murmured.

I poured him a bowl and set it on the table in front of him.

"Do you want some juice?"

"Please, Mama." He lifted his spoon with great

effort, nearly missing his mouth because his eyes were half closed.

I smiled: just like me, he hated mornings.

I watched my cell anxiously for the rest of the day. Every Saturday went like this, though most of those Saturdays I didn't receive the call I was waiting for. It was never guaranteed. Weeks at a time could go by without me talking to him.

I was almost glad that it never rang because that meant that he was fine. It was those times that the phone rang and I wasn't expecting a call that made my heart would stop for a beat: my breaths quickening as I would start to panic.

Eli always sat next to me watching his cartoons, his eyes flicking from the phone to the TV every couple of minutes.

"Today?" Eli asked.

"Maybe," I said, unsure. He knew as much as I did.

We didn't move for hours, scared that we might miss the call. I was just about to give up when the loud noise of the phone rang out.

I snatched it up, fumbled for a couple of seconds then hit the answer call button.

"Corey?" I asked, breathless. Eli sat up straighter, his eyes wide.

We hadn't talked to Corey in over two months now,

and I hadn't seen him for four years. Being in the Special Forces meant that he was away on missions a lot, not only that but we wouldn't hear from him for months at a time.

"Hey, lil' sis," his deep voice came across the line along with crackles, a telltale sign that he was half way across the world.

"Corey," I sighed. "It's so good to finally hear your voice."

"Yours too." He chuckled.

God, I missed that sound. He had an addictive kind of laugh, you couldn't help but laugh along with him. I could imagine the way his eyes would squint and that weird sniffle he always did afterward.

"Put me on speaker phone," he said. I nodded even though he couldn't see me and tapped the button on the screen.

"You're on," I said and placed it on the table.

"Eli?"

"Hi, Uncle Corey!"

"You sound so big," Corey said, his voice rising an octave.

Eli looked at me, a grin spread wide across his face.

"I am big now. I start school Monday," he said and puffed his chest out.

"You do?" Corey asked.

"Uh-huh."

"Wow." Corey chuckled. "You looking after Mama?"

"Yep." Eli nodded emphatically.

"Take some photos of your first day and send them to me, yeah?"

"Okay, Uncle Corey"

"I need to talk to your mama for a minute, Love you Eli."

"Love you too, Uncle Corey," Eli answered and shuffled back on the couch, turning his attention back to the TV.

"Kay?" I detected a subtle tone in Corey's voice and picked the cell up.

"Yeah?"

"I'm off speaker?"

"Yeah." I stood and moved into the kitchen. This was always the part I hated most: after he had talked to Eli came the interrogation.

"You good?" he asked. He always did, but I couldn't say anything but yes. What would he be able to do if I said no? It wasn't like he could come home at the drop of a hat.

"Got any plans for when Eli goes to school?"

I looked around the kitchen for an answer. I had been thinking of getting a job, but just the thought of approaching that subject with Max had me breaking out into a sweat.

"What about getting a job?" Corey asked, like he'd just read my mind.

"Maybe," I whispered.

"Kay, you're twenty-two, there's more to life than just being a mom."

"I know that." I sat up straighter.

I knew there was and I knew that I wanted more for me and Eli than to stay in this rundown apartment. But how was I meant to achieve that? Max would never let me get a job. Countless times he would say, "your job is to be here, as and when I say."

"Look, I haven't got long left." He murmured something to somebody before saying, "Let me give you my buddy's number, I hear he's looking for some office help."

I searched for a pen and ripped a scrap of paper from the corner of a bill and jotted down the number as he reeled it off.

"How are you?" I asked before he got off.

"I'm good, sis. Be home in a few months." I breathed a sigh of relief.

"I miss you."

"I miss you too," he choked out "Take care of my nephew."

"I will."

"And yourself." I didn't answer that time.

"Love you."

"Love you too, lil' sis." Then the line went dead.

I pulled the cell from my ear and dropped it to the table. The smile on my face uncontrollable.

Chapter Two

COME MONDAY MORNING I was a nervous wreck, I'd spent every moment cherishing Eli. Knowing that I wouldn't see him for a few hours each day felt unbearable. I'd never been away from him for more than a few minutes at a time or on the odd occasion that Max would take me out.

He was busy though so that didn't happen often.

Working a full day at the local garage, he would then wind down for a couple of hours at the end of the day in the bar across the road.

He deserved to do that, after all he was the only one working. Which brought me to the same conclusion: if I was earning money maybe things would get better.

I hadn't decided what I was going to do with the

number that Corey had given me. I could feel it burning a hole in my pocket; it hadn't been out of there all weekend as I didn't want to risk Max seeing it.

I had to make a decision... and soon.

I strapped Eli in his seat and jumped into the driver's side, going through the motions, trying to not breakdown into tears.

Eli talked all the way there, while I couldn't bring myself to say much more than "hmmm" or "yeah."

I pulled up in front of the preschool, the windows covered in a painted jungle scene. It had only taken us about ten minutes to get here from the apartment: that put my at ease that I'd be close by.

I'd only been here once for a meet and greet and Eli had loved it. I kept telling myself that: that he'd enjoy it and not even think about me while he was there, but I couldn't say the same for me.

Eli needed to be with other children, only having me to occupy his time wasn't enough anymore. He needed to make friends his own age, he needed to play, and to be silly. Having your mom as your only friend was kind of sad. Luckily, Max had agreed with me that he needed to get out from under my wings. Though he didn't say it in quite that way.

I clutched the steering wheel, my knuckles turning white as I stared at the door, my body not moving an inch.

"Come on, Mama," Eli moaned, squirming in his seat.

"Okay, sweetie," I blew out a big breath, unclipped my belt, and opened the door, trying my hardest to put on a brave face.

Eli jumped down as soon as I opened his and raced to the front door.

"You excited?" I chuckled.

"Yeah!" he shouted. I shook my head and smiled wide.

It didn't take long for Eli to settle. His play teacher, Miss Cooper, was there to greet us and took him into one of the play rooms, but not before I held on tight to him and gave him a sloppy kiss. I knew that it was silly, but when you've spent almost every waking minute for the last four years with someone, it felt like I was losing a limb.

Maybe not to that extent, but that's how I felt.

I shuffled out of there and drove home on autopilot. I just needed to get through the next four hours. They'd go quick... right?

Turns out four hours can go by at a snail's pace. I'd cleaned the apartment from top to bottom, sorted out all of mine and Eli's clothes into piles of keep, throw and donate.

I even had time to have two cups of coffee.

I almost punched the air when it was time to leave to pick him back up. I couldn't get out the door fast

ABIGAIL DAVIES

enough. The drive there took longer than this morning and I was urging all the cars to get off the road.

I needed to pick my son up. Didn't they get that?

I ran at Eli when he came through the doors. I must have looked crazy, all the other children that came out were running to their parents and there I was running *to* my child instead of waiting patiently.

But I didn't care.

"I missed you so much!" I bent down, squeezed him tight then lifted him up off the floor.

"Mama!" I buried my face in his hair and breathed him in. I didn't bother putting him down until we were back at the car.

"Did you have a good day?" I asked, buckling him into his seat and leaning back.

"Yeah, I played with my new friend, Andre, he likes Spiderman too," he said with a firm nod.

"Well if he likes Spiderman then he must be nice." I grinned.

"Uh-huh, my other new friend Ryan said that he likes Batman." He shook his head. The idea of liking Batman over Spiderman was obviously a "friend crime."

"Did you play with Ryan?"

"Mama." He rolled his eyes. "I just told you he likes Batman."

"So that's a no?"

"Yep."

I closed his door and rushed around to the driver's

18

side, hardly containing myself. I felt like doing a happy dance.

"What else did you do today?" I asked as I pulled out of the parking lot.

"Dunno." He shrugged.

That was all that I could get out of him. I tried asking him specific questions but all I got back was a shrug of his shoulders. *Typical.* I was looking forward to a minute by minute rundown. Guess I wasn't getting that anytime soon.

We walked up the stairs back at the apartment block, Eli still chatting away. My problem was that he wasn't telling me about his day but about the cartoon that he watched a week ago.

Several times I tried to get a word in, but each time he would just keep talking. It made the silence when he was gone that much worse. I didn't realize how much he talked until I spent time on my own.

"Can we go see Miss Maggie?" he asked.

"Sure." I nodded as we started on the last set of stairs.

Miss Maggie is one of the ladies who lives on our floor. She came around and introduced herself when we first moved in. When I opened the door and saw an old lady with gray hair, I expected her to give me a cake or something to welcome us.

Instead, she firmly told me that she may be old but she didn't act like those "old farts" in the next building over. She told me to expect loud music to come from her apartment and not to dare complain.

She started to come around more often, and as Eli got older he soon bonded with him and his love of cartoons.

Max had put a stop to her coming around once he found out how often she visited, but that didn't stop me from going and seeing her a couple of times a week. I preferred to be in her apartment anyway.

Eli knocked on the door and pushed it open like he always did.

"Miss Maggie?" I always made sure that she knew who was coming inside. Not for her sake, but for mine.

Once I came in and didn't "announce" myself as she would say. I nearly got smacked around the head with a baseball bat. Suffice it to say that I always "announced" myself now.

"Kay? Eli? That you?" she asked.

"Yeah!" Eli shouted back, running down the hall-way. There were two reasons he loved to come to Miss Maggie's: to watch cartoons and to see her cats.

I walked down the short hallway and into the small living room. The apartment wasn't big, but then there was only Miss Maggie. All the furniture was circa nineteen seventies, complete with a crochet blanket on the back of the couch.

Photos lined most of the walls, and if you followed them in the right order it showed Miss Maggie's whole life in time order. I loved to sit here and look at them, especially the black and white ones. They all held a certain history that I found fascinating.

When I walked into the living room, Miss Maggie was listening intently to Eli. I gave her a kiss on her cheek and headed straight for the kitchen.

"So, I think he's going to be my best friend." I heard Eli say.

"That's really nice, dear. What's his name?"

"Andre, and we played with the trains as well."

"And what about the other young man?"

"No way!" Eli shouted back and I could imagine the outrage on his face.

I rolled my eyes and switched the kettle on and pulled two cups down from the green cupboard, placing a tea bag in each. Earl Grey: I hated the stuff.

My lips pursed as I poured the water over the tea bags: just the smell of it made my eyes water. I was a coffee girl and nothing would ever sway me from that.

I carried the cups in and placed them on the small side table next to Miss Maggie. Eli sat in the middle of the couch both cats sprawled over his lap; so, careful not to disturb them, I sat down gently. Henry, the ginger one, lifted his head and meowed at me. One of those "don't come any closer" kind of meows.

I never left here without a scratch from at least one of them.

"How was your day, dear?" Miss Maggie asked, picking up her tea and taking a sip.

"Lonely." I huffed and sat back.

"I bet; it's a big change."

"Yeah." I picked my tea up, grimaced when I took a sip and put it back down. I really needed to start bringing some coffee with me.

"So, what are you going to do with all that spare time, dear?" I huffed out a huge breath. That was the question of all questions.

"I don't know, Miss Maggie. I'd like to maybe get a little job." I shrugged.

My hand fluttered over my pocket, the number still safely tucked away. I wanted to call, I probably wouldn't even get the job. But the fact that it was still on my mind spoke a thousand words: I just didn't want to go behind Max's back. Was it even worth broaching the subject with him?

"That would be nice. You need to get out and have something of your own."

I moved my eyes from Eli to the cartoon that was playing on the TV. I did need something; Eli couldn't be my whole life. I needed something for *me*.

"Corey said that his friend was looking for some help in his office."

Her eyes widened at the mention of Corey. She always loved to hear about him and knew that I waited every Saturday for his call.

"Corey finally called?"

"Yeah," I answered, fidgeting in my seat.

"Is he okay?"

I nodded and looked at the picture that sat next to

the TV. Miss Maggie and her husband stared back at me, both with giant smiles on their faces, her husband dressed in his army uniform. She knew better than anyone what it was like.

"Well, what are you going to do?"

However much I liked to think I wasn't sure, deep down I knew my answer.

I just had to admit it to myself.

WE STAYED WITH MISS MAGGIE FOR AN HOUR AND then went over to our apartment. Eli sat drawing at the table in the kitchen while I made dinner. I hadn't been able to get my mind off getting a job so I'd finally decided that I would broach the subject with Max.

I just had to do it in a way that wouldn't cause him to think I was overstepping my boundaries. Any little thing I said could set him off, I had to tread carefully.

I knew deep down that he wouldn't want me to get a job, but I had to say something, even if it was just to tell myself that I had tried. That might be enough to put it to rest in my mind. At least that's what I keep telling myself.

The apartment door banged open making butterflies take flight on my stomach before I figured out what I would actually say to him.

I wiped my hands on a towel and picked up the plates, my hands shaking so hard the pasta nearly slipped off them. I made it to the table just in time not to drop all the food.

I inhaled a deep breath, willed myself to calm down, and went back for the drinks.

He walked in as I was sitting down. I couldn't get a read on him, which was worse than when he was angry. *At least then I knew what to expect.*

His boots stomped along the floor as he crossed the small space.

"Hi, Max."

He grunted in answer and sat down next to the window, picked up his fork and shoveled pasta into his mouth.

"Eli had his first day at preschool today." He stayed silent. I did this all the time, I always ended up talking to myself. I'd stayed silent once, which he took to mean that I was hiding something, so now I always made sure to tell him everything we had done that day no matter how small it was.

I moved the pasta around my plate, not hungry in the slightest.

I slid my eyes to Eli, his head was down while he picked up a piece of pasta and placed it in his mouth. I hated seeing him like this, the contrast from a couple of hours ago to now was unreal. It was becoming more and more obvious how Max affected Eli: he'd started to go silent whenever he was around. His movements would slow down, almost like he knew that if he moved too fast he'd gain unwanted attention. If it was just me and Eli, he would have shoved all of his pasta in his mouth much like Max was doing.

"So..." I waited for Max to look up. When he didn't I went ahead anyway. Now was as best of time as ever. "I've got all this free time, now that Eli is at preschool," I said lightly.

His head snapped up, those eyes pinning me in place. I gulped at the intensity, knowing better than to look away. I shouldn't have said anything; the grunting should have been warning enough.

His eyes darkened, the angry swirls told me that I should have kept my mouth shut.

"And what do you want to do in this free time?" he asked calmly. *Too calmly*.

This was where I needed to change the conversation, not say what I wanted to say. To divert his attention elsewhere but my mouth moved before my brain could stop it.

"I was thinking." I clutched my hands in my lap "Maybe I could get a job?" I rushed out.

He shoved another mouthful of pasta in his mouth, chewing slowly all the while watching me intently.

"Your place is here." The vein in his neck started to pulse.

"I know—"

"No, you don't fucking know!" I gasped, my eyes flying to Eli who was watching me with wide eyes. "I've told you time and time again. Your. Place. Is. Here!" He slammed his fist on the table.

"Mama?" Eli whispered. I reached over and held his hand, trying to reassure him while not taking my eyes off Max.

"To cook me dinner and clean this shithole!"

"Max," I pleaded.

He stood, the chair slamming to the floor with a crack that echoed around us and had both Eli and I flinching.

"Do you need to be reminded of your job here? Hmm?" he gritted out, his jaw clenched tight as they vein in his neck pulsed so hard I was afraid he'd combust.

"No, Max." I sat up straighter. "I-I'm sorry."

He moved around the table taking slow, measured steps before stopping next to my chair. He stared down at me for a beat

"You need to learn what is appropriate to say to me." He lifted his hand and I braced for the impact, sure that the pain would come any second. His eyes shined with mirth before he laughed and muttered, "I'm outta here."

I stared at him as he walked away, stunned that I hadn't been corrected.

The air was thick with tension until we heard the front door slam shut. Eli watched me with knowing eyes that were filled with questions, but I didn't know what to say. Whether I should explain that I shouldn't have said anything: that I knew it wouldn't go down well but I couldn't help myself. I needed to learn to control myself better. I'm better than I used to be, but I still had the odd slip up here and there.

"I'm sorry, sweetie." I picked up my plate, stood and emptied it into the trash. I hadn't eaten a single thing: I wouldn't be able to until at least tomorrow. My stomach was all kinds of twisted.

"It's okay, Mama," he replied, his voice soft and sad.

I turned to see him eating and smiled before walking back over to him and placing a kiss on his head. I sat back down, listening intently when he started to talk about his new friend again. He shouldn't have known that I needed a distraction, but I was glad to have one.

It didn't take him long to get back to the little boy that I knew so well.

Max didn't come home until late that night. I half expected him to come into the bedroom, even if it was to only correct me, but as I listened to him stumble into the living room, it was obvious that he was wasted. His snores followed a couple of minutes later and that's when I allowed myself to relax slightly.

Chapter Three

Eli had been at preschool for a couple of days now and he loved it. Every day he would have a new story to tell me about or another new friend that he had made. I looked forward to all of the stories that he told me; I soaked everything in and it amazed me how much he had blossomed in just a few days. Being around other children was good for him, I just never realized *how* good it would be.

Me, on the other hand: I was lonely and bored. All I did was sit in the apartment and watch the hands on the clock tick by.

In the last four years, I hadn't had anytime to myself, and now suddenly I had too much time.

I'd been sitting at the kitchen table for ten minutes now, watching the clock as the seconds ticked down. I could have sworn it was slow. I'd even checked it twice in case it needed new batteries, but it didn't.

I slumped down in my chair: I had nothing to do and nobody to go and see. The only people that I spoke to were Eli, Max, and Miss—

I jumped up out of the chair. Why hadn't I thought of that before? Miss Maggie would keep me company.

I ran to the apartment door, shoved my feet in my Chucks and grabbed my keys. The door slammed shut behind me but I didn't care, I had someone to speak to!

Racing down the hall, I knocked on the door and then pushed it open.

"It's me, Miss Maggie!"

"Oh... hi, dear." She smiled when I rushed into the living room and I planted a kiss on her cheek.

I was full of excitement because I never got to talk to Miss Maggie on her own. I always had to watch what I was saying because of little ears. But now I could say anything that I wanted: not that it would be much, all I had to talk about was Eli.

"Tea?" I asked.

"That would be lovely."

My feet moved quickly and I willed the water to boil faster, I couldn't wait to talk to someone.

"How's your day going, dear?" Miss Maggie shouted into the kitchen. I poured the water over the teabags and then went back into the living room.

"I'm so bored," I huffed.

"I bet." She took the cup from my hand as I sat down. Henry hissed at me but I smiled wide at him: I was even glad to see a cat that hated me.

"I didn't realize how much everything revolved around Eli." I wrinkled my nose as I took a sip of the tea. "Now that he's at preschool, I've got nothing to do."

"What about that job that Corey told you about?"

I shifted in my seat. How was I going to say that Max didn't want me to work? That my place was at home? The more I thought about it, the more I realized how old fashioned it was.

Sure, that choice suited some people; those who had other Moms as friends that would meet up and let all their children play together. But we never had that: Max didn't want us to be judged. I understood, as a teen mom I knew what people thought, it was written across their faces.

But now it was different, I was older and I needed to get out of that apartment, for my own sanity. Being shut inside on my own all day wasn't good for me.

"Max doesn't really want me to work, he'd rather I stayed at home."

Miss Maggie's brow lifted as she studied me for several minutes. I shifted in my seat waiting for whatever she would say. "And what do you want, dear?"

It sounded so foreign to be asked what I wanted. I didn't have to think about it because I knew what I wanted, there was no question about it.

"I want to work," I said with a firm nod.

I had thought that if I tried to talk to Max about it, and he said no that I would be able to put the thought out of my mind. But I couldn't. If anything, it made me want it more.

I wanted to be around other people; I wanted to keep busy; I wanted more. More than what my life had become. I didn't want to sit there all day waiting for Eli and Max to come home.

I hadn't been able to throw the number away, the small piece of paper still sat safely in my pocket.

"You sound pretty sure."

"I am." I was.

I hadn't been this sure about anything since I found out I was pregnant. Several people had given me options: abortion, adoption. But I knew from the time that I saw that plus sign on that stick that I wanted to keep my baby. I had made my decision before I'd even talked to Max. I never expected anything from him, I thought he would walk away, but when my dad kicked me out, he was there for me. He made sure that I had somewhere safe to stay.

"I think you know what to do, dear." She sipped at her tea and I furrowed my brows.

How would I be able to work when Max had said that I couldn't? The only way that I'd be able to do that was to keep it a secret from him. *Would I be able to do that?*

It felt wrong to go behind his back, but it was the only way that I could see how this would work.

One thing I was sure of was that I had to try.

I jumped up, startling Henry who hissed at me again. Miss Maggie smiled: she knew what I was going to do without me saying a word.

"Thanks, Miss Maggie." I kissed her cheek and rushed back to my apartment.

A quick check of the time told me that I had enough time to call the number before I had to go and pick Eli up. I pulled the crumpled bit of paper out and punched the numbers into my phone before I could change my mind. I paced the small space in the kitchen as I bit the side of my thumb, my nerves rattling through me.

It tone sounded twice before the line connected.

"Yo." I opened my mouth to say something but nothing came out. "Hellloooo?"

"Uh, hi?" I croaked, I cleared my throat and tried again. "I was told that there's an office job and was given this number," I blurted out.

"Thank God!" the deep voice said. I raised my brows and felt the corners of my mouth lift into a small smile.

"Can you answer a phone?" he asked in a serious tone.

"Uh, yes."

"Here's the big question." Two beats of silence and then, "Can you operate a computer?"

"Yes," I said, more sure of myself as I nodded as if he could see me.

"Fantastic!" There was a loud noise in the background, much like the sound of someone who clapped their hands and I winced, caught off guard.

"Come in tomorrow for an interview with the boss."

"Tomorrow?"

I waited for him to say something else, but all I heard was shuffling on the other end.

"Hello?"

"Shit, sorry. Yeah tomorrow. That good?"

"Erm... sure." I hesitated: was it too soon? Was I doing the right thing?

He rattled off the address and then told me to be there at ten.

"Don't you need my name?" I asked.

"Oh yeah." He chuckled.

I laughed. "Okay, well my name is Kaylee." I purposely left out my surname, I didn't want to get this job because of Corey, I wanted to do it on my own merit.

"See you tomorrow."

"Bye," I said and pressed the end call button.

My stomach dipped. I had an interview for a job.

I jumped up and down, not being able to contain my excitement.

I was getting a job! Well, I had to have the interview first but I *could* be getting a job.

It may have been a small thing, but to me it meant much more than I could ever explain.

———

I WAS SO NERVOUS THAT NIGHT THAT I WAS oblivious to anything that was going on. I'd put Eli to bed and was now sitting in the kitchen. He'd kept my mind occupied from the time I had picked him up from preschool until his eyes closed and he went to sleep. Only now that he was in bed, my mind ran rampant.

I'd been so focused on whether I should phone the number that I had forgot I'd have to have an interview and actually meet them. It was all an idea in my mind, one that I didn't think I would go through with.

Max wasn't home yet, and normally I would be focused on what I had to have ready for when he walked in the door: his dinner and a bottle of beer.

Today my mind was elsewhere, questions spinning around in my mind like the vortex of a tornado: What would I wear? I owned the bare minimum of clothes, I wasn't sure I had anything that would be suitable for an interview. Would they like me? Would they figure out who I was? Was I brave enough to lie to Max about this whole thing?

Maybe I wouldn't go.

I'd be around people that I didn't even know if I

went through with this. I just couldn't decide whether that was a good thing or a bad thing.

No. I *needed* to do this. I had to do this: for myself, for Eli.

I jumped out of my skin when the apartment door slammed shut, my hearting beating in my chest erratically. I heard a thump on the wall and then he muttered something unintelligible to himself and I sighed. He was drunk again. I only hoped that he would leave me alone—

"Where's my woman?" he shouted.

Maybe not.

"I'm in here, Max."

His footsteps pounded and then he pushed open the kitchen door and grinned at me. His faced masked with that sinister look that I knew all too well: it almost always meant that he wanted to get laid. I willed my eyes to stay open and centered on him, knowing that I'd have to lay there while he got off. I'd disappear to my happy place while he did, pretending that none of it was happening. The upside was that he touched me in a gentle way: it was one of the few times that he would touch me like that.

But there were times he wasn't gentle: it was those times I dreaded.

He stumbled forward, leaned against the kitchen counter and opened his arms to me.

"Come're, baby."

I stood and went to him without any hesitation;

this was a delicate situation and I had to tread carefully. Keeping my face impassive so that I didn't show how much I hated the smell of beer and smoke that he reeked of, I stopped a couple of feet in front of him.

His rough hands yanked me closer before he grabbed the sides of my face and crushed his lips against mine. The taste was even worse, the stale beer mixed with mint that he tried to mask the smell of made me heave.

I tried to pull away, but each time he would hold me tighter while crushing me to his body with bruising force. I needed to breathe clean air; the smell and taste was too much.

His hands started to wander down then landed on my butt, pulling me even closer to him. I could feel his erection through his jeans as his fingers dug into the soft flesh, sure to leave purple bruises.

Gasping when he let me up for air, I stepped back and struggled out of his hold.

"Come back, baby." I took another step back, intent on warming up his dinner.

He tried to step forward, but ended up slumped back against the counter. His face turning red as his hands clenched into fists at not being able to control his own body.

"Now!" he sneered.

"I'll warm your dinner," I told him softly.

"I don't want no fuckin' dinner." He adjusted

himself. "I want you. Here." He pointed to his tent in his jeans.

I hesitated, just long enough for him to see. He narrowed his eyes at me, the air becoming thick with tension. I should have just gone to him.

Maybe he *was* right? I never did learn.

He shook his head, his green eyes darkening with an unspoken threat.

"You'll never learn, will you?" He didn't slur this time and I furrowed my brow. He sounded a lot less drunk than he had only minutes ago.

"I just wanted to warm your dinner," I answered in a small voice.

He shot forward, this time not wobbling in the slightest as his hands wrapped around the top of my arms. He pulled me up to his face, my feet dangling off the floor.

"When I say jump... You say?"

I winced at the grip that he had on my arms and he squeezed even harder when I didn't answer him right away.

"How high?" I squeaked.

"That's right." He smirked. *I hated that smirk.*

"I-I-I'm sorry, Max." I willed the tears to stay back.

He gripped my arms harder still and this time I squealed out loud. I was sure that he'd break the bones if he didn't let up; I could hardly breathe through the pain.

He made a noise in the back of his throat, closed

his eyes and tilted his head back. He enjoyed this, I was sure he had waited until I cried out in pain.

I knew better than to struggle so instead I kept still, biting my lip to take my mind off the pain in my arms.

"I'm feeling in a good mood," he said, then opened his eyes, the emerald green connecting with mine and sparking with mirth. "I'll let you make it up to me."

"Okay," I whispered. All I wanted was for him to let me go.

"But..." He brought his face down to mine, our noses touching. "This is the only time that I'm gonna to let you do this."

I nodded and breathed a sigh of relief when he let my arms go. It never helped with the pain but I still rubbed them in an automatic response. I'd have bruises there in the shape of his fingers in the morning.

"Next time you won't be so lucky," he gritted out, the warning clear.

I looked down at the floor. He liked it when I did that: submitted to him. I had to diffuse this situation somehow. It could get much worse than it already had; a fine line sat between when he was annoyed and when he was angry.

This was annoyed Max.

I didn't want angry Max.

I'd encountered him a couple of times, each time worse than the one before. I didn't want to think about the next time he'd rear his ugly head.

"Good girl," he murmured, his hand cupping the side of my face softly.

I saw movement out the corner of my eye as he undid his belt. I flinched at the sound of the metal buckle and watched his grease stained fingers as they undid the buttons of his jeans methodically.

"On your knees."

This was the worst part. I would have preferred him to hit me rather than having to do this. By the end of the night my throat would be sore and I'd most likely bring up any food I had eaten that day.

I'd have to be extra careful when I washed my hair, and I'd also have to wear my hair down because my scalp would be sore from where he would yank on my hair.

I took a deep breath then got down onto my knees as my eyes closed on their own accord. I was halfway to my happy place when his hand wove through my hair and pulled. I wouldn't be seeing that tonight; I'd have to endure every minute of it.

At least I wasn't thinking about my interview tomorrow.

The only silver lining on this dark cloud of a night.

When I woke the next morning, the bed was empty and Max was gone. I rubbed my eyes, aware that I'd definitely have bags under them: just what I didn't need today.

He'd kept me up most of the night, letting me "make" it up to him. I'd thought that I would be done after the kitchen incident, but I was wrong. At some stage, I'd gone to my happy place and hadn't come back until he rolled away from me and filled the room with his snores.

I shook my head; I was in desperate need of a shower and a cup of coffee before I even entertained the thought of what I had to do today.

I stumbled out of bed and into the bathroom, stepping into the shower before I turned the knob to let the water wash over me. I kept my feet planted to the bottom of the tub and let the cold water prickle against my skin. All the dirt and grime from last night swirled down the drain. I stared at the vortex it was creating, wishing that it could take away my memories like that too.

Dark purple, finger shaped bruises wrapped around my arms in a band, the skin so tender and sore. Just lifting my arms to wash my hair took all my effort.

My scalp burned from where Max had gripped my hair painfully. He liked to do that: to lead me wherever he wanted to take me.

I wasn't in the best shape to go to an interview, but if one thing was clear, it was that I needed to get out of here, even if only for a couple of hours a day.

The walls were closing in on me, I had to have something just for *me*.

I finished up in the bathroom and padded into the bedroom. It had once been a savior from all the other rooms in this apartment. Nothing ever happened in this room, nothing bad anyway. The only time Max ever came in here was to get clothes or to sleep in the bed on the odd occasion. He'd taken to sleeping on the couch for the last couple of months.

He had never hurt me in this room.

That changed last night.

I grabbed some clothes, threw them on and went through the next hour on autopilot. I gave Eli his breakfast, got him ready and dropped him off at preschool.

Before I knew it, I was stood in the doorway of the bedroom again. It looked so different from what it did only yesterday, I may as well have been looking inside a stranger's room.

The metal bed that sat in the middle was covered in a mess of sheets, a glass of water sat on the bedside table that had once been a stool. I didn't recognize it, it looked so... different. The walls somehow seemed darker, the room smaller.

I crinkled my nose at the smell of stale sweat and grease that permeated from everything. Moving forward, I opened the window as far as it would go and stood back, closing my eyes and taking a deep, calming breath.

This wasn't how things were meant to be, life wasn't meant to be this hard—this draining. I didn't know a lot about relationships, I'd only been around my mother and father for the first seven years of my life, but I did know that it wasn't meant to be like *this*.

How had I let things get this bad?

I closed my eyes and remembered the way my mom would smile when my dad walked in from work, how she would close her eyes when he kissed her cheek and burrow into his chest as his arms wrapped around her.

It was a happy home. That much I do remember. I would rush home from school every Friday knowing that we would bake cookies. It was time that I got to spend with Mom on my own. She always made sure that me and Corey had time with just her or Dad.

Dad always took me into the woods on mini adventures, we'd pack a bag then explore for the whole day. Once, we even camped in the woods.

I never knew what they did with Corey. Whatever adventure we had been on, I was meant to keep it a secret, but I was never good at that. Corey could get it out of me within minutes of us walking back in the door.

Everything changed when mom was diagnosed with cancer, it was worse than all the doctors had thought. We only had seven of the twelve months with her that they had predicted. But those seven months were full of memories: both good and bad.

I shook the past from my head, pulled my cell from my pocket and checked the time. I had ten minutes before I needed to leave. I headed straight for the wardrobe and picked the best skirt and tank top out that I owned. It was a simple blue stretchy pencil skirt paired with a white tank top that I would tuck in to look more professional.

That's where it stopped, I had no other shoes apart from my black Chucks so I shoved my feet in them and slipped my arms into my light gray cardigan to cover the bruises on my arms.

I stared at my reflection with indifference, the girl who stared back wasn't who I remembered. My dark brown hair was tamed into submission, still damp but not the frizz ball that it would become once it was dry. My face was clean of makeup because that's how I liked it. I could never do all that fancy shading on my eyes and my eyeliner would always end up with a wobble in the middle.

I leaned forward, popped my eyes wide and stared. My dark blue eyes were dull, the white that surrounded them bloodshot. I took a deep breath and collected my things and made my way of the apartment.

Locking the door behind me I noticed Miss Maggie standing in the doorway to her apartment.

"Oh, hey, Miss Maggie." I pulled my bag over my shoulder.

"You off anywhere nice?"

"Interview." I whispered and looked down, my eyes refusing to meet hers. I was sure that she'd be able to see all of the things I did last night written across my face. The thought of Miss Maggie knowing made me feel sick.

I wasn't a prude in any way, but some of the things that Max had me do made me feel ashamed. It was for an easy life that I did as he said, which made it even worse because I hadn't put up a fight.

I'd gone along with everything and that made me as bad as he was.

"Good Luck," she said in a sing song voice.

"Thanks." I waved and rushed down the stairs.

Chapter Four

I PULLED up in front of the large metal gates at the end of a private road, pressed the button on the little speaker box and waited. Looking out of the window, I noticed an eight-foot metal fence that lined the property as far as I could see. It was the most secure place that I had ever seen.

"Yeah?" a voice boomed through the speaker.

I cleared my throat and leaned closer to the speaker box. "Hi, I'm Kaylee. I'm here for the interview."

I was proud that my voice sounded confident because my hands had started to shake half way there. I was glad it was only a twenty-minute drive; any longer and I would have had to pull over to get myself together.

The gates swung open and I drove through: a collection of cars were straight ahead so I parked next to them. There were SUVs, vans with company logos on the side and even an old clunker of a car circa nineteen eighties.

The place was huge. All of the cars were parked outside a big warehouse and I could make out at least two other buildings farther back. I squinted, trying to make out what they were. Houses?

Woods surrounded the whole place, the fencing seeming to weave in and out of it: the trees and smell reminded me of my dad. I shook that thought from my head as soon as it popped in. That was the last thing I needed to do, I'd spent way too long in the past this morning. I needed to look to the future.

I pushed my car door open and jumped out, pulling my bag with me. Swiveling on the spot, I searched for some sort of sign as to where I was meant to go.

"Can I help?" I jumped, my hand flying to my chest.

"Crapstickles!"

"Crap what?" I looked to the voice and did a double take.

Standing a couple of inches shorter than me, which is saying something because I was only five foot four, was a girl with lavender hair that sat in a side braid and eyes rimmed with black glasses. I instantly liked her because she gave off a welcome vibe and her light brown eyes showed kindness and warmth.

"I'm here for an interview," I squeaked.

She stood with her feet hip width apart, arms loose at her sides as she studied me from head to toe. She tilted her head, staring into my eyes before nodding after a couple of seconds.

She pointed to the end of the warehouse. "I'll take you in."

I followed behind her, rushing to keep up with her quick pace. She turned the corner of the warehouse and pulled open what looked to be a heavy metal door.

"In here," she said and waved her arm.

I stepped inside cautiously, not knowing what I would find. Corey hadn't told me anything about the place and I realized that I probably should have asked more about it instead of jumping in head first without any knowledge.

I scanned the warehouse: to my right there was a table with six chairs around it, the open space in the middle of the vast room was covered with gym mats. We walked past the mats, then past two doors. The first one was open so I peeked in: a small kitchen with a sink and a coffee machine. I nodded to myself, that was a must. Coffee.

"I'm Kitty by the way."

"Kay," I said to the back of her head, continuing to look around with wide eyes.

The second door looked nothing like the others,

made from some sort of steel, and a small screen sat next to it.

She knocked on the third door then waited. I scanned the back part of the warehouse, several computer screens lined the wall opposite the doors, they were all attached to one keyboard. Next to it sat several gym machines.

"Come in!" a gruff voice shouted through the door.

Kitty opened the door and said, "Interview." Then she waved me in and shut the door behind me. I whipped my head back and caught the tail end of a wink.

I stood and waited for him to lift his head, my gaze roaming around the room. The walls were off white with sun streaming through a skylight in the middle of the ceiling. Photos scattered along the walls, all of them filled with people in uniform. A small couch sat in the corner with two desks opposite it.

My eyes moved back the man who sat at the back of the room behind his own desk. This one larger than the others and the only one that had a desktop computer.

I could only see the top of his shoulders and forearms but from what I could make out he was ripped. He wore a black t-shirt, stretched across his muscles. Tattoos danced down his arms, one side black and gray the other side full of color.

He lifted his face up toward me and pulled off the beanie hat that sat on top of his head. His large hand running through his light brown hair, trying in vain to tame it.

"Kaylee?" His deep voice vibrated through me. This man screamed danger. The good kind—wait, was there a good kind?

"Yes?" I croaked, clearing my throat. "Yes," I said, louder this time, more sure of myself.

He raised his brows at me, tilted his head to the chair opposite him then scribbled something down on a piece of paper.

I moved forward, sat down in the chair and wiped my hands on my legs. My palms had never sweat before and now was *not* the time for them to start. He carried on scribbling on the paper for several more seconds then lifted his head up.

"So..." He leaned back in his chair. "You want a job?" He crossed his arms, his muscles moving in a way I'd never seen before.

"Yes." I answered, my head nodding at him awkwardly. I could feel my cheeks heating from his intense gaze.

"Have you worked in an office before?"

"Yes. I worked the reception desk at a small hotel until I was eighteen." Hotel was a stretch, but experience was experience, right?

"And how long ago would that have been?" Was he asking how old I was?

"Four years ago." I said, shifting in the chair nervously. He scanned me, much the same as Kitty had outside. His chocolate brown eyes held me captive. Assessing me, seeing down to the depths of my soul.

I couldn't handle how he was looking at me so I looked away and cleared my throat.

"That makes you twenty-two?" I nodded in reply. "Any other experience that would help you in an office."

"I can organize things." That was lame but I had nothing else to give him. When I worked at the small hotel, I never had to have an interview, they were friends of my mother's so naturally they gave me a job. I'd loved working there but I had to give it up when I had Eli.

"Organize things?" he repeated.

"Yes, I have to organize a four-year-old every day, and let me tell you, it's not easy to do." I laughed at that, the sound shrill to my own ears.

Trying to lighten the mood was *not* working.

"You have a kid?"

"Yes, is that..." I clutched my hands in my lap. "Will that be a problem?"

He narrowed his eyes at me. I had come across this look so many times: judging. He was working out how old I would have been when I had Eli, thinking that I was some kind of slut to get knocked up while still in high school. Yes, I may have got pregnant at a young age but I did everything I could to care for Eli.

"No," he finally answered. "As long as it doesn't interfere with your work."

"It won't." I said, breathing a sigh of relief.

"The job involves answering phones, booking meetings..." He shuffled some papers on his desk. "General filing, that sort of thing."

"I can do that," I said, confident that I could.

"Here's what I'm gonna do." He leaned forward, interlocked his hands and rested them on the desk. My eyes glued to the way the veins popped in his forearms. "I'm gonna give you a month's trial."

"Really?"

"Yeah, see how you get on." I smiled wide, I actually got the job.

I. Got. The. Job.

"Besides," he continued, then shrugged, "I'm desperate for the help."

"I can start tomorrow, if you need me to?" I said, then cringed at how eager I sounded.

He chuckled at that, picked up the papers that he had been looking for and held them out to me, I shuffled forward in my chair and took them from him.

"Fill those in and then I'll take you on a tour of the place."

I took the pen that he offered and scanned the forms feeling his eyes on me the whole time.

I left my name blank to start with and filled out all of the other stuff first. Just basic information and references, I put down the hotel information and added

Miss Maggie as another reference—she was the only other person that I could think of.

The only thing left to fill out was emergency contact information and my last name. I held the pen over the paper, ready to write it down but when I looked up he was watching me intently.

I knew he'd recognize my surname straight away.

"Erm..." I leaned back a little, my eyes looking anywhere but at his. I traced the white "MAC SECU-RITY" logo on his chest of his t-shirt.

"Yeah?"

"So, I erm... well... you see."

"Goddammit, woman, spit it out." My gaze shot to his, sure to find him pissed at my ramblings but he wasn't, instead his eyes held laughter. I hadn't expected that.

I blew out a breath, causing the hair that had fallen over my face to fly in front of my face. I pushed it away, then clutched my hands in my lap.

"I was given your number by my older brother. He was the one who told me about the job."

"Yeah?" His eyes narrowed as he watched me intently.

"I didn't want you to give me the job just because of my brother, but I thought that you should know."

It was ironic how I felt the need to be honest with him, yet I was lying to Max about being here like I would be every single day.

"Okay, shoot. Who's your brother?" His fingers

drummed on the desk to some imaginary beat as he waited.

I cleared my throat before answering, "Corey Anderson."

His fingers stilled, the air in the room sucked out at his silence. Butterflies swarmed in my stomach because I was unsure how to take him. I sucked at reading people.

Corey never told me much about his work friends, in fact I couldn't even tell you any of their names. He said he liked to keep family and work separate, but I had a feeling that wasn't the real reason. He always had this irrational need to protect me.

"Corey Anderson?" he asked, his eyes wide and his jaw slacked.

"Yes." I nodded.

"Corey has a sister?"

"Huh?" My brows furrowed. What did he mean?

"He never told us." He stared over my head, almost like he was talking to himself.

"Well, he told me that his friend needed help in the office and gave me your number," I rambled on, he wasn't listening though.

I placed the pen on the table, picked my bag up from the floor then got up out of the chair.

"Look, if it's going to be a problem then I'll just leave." I spun around and made it halfway before a hand grabbed my arm. Right where Max had left bruises.

I squealed in pain then slammed my hand over my mouth as tears pricked behind my eyes.

He let go of my arm so fast almost as if I had burned him and stared at his hand in confusion.

I tried to catch my breath but the throbbing in my arm made it impossible.

"Fuck, I'm sorry." His face paled "I never..."

"It's fine," I said through clenched teeth. My lips lifted in an attempt at a smile which I'm sure came out more like a grimace.

"It's not going to be a problem." He cleared his throat and stepped away from me. "I was just shocked, we all thought... never mind," he said, shaking his head.

"Are you sure it's not going to be a problem?"

"Certain." He smiled, revealing straight white teeth.

"Okay." I took a deep breath: the throbbing wasn't as bad now. "But can we not tell anyone else?"

"Kay—"

"I just don't want to be known as his little sister." He studied me in that intense way again and I couldn't help but squirm under his gaze.

"Okay." He nodded.

"Okay." I repeated.

"Let's take a look around, introduce you to the guys, then you can be on your way."

He opened the door for me and waved me out, stepping out behind me. He showed me all of the areas of the warehouse: the computers were Evan's department, he was the one I had spoken to on the phone yesterday and I'd meet him tomorrow.

He also said that I could use any of the gym equipment any time I wanted. I laughed at that, the idea of me and exercising was a joke. My legs ached from climbing the four sets of stairs to my apartment every day, I told him this to which he said, "The offers there," and carried on with his tour.

"We have a meeting each morning to go over active or new cases. It starts at nine, I expect you to be here to take notes."

"Okay." I followed behind him, watching the muscles ripple in his back each time he moved.

"Kitchen, office, and safe." He pointed to each door and headed to the one that he said was a safe.

"It has a palm reader as a lock."

"What's in there?"

He turned, his brow lifted. "What do you think is in there?"

"I dunno? Files?"

He laughed so loud and unexpected that it startled me. I felt my own lips lift as I watched his whole face open up, the fierce mask that he'd be wearing disappearing.

"Weapons." I jumped at the voice and spun around. Kitty was stood behind me. Again.

"Jeez, are you going to do that all the time?"

"Should always be aware of your surroundings."

She grinned. I stuck my tongue out at her, shocked at my own response. It was so unlike me. I didn't know what possessed me to do that, but I couldn't stop it. She mustn't have minded though because she winked at me then walked off into the kitchen.

"You've met Kitty," he said. "That's Luke." He extended his arm, pointing over at the door as a man came through it.

He was as big and ripped as— "Wait." I laid a hand on his arm. "What's your name?"

He furrowed his brow at me, his gaze flicking from my hand to his arm. "What?"

"You haven't told me your name."

"Tyson Mackenzie."

"Or just Boss!" Kitty shouted, coffee in hand as she walked from the kitchen to the office.

"Luke!" Tyson called out and he looked over at us then. "This is Kaylee, the new office girl."

"Lady," I interrupted. Ty looked down at me, lifted the side of his mouth into a smirk and shook his head.

Luke scowled, his ice blue eyes narrowed at me. He ran his hand through his slicked back blond hair, grunted, then walked right past us and into the office. I followed him with my eyes, confused. I looked back to Tyson, his eyes focused on his arm where my hand still lay and I frowned.

"Sorry," I whispered and moved my hand slowly. He shrugged and walked forward so I followed him, stopping as he opened the metal door.

"Monday? Be here just before nine."

"Sure." I pulled my keys out as I walked through the door, turned back and lifted my hand above my eyes to shade from the glaring sun. "Thanks for giving me a chance."

He nodded in reply and leaned against the door.

I turned, headed for the car and checked my cell. Time had flown by: I'd only just make it back in time to get Eli.

I heard the sound of the metal door shut just before I got in the car and stopped, looking around at the place. There was something about it that felt... I couldn't put my finger on it.

It just felt *right*.

Chapter Five

WE VISITED with Miss Maggie after I picked Eli up from preschool. Eli and Miss Maggie spoke most of the time about the superhero movie she had watched that day while I did nothing but think about the people I had met at MAC Security.

They all seemed nice; though I wasn't sure quite sure about Luke yet: there seemed to be something about him. What that was, I wasn't quite sure yet. Having another woman there was a relief, that wasn't the only thing that put me at ease though but also being known as more than Corey's little sister.

All throughout school, that's all I was known as, "Corey's little sister." Everyone stayed away from me, *especially* the boys. Max had been the only one brave enough to approach me, but even that hadn't been until Corey graduated high school. The most frustrating thing was that we hadn't even attended the same school. Corey was only three years older than me, but he was a whiz at school and was moved a grade above pretty early on.

I was in a constant daydream for the rest of the night, I was there in body, but my mind was still back at the warehouse when Max came home. Even when he walked in, the smile on my face couldn't be moved: *I had a job!*

He ignored me, ate his dinner in silence and went to sleep on the couch. It was a welcome reprieve after the night before. I honestly didn't know if I could stand to talk to him without saying something that I would later regret.

My good mood seemed to rub off on Max over the next couple of days, either that or he felt guilty about what he did that night because he offered to take us out on Saturday night, and we had the best time. I hadn't been this happy in so long.

It was funny how the little things could change your whole perception. If I'd known this was how it was going to feel, then I would have tried to find a job sooner. I still had to start the job and do a day's work, but at this point, I was looking forward to it immensely.

By Sunday night, butterflies were swarming my stomach and I had that first day of a new school feeling.

I'd already planned in my head what clothes I would wear, how I would do my hair and I even tried to practice applying eyeliner in a straight line. After the third attempt, I scrubbed my face clean and decided I would forgo the makeup and stick to what I knew how to do best and go fresh faced.

They all wore combat pants or jeans and a t-shirt with MAC SECURITY on it. But I didn't want to look they them. After all, I was going to be working in the office so I decided I would wear something similar to what I wore at the interview.

The bed shifted as Max slid in next to me. "You good, Kay?"

"Yeah," I answered automatically before turning my face toward him. "Why?" I moved on to my side fully, only being able to make out his profile in the pitch-black darkness.

"You seem, I don't know, different," he replied softly.

My eyes widened. "Do I?"

"Yeah." I felt him shift closer to me and blew out a big breath. I didn't know what to make of him sleeping in the same bed as me again: this made it two nights in a row.

"Everything's fine..." I paused before I said, "Night," and rolled over before I closed my eyes. The sooner that I was asleep the better.

"Night."

I woke up early the next morning; Max was already gone so it gave me time to get all of my things ready for the day. I started by packing me a lunch, much like Eli's, and jumping in the shower. I had my hair dried and hanging in loose waves by the time Eli stumbled out of his bedroom, still half asleep.

I fixed him some breakfast before I went back to my room to finish getting ready.

Choosing a maroon skirt and another tank top, I tucked it in and shrugged my gray cardigan on before I looked down at my feet as I pushed them into my Converse. Mental note: get some better shoes with my first paycheck.

"Eli!" I found him some clothes and went to the bathroom. "Come on, sweetie, wash and teeth," I said as I sat on the edge of the bath. He padded down the hallway and when he stumbled inside, I passed him his toothbrush and watched as he brushed his teeth. Grinning widely, he scrubbed at them, toothpaste flowing out the side of his mouth and down his jaw.

"You look pretty, mama," he said once he spat the toothpaste out.

"Aww, thanks, sweetie." I washed his face and then ushered him to his bedroom to get him changed. "You look handsome," I said after he was dressed.

"I know." He rolled his eyes and sauntered into the

hallway to put his shoes on and I followed, chuckling to myself.

We made it out the door five minutes early and I mentally gave myself a pat on the back for having our routine down and it only being the first day.

I pulled out of the preschool parking lot half an hour later: I was running right on time.

When I got to the gates of the compound, I pressed the buzzer and they opened up for me. Parking in the same place I had last week, I reached over for my bag, climbed out of my car and started to make my way to the other side of the warehouse and toward the main door. I had to use all my strength to open up the big metal thing. That would be workout enough. *Jeez, why did it have to be so heavy?*

Walking in, I found the warehouse empty so I made my way toward the back and to the office before I knocked on the closed door.

"Come in," the deep, gravelly voice greeted.

I pushed the door open and found Tyson sitting behind his desk, his fingers jabbing at the keyboard violently. He was practically attacking the thing.

"Goddamn computer!" he roared, before pushing back on his chair. The momentum sent him flying back and at the last second before he hit the wall, he slammed his boots down on the floor causing the chair to come to an immediate stop.

His ran his hands over his face and through his hair before he slid his eyes over to me.

"Morning," I whispered unsure.

"Morning." He looked back at the computer screen, clicked the mouse a couple of times and stood, frustrated still painted over his features.

"You can put your things in there." He pointed to a cupboard behind his desk.

I moved forward, slid past him and put my bag inside. When I turned around he was sitting in the chair that I had sat in for my interview.

"Sit," he said and tilted his head to the seat behind the desk that he'd just got up from.

I pointed to the seat. "There?"

"Yeah, we're gonna share a desk."

"Oh, right." I sat down in the chair after a beat, amazed at I sank into it. It was one of those ones that they have in fancy offices: the ones with backrests, covered in buttery soft leather.

"You're early," he commented.

I shrug. "I wanted to make a good impression."

He cocked his head to the side and watched me intently: the same way that he did last week. It unnerved me, but I ignored it and focused on the pile of things sitting on the edge of the desk, a note stuck to the top with my name on.

"They're for you."

I stood and reached out to pick up five notepads, each with a label on the front: Meeting, Tyson, Kitty, Luke, and Evan. Underneath was a hardback diary, the sort that had a page to each day. Then there were a bunch of printed papers.

"You need to keep track of all our comings and goings. The diary is to be used to book any appointments."

I held up the papers. "And these?"

"That's your contact information, a non-disclosure agreement and your job description."

"Non-disclosure?" I asked, my brows drawing down into a frown.

"Yeah, it's straight forward. You can't say anything about the cases or what goes on here."

"Okaaay..."

"You'll be given access to everything we have access to. Apart from the safe. You're gonna know things that a lot of people would like to know." He leaned forward, continuing, "Things that are dangerous."

"Dangerous?" I squeaked.

"You won't *be* in any danger. But you need to know that what we do here is important." His chocolate brown eyes held mine, a warning loud and clear in their depths.

"And what is it you actually do?"

He leaned back in his chair and stretched his long legs out. "You'll find out soon enough."

I read and signed both contracts and put my job description back on top of the pile.

"Ready for your first meeting?" Tyson asked,

standing up and pulling the book that had "Meeting" written on the front from under all of the papers. I stood, pen in hand and took the pad from him before I clutched it to my chest, nodding.

My eyes were level with his chest as he towered over me so I tilted my head back to meet his eyes. "Ready as I'll ever be." He smiled then, his teeth glinting in the sunlight that streamed through the skylight above us.

"Come on." He flicked his hand toward the door and followed me out.

Kitty and Luke were already sitting at the table when we approached. Kitty lips were spread into a grin as she looked at me, so I smiled back before I turned my gaze to Luke. His attention was fixed on his cell, his fingers flying across the screen until Tyson sat down at the head of the table.

I slowly took the seat next to him; opposite Kitty and Luke.

I watched out of the corner of my eye as Tyson pulled off his beanie hat and ran his hands through his brown hair. Placing the pad on the table, I opened it to the first page and wrote the date on the top left-hand side.

"Okay, guys. First off: any finished cases?" Tyson asked them.

My gaze pinged around the warehouse, expecting to see Evan. I zoned in on his work area, but all of the computer screens were switched off, the chair pushed neatly under the table.

"I finished up the 'Knights Case' last night." Kitty pulled a folder off the top of the pile that sat in front of her before she held it out to me. "Just needs to be written up."

I took the folder and placed it next to me. "Okay." My voice was small and unsure. Written up?

"Luke? Any luck with the Jakeman case?"

"No, Boss," his deep, rough voice answered. "Still following leads."

Tyson nodded, shuffled through the papers in front of him and handed out one to each of us.

"Charlie asked me to look into this," he said as way of explanation when I raised my brow is silent question. I scanned it, not able to make much sense other than it was a man they suspected of running a drug ring. I was about to ask who Charlie was when Tyson carried on talking.

"He caught one of the dealers and they gave up some information." He pulled something out of the folder, spun in his chair and stuck a photograph on the wall. It was a mug shot, taken when the person was arrested.

The first thing that jumped out was the man's eyes, almost black with pure evil seeping out. His neck was covered in tattoos, climbing up the side of his face. He was the kind of person that would make you feel like you needed to cross the street so you wouldn't have to walk past him.

"Phillip Shore."

"His info any good?" Luke asked.

"That's what we need to find out." He looked at all of us in turn. "Charlie suspects it's one of the cartels."

"What do we know so far?"

"He says that he can give dates and times of shipments. The first one is happening in two days." Tyson raised his brows at Luke, a silent conversation taking place.

"What does he need us to do?" Kitty asked.

"Watch the trade take place, then report back."

Kitty nodded. "I'll scope out the place and set up surveillance."

"Take Luke with you: we work in teams for this one." They both nodded at Tyson in agreement before talking about all of their active cases.

I took notes and found that I was pretty good at writing in shorthand, at least what *I* considered shorthand.

Corey and I had invented a secret code when we were kids where we swapped letters around and made new words. It was a brilliant way to send secret messages to each other. Corey had said that it was practice for when he grew up and became a spy. I used to laugh at that, thinking that we would have no way to use it. But the older we got, the more I found I used it.

Secret text messages were sent frequently; he even wrote to me a couple of times a year using it. It always made me laugh because it was never anything important, mainly just silly little things like what he ate for dinner or how much he missed chocolate cake.

I found that using the code while taking notes of the meeting was much easier than writing every single word they said.

Once the meeting was finished, Kitty and Luke headed out to scope the meeting point and I followed Tyson back into the office. He sat opposite the desk again so I sat in front of the computer and moved the mouse to bring the screen to life.

"You've got access to all of the files."

I looked up at him confused. "Sorry?"

"We all have our own system on the computer, I'm the only one who can access all of them, and of course, you can now as well."

I kept my gaze connected with his. "Okay."

"Every case report needs to have two copies." He leaned forward in his chair, bracing his arms on his thighs. "One saved to whoever did the case and the other on the main system"

"What if it's a joint case?"

His lips lifted at the corners. "We each get a report then."

I nodded in reply and then pushed up out of his seat before he moved around the desk and leaned over me.

What was he doing?

His aftershave wafted around me—musk and spice —and I couldn't help but breathe it in. I'd never smelled anything quite like it.

Car grease was all that I was usually surrounded with on a man. I mean, don't get me wrong, there was something to be said about a man who smelled of car grease, just not when it was mixed in with beer and all that came after that.

I flicked my gaze to Tyson as he held out a yellow post it note. Reaching up, I took it from him.

"Username and password," he grunted.

"Oh, right. Okay." I typed it in while Tyson stood at my back, shivering as his breath fanned across the back of my neck.

"Cold?"

"No." I shook my head and moved the mouse over the screen, opened a blank file and reached across the desk for my notepad.

I decided that it was better for me to do it how I thought it would be best, rather than try to copy what had already been done. If Tyson didn't like it then I learn how do it his way.

"What's that?" His large hand gripped the end of the notepad and pulled it out of my grasp. His brows furrowed as he read all of the secret code and I smiled to myself, knowing that he would never be able to understand it. "What the hell is this?"

"It's the notes from the meeting." I curled my

fingers around the edge of the pad before pulling on it. "It's code." I shrugged.

I started typing as silence surrounded us, but I didn't let it bother me, instead I carried on creating a new system for me to work on.

Finally, he murmured, "Corey."

I looked up at him and gave him a small smile as an answer before I went back to typing. I'd have to explore all of the documents after this and look at how the reports are written up before I handle the folder Kitty gave me.

I felt rather than saw Tyson move from behind me, his combat boots thudding along the floor.

"I'll be back in a couple of hours," he said from the doorway.

I tilted my head back, meeting his eyes. "Okay."

"You'll be okay?"

"Yes," I said, confident that I would.

As soon as he was gone, I leaned back in the chair and blew out a big breath. Impressing the boss was my main goal, I wanted this job to work out, not just for me but for Eli too. I wanted to make something of myself.

Scanning the photos on the wall, I landed on one of Tyson and Corey standing with their arms around each other as they grinned wide.

I felt my own lips lifting into a matching grin. I think that would be my new favorite picture.

Chapter Six

Tyson seemed happy with the way that I wrote the reports at the end of my first day, so I'd say it was a success. It may have been a small thing to anyone else, but to me it was huge. To have someone be impressed with something that I did and to feel valued; it was a big deal.

My second day went even better than my first. I took notes at the meeting like I had the day before, using my secret code once again. My stomach dipped when I noticed Tyson watching me as I wrote, a grin on his face. He always seemed to wear a fierce expression, but when his lips lifted, his whole face changed.

I shook my head, looked back down at my pad and concentrated on the meeting. Kitty was telling Tyson what she had found when she checked out the meeting point they talked about the day before.

"It's gonna be a nightmare to watch it. The only viable option is the building there." She pointed to an area on the map she placed on the table, and then set down several photographs next to it.

I leaned forward to get a better look. The first was a photo of the building, it looked like it had once been a factory of some sort but it was now derelict and long forgotten about. The second photo was taken from a window inside the building, you could see almost everything from that viewpoint. The problem was, there were so many hiding places that any meeting could be easy to miss—even I could come to that conclusion.

"It'll have to do," Tyson finally said after staring at them for a few tense minutes.

They arranged what time they needed to set up and be in place tomorrow night to watch the exchange take place, then Luke and Kitty left to set up the rest of the equipment while me and Tyson went back to the office.

I knew what I needed to do by now, so I started typing up the meeting as Tyson pulled open the drawer to the filing cabinet to the left.

"What's it like?" It was out of my mouth before I'd even registered that I'd spoken.

"Hmm?"

"To do what you do?" The sound of the drawer

shutting sounded around us before he turned to face me. His chocolate orbs watched me, the tension around them unmistakable.

"Dangerous," is all he said, before he spun around and walked out.

I looked down at the mouse my hand was sitting on, afraid that I had offended him. I really did need to think before I spoke. It was an innocent enough question, but he obviously didn't like it.

I just found it so interesting what they did here. I knew that I hadn't scratched the surface with what they did and I couldn't help but be drawn to it.

I spent the next couple of hours typing things up, at one stage I went into the filing cabinet to put something away and decided that I'd re-organize it. First, I made piles for each person and then I put them all in alphabetical order.

It wasn't until I'd nearly finished that I hoped Tyson didn't mind me changing things about. I was the one that was working in the office all day, so it made sense to me that I organized it in a way that made things easier for me to find things.

Bending down to put the last file away, I froze as I heard someone say, "Daaaammmn, that's a fine sight."

I spun around, the files scattering along the floor as my eyes connected with his. He was leaning against the door with his feet crossed at the ankles and his arms folded over his chest. A wide grin spread on his face as his honey eyes scanned me from head to toe.

"You scared me."

I narrowed my eyes as he grinned wider.

I didn't know what it was about him, maybe the way he watched me with laughter in his eyes or the fact that he hadn't moved a step toward me, but I felt a smile lift up my own lips.

He wasn't as big as Tyson and Luke: his black skinny jeans showed his athletic legs up into a narrow waist, built much like a swimmer. A black t-shirt with a thunderbolt in the middle covered his wide shoulders.

"Evan." He pointed a finger to his chest then turned it on me, raising his brow. "Kaylee?"

"Yes." He lifted his other brow in response and I word vomited, "Nice to meet you?"

He laughed, a sort of uncontrollable laugh that took over his whole body. I didn't see what was so funny so I huffed and bent down, picking the files up from the floor, all the while his laughed bounced off the office walls.

By the time I'd put the last files away and sat back down in my chair, I'd had enough of the sound. I hated being laughed at.

"What the hell are you laughing at?" It came out more abrupt that I meant it to, and for a second I regretted saying it; fearing what would come from speaking to a man like that. Then I reprimanded myself, because I haven't once felt unsafe here.

He stopped abruptly, tilting his head and taking

me in before slowly moving toward me. Keeping my eyes on him, I watched as he perched on the edge of the desk, his curious eyes assessing me.

From this close, I could see the swirls of gold mixed in with the darker honey tones in his eyes and I also got a closer look at his other features: his nose was straight, lips thin, but he was handsome in a quirky kind of way.

"Stop staring," I said through clenched teeth wanting nothing more than to shuffle nervously.

He didn't, instead he put his elbow on his knee and rested his chin on his hand as he continued to stare at me.

"Seriously," I huffed, my voice getting smaller. "Please stop staring."

"You look familiar," he commented.

"Do I?" I moved the mouse on the desk, bringing the screen to life. Although I hadn't got a clue what I was going to do on the computer, but it made me at least look like I was busy.

I'd finished all of the reports handed to me in the meeting this morning, and I'd organized the filing cabinet. There wasn't anything else to do but answer the phone, but considering it hadn't once rang since I started yesterday, I somehow knew that I wouldn't have much else to do.

"Yeah, you do." He tilted his head the other way. "Do I know you?"

"I don't think so."

Starting to feel even more uncomfortable at all of his attention, I stood up and walked out of the office toward the kitchen.

Coffee. That's what I needed.

I switched the machine on and reached into the cupboard for a cup.

"You want one?" I asked, knowing that Evan had followed me in. I remembered what Kitty had said that first day we met about at being aware of my surroundings; I was getting better at it.

"Sure."

I could feel his eyes on me as the coffee brewed but neither of us said a word.

"I don't think I do know you," he announced all of a sudden. I shook my head, picked up the first coffee and handed it to him. "I think I'd remember you if I did." He winked as he took the cup out of my hand.

"Excuse me?" I choked.

"And you would definitely remember me." His brows did a dance on his face, up and down, up and down.

"Ugh."

"What?"

Damn, did I say that out loud? I really, *really* needed to learn when to keep my mouth shut. For many years I had watched what I said, making sure to not say anything that was deemed "wrong." But two days into a new job and I couldn't seem to keep my mouth shut.

I could see that it was going to get me into trouble so I needed to keep reminding myself of the lessons I learned at to conceal how I was feeling and to not voice the thoughts in my head.

Corey always said that my mouth would get me into trouble one day: he was right. Those first few months after I first had Eli and Corey had gone back on tour were a nightmare. I never knew when to keep my mouth shut, always saying the wrong thing at the wrong time—or right time depending on whether you were me or Max.

I thought that I had control over it—my mouth. Evidently, I didn't.

"Sorry." I ducked my head, trying to paste on the mask that I had perfected.

"Hey."

Evan came forward and I saw his hand reaching up. Out of the corner of my eye. I tried my best not to flinch, but there was nothing I could do to stop the natural reaction. His hand stilled in the air, silence spreading between us.

I shuffled my feet on the spot, not knowing what to do or say and feeling like I just showed him a part of me that nobody knew about.

"Come with me." Bringing my eyes back up to his, I watched his back as he walked out of the kitchen and waved his arm at me to follow him. "Come on!" he shouted through the kitchen door when I still hadn't moved.

Taking a deep breath, my legs shuffled forward as I made my way into the main part of the warehouse. I stopped at the edge of the mats that took up the middle of the space toward the back where the gym equipment and Evan's desked sat.

Evan was rummaging through a small cupboard I'd never noticed before he lifted something in the air, shouting, "Aha!" Standing up, he walked toward me, over the training mats and came to a halt in the middle.

I stayed at the edge, not knowing what he was holding in his hands or what he was doing.

"Come on." He rolled his eyes, beckoning me forward.

My head swung left and right, but there was nobody else here: only me and Evan. *Where was everyone?*

Biting my lip, I decided that I didn't want to make him mad, so I moved toward him. When I came to a stop a couple of feet away from him, he held up both of his hands that were covered some sort of pads.

"Hit me," he demanded.

My eyes widened as I choked out, "What?"

He clapped the pads together, the sound echoing throughout the warehouse.

"I don't—"

"Go on," he taunted, "Like *Nike* say: Just do it."

I shook my head, taking a step back. "No, I don't want to."

"If you're gonna work here you're gonna need to at least be able to throw a punch."

"That—"

He huffed at me and moved closer. "Make a fist, thumb always on the outside."

I blew out a breath and did as he said. This was the most awkward thing that I had ever done. I'd never hit another person, I'd *never* wanted to inflict pain on another. I knew what it felt like to be hit—to be hurt—I didn't want anyone else to feel that.

"Now... hit the pads." I rolled my eyes and hit the pad softly to satisfy him.

He chuckled. "Really? That's all you got?"

My nostrils flare; that chuckle really got my back up so I hit the pad again, this time a little harder.

"That's it," he encouraged and started to move around in a circle. "Now with your left hand."

I hit the pad again and each time my knuckles made contact with it, I felt a little better—more confident.

"Woo! That one had some power behind it."

I smiled and hit the pad again. And again. And again. I never knew I could feel this way—this strong.

"Okay, Okay!" He backed away, hands held up in the air in surrender. "I think that's enough for today." He smirked, his eyes shining with something that looked like determination—but determination for what I wasn't sure of.

My gaze flicked down to my knuckles that were

red from where I had punched the pads. Evan moved closer having seemed to have followed where I was looking before he pulled the pads off his own hands.

"We'll get you some gloves. They'll protect your knuckles."

"Oh, I don't need gloves." I shook my head, already dismissing the idea.

He frowned. "Why?"

"Because I won't be doing that again."

"Kaylee," he said on a breath, shaking his head as he went back to the cupboard and placed the pads inside. "You'll be doing that regularly." He walked across the warehouse, pulling the door open and disappearing, not giving me a chance to correct him.

I didn't want to learn how to throw a punch—I didn't want to inflict pain on anybody.

But I couldn't deny the rush of adrenaline as I hit the pads with my knuckles, feeling like I have a little bit of control.

I GOT TO THE GATES THURSDAY MORNING AND clicked the button on the fob that Tyson had given me yesterday. I hadn't wanted to have responsibility over the security of the compound but he had insisted, saying that I needed to be able to get in and out as and when I was needed. It was a small fob that could be put on my keys, but I decided to hide it in the car instead. I couldn't risk Max seeing it, I'd never be able to explain what it was or where it gave me access to.

Max had been a different person this past week. He hadn't gone out for a drink after work every day, instead he came home and spent time with me and Eli. He may have only sat on the couch watching TV, but the fact that he was there and not out with his friends was a good thing.

I could feel things changing for the better. My job was going great and things at home were better than they had been in a long time. I was sure that if things carried on then I'd be able to tell Max about the job and that he'd be okay with it. Maybe he would even be proud that I was doing something with my free time and appreciate the extra money.

I parked in my usual spot on the compound and walked to the metal door, pulling on it but it wouldn't budge. I knocked on it for several minutes but no one answered. Looking around, I couldn't see anyone, but all of the cars were here so that meant that they had to be somewhere on the grounds.

Then I realized that they had all been on a surveillance mission. They probably didn't come back until really late.

I looked left then right, trying to decide what to do. Tyson had given me the key fob to open the gates but nothing to open the warehouse door. I decided I'd head towards the other side of the compound where the houses were to see if I could find anyone.

I walked across the gravel, getting closer to the buildings that sat at the back of the compound. The first day I could only see two, but now that I ventured closer I saw more. Two more to be exact.

The first was a wooden cabin and next to it was an average sized house covered in blue-gray siding. A little way back was a small cottage with flowers climbing up the outside walls and pots lining a small walkway up to the front door.

I swung my head at the sound of a door closing. The last house was the biggest and that was the one that someone had just excited. Tyson jogged down the steps and halted when he saw me. I flicked my eyes to him then looked back at the house. A swing sat on the wrap around porch, the siding white with dark-blue trim around the windows.

It was the kind of house that you only dreamed of, the kind that you wanted to make into a home, bake cakes, and sit on the porch to watch the sun go down or even the sunrise early in the morning with a cup of coffee and a pastry.

"There was no one in the warehouse," I blurted out when he approached me.

He walked past me and toward the warehouse. "Yeah, didn't get back until four this morning."

"How did it go last night?" I had to jog to keep up with him and his long strides.

"Good," he replied as he unlocked the metal door.

He held it open for me so I ducked under his arm

and went right to the kitchen to start the coffee machine. I heard his boots stop outside the kitchen briefly then carried on into the office.

When I walked into the office, I handed him a coffee where he was sitting on the couch. I made my way toward the desk and switched the computer on.

"Come sit."

I looked at him, unsure as he patted the seat and nodded to it.

"Over there?"

"Yeah." He rolled his eyes. "I'm not gonna bite."

I shuffled over to him and sat on the other side of the couch; a seat separated us but it was nowhere near enough space. Something about Tyson drew me to him, he exuded danger but at the same time screamed safety. He was a potent mix of both and it called to me in a way that I had never felt before.

"Let's talk."

"About what?" I raised a brow and turned to face him.

"Tell me about yourself." He drummed his fingers on his knees and I watched them as they tapped the same beat that he did every day. The way his long fingers tapped on his knee mesmerized me.

"What do you want to know?" I whispered, unsure.

"Anything." I looked up into his eyes, the chocolate brown depths held me captive.

"Well." I rubbed my hands down my legs. "I have a son."

"Yeah, you told me that already."

"Right." I cleared my throat and took a sip of my coffee "His name's Eli."

"You with his dad?"

"Excuse me?" My muscles locked and my back straightened as I reeled back. "Of course, I'm with his dad."

His eyes widened at my tone. "Whoa!" He held his hands out in front of him. "Just asking."

I closed my eyes, cursing myself for the way I spoke to him. "Sorry." I dipped my head down the apology coming out of my mouth automatically.

"Hey." The couch dipped next to me as he moved closer, and I took a deep breath as his aftershave wafted around me. "You don't need to apologize."

My cheeks heated from his stare as silence surrounded us.

He cleared his throat after a beat. "You heard from Corey lately?" I was thankful for the change of subject and jumped on it, afraid that he'd ask something else about my personal life.

"A couple of Saturdays ago." I looked up at him from under my lashes. "I don't know when I will again though."

"I know." He leaned back, his long legs stretched out in front of him. "It can be a long time between calls."

I forgot that he had done the same, that he had spent months at a time without talking to his family. I suddenly saw him in a new light. I'd only seen him as a boss, but now I could see him as Corey's friend, and it made me feel that much closer to Corey.

"Can you tell me about him." Tyson raised his brows. "Corey… what he was like over there."

"You miss him," he said it as a statement.

I nodded. "He's my only family. Apart from Eli."

Ty opened his mouth, closed it and shook his head.

"Please, Ty." I swallowed against the lump in my throat. "I haven't seen him for so many years and I haven't spoken to anyone else that knew him in such a long time."

His eyes flashed. "I like that."

"Like what?" I asked, confused.

"You calling me Ty."

"I did?"

"Yeah." He smiled at me, I hadn't meant to call him that but if felt so natural. The rest of the guys called him "Boss" but that didn't feel right coming out of my mouth.

He went on to tell me all of the pranks that Corey used to pull on people, how he was one of his best men in his unit as well as one of his best friends. I listened intently, and at some point, I leaned back and watched Ty talk.

His lips moved in time with his hands, every few

sentences he would chuckle at something then tell me what had made him laugh.

Then I started to tell him what Corey was like as a child; he laughed at some of the things we used to get up to. He especially liked it when I told him how we came up with our secret code. He leaned his head on the back of the couch, turned to face me and watched me the way I had with him.

It felt so easy to talk to him.

I made sure to only tell him the good parts, leaving out all of the bad things that had happened to us. Like when my mom died, which in turn caused my dad to change. He left us, preferring to sit with a bottle of whatever alcohol he could get his hands on. Even though he was there physically, he had left in every other way. Corey wasn't just my brother, he became my father, mother, and most of all, my best friend.

It wasn't until I heard the soft snores that I realized Ty had fallen asleep. I watched him for a couple of minutes, the way his full lips would move with each exhale. I followed the line of his nose, the slight crook in the middle where it must have been broken at some point. My fingers itched to reach out and see if the scruff on his face to see what it would feel like.

Closing my hands into fists and careful not to disturb him, I lifted up off the couch. I couldn't find anything to cover him with so I pulled my cardigan off. It flowed down to my knees so would work well as a small blanket. At least small for him anyway.

I caught sight of the bruises on my arms as I went to cover him, I didn't want anyone to see those. There'd be no disputing what they were so I shrugged my cardigan back on and looked around for something else to cover him with. Not being able to see anything I could use, I walked over to the desk instead.

I sat at the computer, determined to do something, but my attempts were futile. There was no meeting and no files to type up so I spent much of the next few hours watching Ty sleep.

Chapter Seven

IT WAS FRIDAY, the last day of my first week, and I felt fantastic. The job was amazing; if I'd known how much having a job would change my outlook on everything that I did, I would have gotten one sooner.

I came into work with a massive smile on my face because my morning had been great. Max had left me a note to say that he was taking me out tonight and Eli was looking forward to going to preschool. They were doing some sort of art project that he was super excited about. I didn't know exactly what it was but I'd be able to see it when I picked him up.

On my way inside, I hummed the tune that I'd been listening to in the car, my shoulders moving up and down to the beat that was sounding in my head.

I hung my jacket on the hook in the office and

then dropped my bag off at my desk. Pen and pad in hand, I continued to do a weird bopping dance combination as I went into the kitchen and switched the coffee pot on. Spotting Evan coming in out the corner of my eye, I smiled and he grinned as he moved his shoulders up and down in the same way that I was.

"What are we dancing to?"

"I don't know." I grinned.

He moved closer, his legs doing something different to his arms and I couldn't help but laugh at how silly he looked. He grabbed my hands, pulling me closer and moved us around in circles then out of the door and into the main part of the warehouse, laughing uncontrollably all the way.

He pulled me closer, his hand resting on the small of my back while his other held my hand and I asked, "You dance ballroom?" amazement clear in my voice.

"Yep," he replied, popping the p.

He sang as he led me across the floor, his voice deep and melodic: soothing to the soul.

We both had wide smiles stretched on our faces as he turned me in a circle again. This time my foot caught on the edge of the mat and I reached out, clutching onto Evan's arm, but it was of no use. I was falling.

I screamed and Evan's eyes popped wide then all too fast he spun us around and took the brunt of the fall.

"Ooof." I landed on his chest and Evan groaned as my face smacked off it.

There was two seconds of silence before we both burst out laughing. I pushed up on my hands and held myself over the top of him. I couldn't get myself under control, I was giggling like a schoolgirl. Lifting my hand to my face, I swiped away the tears that were streaming down my cheeks and Evan did the same. I couldn't remember the last time I'd laughed so hard.

"What. The. Fuck."

We stared at each other, both of us becoming silent as our eyes widened. Evan tried to scramble up and in the process knocked me over and I flailed around, landing on my shoulder awkwardly.

"Ugh."

"Evan!" Kitty admonished.

I couldn't face looking at all of them, I could feel their stares on me so I hid my face in the mat on the floor.

"It was all her fault!" Evan shouted at Kitty.

"Was not!" I shouted back, but it came out muffled thanks to the mat.

A large hand gripped my arm and pulled me up with one swift movement. My hands came out and landed on a hard chest. I swallowed, looking up into Ty's eyes; I don't know what I expected to see, but as they danced with amusement I let out a breath of relief.

"Kaylee," Ty said in an amused tone.

"Sorry," I automatically replied.

"What were you doing?"

Evan pointed at me. "She was dancing and you know I can't resist dancing."

"Evan," I warned.

"What?" he scoffed. "I'm the best dancer." He pointed both of his thumbs at his chest, his lip lifting into a smug grin.

I turned my attention back to Ty's hand that was still on my arm, feeling it as it burned through the sleeve of my shirt.

"Come on." He moved back a step, frowning down at his hand when he realized he was still holding it, before he shook his head and turned, walking away.

Evan winked as I walked past him. "Tattletale," I whispered to him.

He gasped, his hand flying to his chest and I shook my head at his theatrics, but couldn't wipe the smile off my face.

I grabbed my pad and pen from the kitchen and sat down at the meeting table. This was the first time I had been at a meeting with Evan so when I moved my eyes to him where he was pulling out the chair on the other end of the table, I just knew he was going to be trouble.

"Charlie said he's gonna take it from here." Ty said as they started to talk about the surveillance from the other night.

"Who's Charlie?" I asked

"My brother," Ty answered but didn't look at me.

It was then that I noticed the dark circles under his eyes and the tense set of his shoulders.

"He's a Sergeant with the local PD," Kitty supplied.

"Oh." Ty hadn't mentioned that he had a brother. He'd asked about me but I'd never asked him. Not that I thought he would have told me because he gave the impression that if he wanted you to know something then he would tell you, and if he didn't then... well, you were left in the dark.

I was given two files to type up: one from Kitty and one from Luke.

"Make sure you do it right," Luke said with a grimace.

"I will." I nodded. He didn't look impressed at all; he hadn't spoken two words to me since I started. I didn't know whether I had done something to offend him or whether he was like that all the time.

"Okay, guys. Get to work," Ty said, his head dropping into his hands.

I hesitated when they all moved; I couldn't leave him here without making sure that he was alright.

"You okay, Ty? You look tired."

"Yeah." He sighed. "I need a word."

"Okay." I swallowed and nodded, my hand winding around each other with nerves.

"I need you to take one of the company cars."

There was no way that I would be able to get away with having one of those cars. Max would find out for sure and it wasn't the right time to tell him yet. I was just starting to feel like myself again—my old self. I couldn't have it taken away from me, not now.

How the hell was I going to get out of this?

"I can't take one of those cars, Ty."

"You will," he warned.

"No really, Ty, I can't."

I tried to keep my walls up, but when it was just me and him, something always happened. They'd start to come crumbling down. I didn't know what it was, but I found it so hard to keep them in place.

He watched me with narrowed eyes for several seconds. The secrets kept piling up, and I honestly didn't know how much longer I would be able to not say anything. I swallowed, my throat dry, not willing to budge on this.

"Fine," he huffed. "But I'm putting a tracker on your car." I opened my mouth to protest, but he cut me off. "No argument." He stood and walked away, ending the conversation.

I sat there for several minutes, debating what to do —what to say. Would Max notice that there was a tracker on my car? And why did I need to have one in the first place?

"Why do I need one, Ty?" I asked several minutes later when I walked into the office.

"Upcoming case," is all he said and laid down on the couch.

He looked so tired and his eyes were already

drooping closed, so I decided that I'd drop it for now, but I wouldn't let it go altogether. I had to know what was going on.

"Why don't you go to sleep for a while?"

"Can't: need to work."

I shook my head and walked toward the desk before I sat down. "You'll be asleep soon anyway."

When he didn't answer, I looked over at him; his mouth hung open slightly as soft snores sounded in the room. Rolling my eyes, a smile lifted the corner of my lips.

I smiled gently, my eyes crinkling at the corners at the sight of him. Finally, I picked up the file that Luke had given me and got to work.

EVERYONE WAS IN AND OUT OF THE WAREHOUSE for the rest of the day so I didn't get a chance to see Ty on his own before I left. I said goodbye to Kitty and Evan then left to go and pick Eli up from preschool.

He stood waiting for me, and as soon as I walked in, he took my hand and dragged me over to his art project.

"Wow, that's really good, Eli."

I hadn't got a clue what it was; I moved my head side to side, trying to figure out what he had depicted. There was paint all over the place and the more I moved my head the more confused I was.

"You like it, Mama?" he asked, his voice unsure.

I looked down at him and smiled wide. Bending down next to him, I pulled him in for a hug. "It's fantastic!"

"Really?"

"Yeah!" I nodded enthusiastically.

"It's me and you." I looked back at it; now that he said what it was, I could kind of see it.

"It's for your office," he said when he pulled back and moved toward the painting.

"It's great isn't it," a soft voice said from behind me and I spun around. Miss Cooper stood behind us with her hands behind her back. My gaze drifted over her, taking in the paint splattered up the front of her apron.

"It is," I agreed.

She was a curvy woman with a soft, blond bob and she rocked the paint that was covering her front. Her kind face broke out into a dazzling smile as she turned and spoke to Eli. "You can take it home on Monday after it's had time to dry," she told him, ruffling his hair.

"Okay," he replied, his cheeks tinging red at her attention.

I held my hand out for Eli and turned around.

"Have a nice weekend," she chirped to the two of us as we walked out.

"You too," I said and led Eli out the doors.

Eli talked nonstop on the way home. He told me everything that he had done with Miss Cooper all day: I think he may even have a little crush on her.

It wasn't until we got in the apartment that I remembered Max was taking me out tonight. I looked down at my clothes, deciding to stay in these as he wouldn't know that I'd been wearing them all day.

I cooked Eli's dinner and sat with him on the couch while we watched cartoons, and that's how he fell asleep: tucked against my side. I'd been so busy this week and with Max being home every night that we hadn't had the time together like we normally did—just him and me.

I startled when the door slammed shut and loud footsteps sounded into the kitchen, so I quickly shuffled forward and picked Eli up.

Jeez. He was getting heavy.

The clock read nine p.m. and I guessed that meant we wouldn't be going out now. If I was honest, I was kind of relieved.

I carried Eli to bed and tucked him in then took a deep breath and walked out of his room.

He sneered when I walked into the kitchen and my stomach dipped. "Hey, baby."

"Hi, Max," I said tentatively before I turned the water on, filling the sink.

I washed the dishes from Eli's dinner, all the while feeling Max's eyes on me. I tried my best to ignore it while I did my tasks and when they were finishes, I opened the fridge, looking inside—mainly for a distraction.

"What do you want for dinner?" I asked with my head still in the fridge.

"What do I want for dinner?" he slurred.

"Yes."

A hand grabbed my arm in the exact place that Tyson had earlier in the day but this touch was much rougher. I shivered and not in the same way that Ty's touch had made me shiver.

"Ouch, Max, you're hurting me. Let go." I moved my arm, but his grip tightened.

"You telling me what to do?" He pulled me closer to him then pushed me back, causing the fridge door to slam shut.

His nose touched mine as he pushed his face closer to me and his green eyes swirled with anger. There were times like this that I wished I couldn't read him so easily when he was angry. It was the only time that I knew what would happen—*the only time I could read him*.

"Answer me!" he roared, spittle flying on my face.

"No, Max, I'm not telling you what to do."

"Tut. Tut." He shook his head and backed away a couple of inches but still kept his hands grasped on my arms.

"I'm sorry, Max." It was an automatic answer when it came to him.

His brows lifted and he let me go. I sagged against the fridge and blew out a breath, but was on alert as he backed away laughing.

I couldn't help but compare it to the laughter that came from Evan. This one was sinister and cruel. He wasn't laughing with me: he was laughing *at* me.

All of a sudden, he flew forward and gripped my head in his hands then spun me around before he slammed my face against the fridge door.

"This is for not having my dinner ready."

"But—" I was cut off when he pulled my head back and slammed into the fridge door a second time.

Pain exploded across my face, wetness trickling down past my eye and rolling onto my cheek. He pulled me back again by my hair, my scalp burning from the force. My mouth opened on a silent scream that I wouldn't allow past my lips, knowing it would only make things worse.

"This one is for not keeping your mouth shut."

He slammed my face into the door a third time.

"You're so selfish," he gritted out. "For making me do this."

He pulled me back and slammed my face into the fridge again, only this time he used twice the force than he had before, then let go. I was sure that he had broken something.

I sobbed at the pain and slumped down the fridge, smearing blood down the front of it.

I kept my head down, not wanting to make things any worse. The first drop of blood landed on the floor, followed by a second drop mixed in with tears as they slid down my face.

"So sick and tired of this," he muttered as he walked away. "You'll never learn."

His boots thudded on the tiled floor, then the carpet in the hallway. The slam of the front door followed him out.

I agreed with him.

I was sick and tired of this too.

Chapter Eight

As soon as I woke up the next morning, the first thing I felt is the throbbing in my eye. I felt like I had the worst hangover in the existence of hangovers. Lifting my head off the pillow, I pushed myself up off the bed, knowing that if I didn't get up right away, all I'd want to do was stay in bed and hide away from the world—from reality.

Shuffling into the kitchen, I started the coffee machine and pushed the door to the living room open, relieved that Max wasn't in there.

He was the last person that I wanted to see right now.

I made my coffee, taking a small sip of the bitter liquid as I walked to the bathroom, needing to do something with my eye before Eli woke up and saw it.

I hadn't checked it the night before, afraid that it would be my undoing. Instead, I went right to bed and cried myself to sleep for what felt like the hundredth time. I'd probably cried enough to fill a flowing river at this point.

Taking a deep breath, I lifted up onto my tiptoes, pushing my face up into the mirror to get a closer look.

My whole eye was swollen with a gash underneath my eyebrow, all covered in a horrible green and purple bruise mixed with dried blood. I dipped my head, not wanting to see it, reasoning that if I couldn't see it then I could pretend it wasn't there.

I turned away, stepping into the shower, needing a reprieve before I tackled covering it. As the water flowed over my body, I thought about what had happened last night. On any other day, I'd know what I'd done to cause Max's anger, but last night was different.

If anyone should have been annoyed, then it should have been me: he was the one who was meant to take us out last night.

Cursing myself as I laid my hand on the tiled wall, I shook my head. I should have known to tread carefully when he came home slurring. It was always worse when he'd been drinking. It did something to him: made him have a short fuse.

I believed when he told me he blacked out when he hurt me because the man that would relish in causing me pain wasn't the man that I knew for last five years ago.

Stepping out of the shower, I wrapped a towel around my body and wiped at my eye with some cotton wool pads. The cut opened, and I stared as the drop of blood trickled down my face. It made it all the way to my chin before I caught it with the cotton pad.

After staring at the bright red that had expanded on the pad, I finally shook myself out of it and rummaged through the cupboard for the first aid kit. I cleaned the cut with some antiseptic and applied some butterfly stitches before cleaning the dried blood around the area as best as I could.

I huffed out a breath; it looked better than it had, but there would be no way to disguise it. My gaze tracked over my arms, the faint bruises having nearly disappeared. That was where the marks and bruises normally were: he'd never hurt my face before, it was always somewhere that I could cover up easily. I frowned; something had changed.

The sound of Eli's bed squeaking alerted me to him waking up so I pushed the first aid kit back quickly, just in time to see him walk down the hallway and past the bathroom.

"Morning, sweetie!" I called as he went past.

"Mornin', Mama," he mumbled back.

I went into the bedroom, threw a t-shirt and leggings on and went to make his breakfast. I hadn't got anything planned today apart from visiting with Miss Maggie and I hadn't seen her since I told her that I got the job.

I cleaned the apartment while Eli ate his breakfast, glad that I could get it done without Max being here. I hadn't had much of a chance to clean it to Max's liking with working all week, and at that thought, I stumbled. *Maybe that's why he was like that last night?*

Shaking my head, I continued cleaning, scrubbing surfaces extra hard and dusting everything in sight. I'd make sure I did better from now on.

Once I'd finished and put all of the products away, I walked into the living room. "Come on, sweetie, let's get you dressed."

"But, Maaaaaaa, I'm watching this," he groaned. I stood in front of the TV and watched his head moved from left to right, trying to see past me.

"Now, Eli." He huffed and crossed his arms. "Come on, we'll go to Miss Maggie's." I smiled.

His eyes widened and he shot up off the couch. There was nothing that got him moving more than the prospect of seeing those damn cats. I wasn't really a cat kind of person, dogs were more my thing, not that Max ever let me have one because he hated them.

I watched Eli brush his teeth in the bathroom, then let him pick his clothes for the day. I smiled at the odd combination of a pair of shorts and a winter sweater, but one of my favorite things to do was to see what he would choose to wear on the weekends.

"Let's go, Mama!" he called on his way to the door.

I followed him out the apartment and went over to Miss Maggie's. Eli headed for the couch as soon as we were inside. He hadn't even sat down before the cats jumped up to him.

When I looked up at the TV I saw the same cartoon that Eli had been watching not fifteen minutes ago.

"Hi, dear!" Miss Maggie waved, not bothering to turn toward me as she was just as engrossed in the TV as Eli was. I'd never seen anyone watch cartoons the way that she did. At least not anyone over the age of twelve.

I made us tea like usual, cursing myself for not thinking to bring over some coffee again before I picked up both cups and sat down on the couch next to Eli.

My mind wandered as I sat there with them, not a word spoken in the room as they both stared wide eyed at the cartoon. I couldn't help but wonder what the guys at the compound would get up to today. Did they have weekends off? I'd never thought to ask.

I found that I missed seeing Ty's face and listening to Evan's silly jokes. I'd tried to tell Eli one the other day but he looked at me like I was losing my mind. I think there was a way that they should be told and I obviously didn't do them justice, but Evan always got it spot on.

I hadn't been able to talk to Kitty much this last

week, but she told me that she wouldn't be as busy next week so we could sit and chat. I smiled at I thought about that: I'd never had a *real* girlfriend.

I'd had plenty of girls who wanted to pretend to be my friend so they could get closer to my brother; little did they know that he disliked them even more when they did that. I was the one person at school who never fit into any of the cliques. I wasn't smart enough for the nerds, too cheery for the goths, not cheery enough for the cheerleaders and not popular enough for the "in" crowd.

"What the hell happened to your face?" Miss Maggie practically shouted.

"Jeez, you scared me," I croaked, my hand flying to my chest.

She raised her brows at me and I moved my eyes toward Eli, knowing that his little ears heard everything.

"I fell." The lie rolled right off my tongue with such ease that it scared me a little.

Her face told me that she didn't believe me, but she knew that there was nothing else that I would say.

That I *could* say.

"So... I finished my first week at work," I said, trying to change the subject.

It would only work for so long, but either way she knew that she wouldn't get an explanation as to what had happened.

I spent the entire meeting on Monday morning with my head down, my face half covered strategically by my hair. The bruise was even darker now after two days of it coming to the surface, and no amount of makeup I tried to put on would cover it. *At least I'd been able to take the butterfly stitches off, that was a plus.*

Max had come home late last night while I was in bed and I had panicked because I the last time I had seen him was Friday. I didn't get up to go and see him —I couldn't because my body wouldn't allow me— instead, I stayed where I was and spent most of the night awake, waiting until he left this morning.

Just the thought of seeing his face made me feel sick to my stomach.

Unlike last week, when everyone would scuttle off to whatever jobs they needed to do, Evan and Kitty stayed at the table talking. Luke headed for the gym equipment and Ty leaned back in his chair looking through some files.

I took my chance to go unnoticed and fled to the office. I turned the chair to the side when I sat down, knowing that the right side of my face couldn't be seen from this angle as I started typing the files up, trying to keep my mind busy to stop my warring thoughts.

"You good?" Ty asked when he came in half an hour later.

"Mmmhmm." I clicked save on the computer and opened up a new blank document.

"Kay?"

I winced at his tone, the subtle undertone to his voice making me on edge. "Yes?"

"Look at me."

I started to type, hitting random keys as I had nothing to actually type up and then I clicked the mouse a few times, making it look like I was doing something important. The vibe emanating off him told me that he knew something was wrong, but I didn't want to have this conversation: I didn't want to lie again. Not to him.

The sound of the door clicking shut echoed around the room, but I felt him rather than saw him move closer to me.

"Kay?" He breathed my name this time, a pleading edge to it. I moved my gaze to the side, watching as his hands landed on the desk and he leaned down in front of me.

"Ty." Click. Click, click, click. Just carry on typing.

"Look. At. Me"

I swallowed at his gruff town before sighing as I realized that I couldn't hide away from him forever.

"Here's the thing," I started as I moved my hands from the keyboard and held them out in front of me. "I fell over Friday night. And...well... you see—"

I turned then, and his eyes zoned in on my eye

light a beacon calling out to him. His jaw clenched as he pulled his hands from the desk and stood to his full height.

"You fell over?" he gritted out.

"Yeah, you know what it's like, right? You're standing one minute then the next thing you know you're face down on the floor." I laughed, the sound shrill to my own ears.

He scanned my face, searching for the truth so I quickly slammed my wall up and was successful this time.

"It happens all the time, you should have seen the amount of bruises I had as a child." I rolled my eyes, wincing at the pain it caused.

I just hoped that he didn't mention it to Corey, knowing that he had gone dark again was a relief in itself. By the time Ty would talk to him he'd have probably forgotten all about it. *I hoped.*

We stayed like that—him watching me, me keeping my wall in place—for what felt like hours. In reality, it was only a couple of minutes.

He narrowed his eyes at me and I smiled at him.

"Right," he finally said. The set of his jaw told me that he didn't believe me one single bit, but there was no way I'd tell him the truth.

"You remember last week when I fell over with Evan?" I shrugged and fidgeted in my seat. "I've always been the same."

He sat down, his head in his hands, his body vibrating with an emotion I didn't understand.

"How was your weekend?"

"Changing the subject?" He looked up at me with a slight smile on his face.

"Not at all." I smiled back. "Do you work weekends?" I asked, genuinely curious.

"What?" His smile grew even more.

"I was thinking..." I leaned forward. "Do you work weekends? You know like go out and be all bad ass?"

"Bad ass?"

"Uh-huh."

He shook his head and chuckled. "Come on, let's go." He headed for the door.

"Go where?" He grabbed his jacket and turned to look back at me with a smirk kicked up on one side of his face.

"Out." He opened the door. "We're not done talking about this, by the way." He pointed to my eye before he walked out of the room and into the warehouse.

I scrambled after him, grabbing my own jacket and purse as I went.

"Evan get the phone if it rings," Ty rumbled.

"What? Why? That's Kaylee's job."

"Ah, don't whine Evan." I pinched his cheek when I walked past him.

"What the—"

"Kay let's go." I looked up at Ty and furrowed my brow at the clenching of his jaw as he watched me.

I rushed forward, ducked under his arm that held the metal door open and waited for him. He walked to the big, black SUV, its rims a matte black and every window tinted. I pulled the door open when the lights flashed, placed my foot on the little step and grabbed the OS handle.

"You okay there, sweetheart?" Ty asked from behind me.

From right behind me.

I turned to find him holding back his laughter and rolled my eyes. It must have been so funny to watch me struggle to get up into this beast of a thing.

"Me and this OS handle got it. Thanks." I jumped into the seat—literally jumped—and Ty closed the door behind me.

I watched him round the front of the car and get inside the driver's side with ease.

"OS handle?" he asked when he turned the key in the ignition.

"Oh. Shit."

"What?"

"Oh. Shit."

He turned his head to me, brows furrowed as his chocolate eyes assessed me.

"The. Oh. Shit. Handle"

"Oh right."

"No." I shook my head, smirking. "Oh. Shit."

"Ha, funny." He rolled his eyes at me then reversed out of the spot. The gates opened up and then we were driving down the private road that led to the compound.

I felt giddy with excitement because I'd never been out of the compound with one of them before. I had to stop myself from bouncing in the seat on several occasions.

"So, what are we doing?"

"Just a quick surveillance thing."

I clapped my hands at that. The thought of watching people who had no idea they were being watched excited me.

Ty stayed silent most of the fifteen-minute drive while I talked nonstop. I told him all about my weekend—minus the Max thing. Eli and I had painted a picture on Sunday, my side was neat whereas Eli's had been a big blob of about ten different colors all mixed together. The result was a dark gray kind of color—it always ended up that way.

"And when I picked him up on Friday, he painted me a picture for the office," I said.

"Yeah?" He pulled the car to a stop on a little side road.

"Would it be okay to put it up in there?"

"Sure." He turned the ignition off, his eyes never leaving the house a few doors down.

"What are we looking for?" I whispered.

"We need to wait until he leaves and then follow him," he whispered back.

"Okay, what does he look like?"

He handed me a photo. The man looked like any other ordinary man, nothing distinct about him. He wore a beige shirt and brown tie in the photo, old glasses sat on his round face complete with a receding hairline.

"What are we watching for?"

"I think he has something to do with an underground ring."

"What like under the ground?"

He cut his eyes to me. "Seriously?"

"What?"

"It's not actually *under* the ground." He shook his head then looked back at the house.

"I know that."

"And why the fuck are we still whispering?"

I laughed then, I had no idea why we were still whispering.

Ty smiled at me and the sight took my breath away as butterflies swarmed in my stomach; I had to turn away to try and stop them. It was happening more often than I'd like to admit, but it didn't mean anything. I could have this innocent feeling over a good looking man, right?

"There he is." I pointed.

Ty waited until he had left in his car, then turned the key in the ignition.

"Ready?" He raised his brows.

"As I'll ever be." I clutched my seatbelt, trying to hold in all of the bubbling excitement at feeling like I was a part of this team.

Chapter Nine

THE NEXT COUPLE of days flew by. Ty continued to take me out on a couple of jobs, and yesterday he had even let me take some photos. It was something that I'd never thought I'd enjoy, but I did. The photos had come out okay, I wouldn't be a professional anytime soon but Ty was pleased with them so that was all that mattered.

We'd spent most of the last couple of days just the two of us while we watched other people. I got to know him a little better and we found that we both loved people watching. I told him that I couldn't stand to do any sort of exercise and he told me that he had to do it every day or he felt like something was missing.

It would explain his big muscles, not that I was complaining. I found myself smiling more and more being around him, especially as he started telling me some more stories about Corey, but after the first day he told me more about himself.—those ones I paid special attention to.

He said that it had never been a question of joining the Special Forces; he'd wanted to for as long as he could remember. I admired him for how hard he had worked to get to where he was today. He asked a couple of times what Eli and Max were like and I told him story after story about Eli. But never anything about Max.

I knew that he noticed but I brushed it off like it didn't matter, and it didn't. I wanted to keep my two worlds separate, the less they knew about Max the better.

By the time we got back to the compound it was time for me to leave to pick Eli up.

"I'll see you tomorrow." I turned in my seat where we were parked outside of the warehouse, facing Ty.

Ty's eyes met mine, and I stared into his chocolate orbs—there was something hidden in their depths that I couldn't quite make out. A gentle smile lifted the corners of his mouth as he whispered, "You're incredible, you know that?"

I snorted. "Yeah. Okay." I reached for the door handle.

"No." His hand wrapped around my arm, soft but firm. "Really."

I faced him, brows raised. "Oh yeah?" I swallowed

past the lump forming in my throat. "What's so incredible?"

"I don't know." He shrugged. "There's just something about you that—" He shook his head as he let go of my arm but I could still feel the burn his large, calloused hand.

His expression was torn, like he wanted to say something but thought better of it. I leaned back in my seat and watched his fingers as they started to drum on the steering wheel. I'd noticed that he had several different "finger drums."

The first was a relaxed one, he did this mostly when we were in the office. The second one was a little faster, mainly when he watched someone, or was thinking about something.

The third—the one he was doing now—was a new one. Erratic.

"Ty," I whispered.

He faced me, his eyes full of confusion and we stayed like that for several more minutes. Staring into each other's eyes, neither of us moving a single inch.

"Kay," he said on a breath, his gaze dipping to my lips and back to my eyes.

I was entranced, I couldn't move even if I wanted to. There was nothing but us, nothing else existed in this moment.

He moved forward, his tongue tracing along his bottom lip and I watched it slide out, imagining how it would feel to have his lips touch mine. Would they be as soft as they looked?

My phone buzzed with my alarm, making me jump as it signaled that it was time to pick Eli up.

I stared wide eyed at him, my chest heaving as I tried to catch my breath, then I scrambled to get out of the car.

"Kay," Ty reached for me but I dodged him, nearly falling out of his stupid SUV.

"I'm sorry," I croaked.

What was I thinking? How had I forgotten all about Max and Eli?

I stumbled to my car and tried to get the key in the lock three times before I could finally pull the door open. I heard his boots crunch against the gravel as he moved toward me as I yanked it open.

I started the car just as he came into sight. Pushing into reverse, I drove out of there as fast as I could.

My hands shook most of the way to pick Eli up as I remembered the look on his face and the feelings flowing through me. That was the worst part: I'd wanted him to kiss me.

I tried to tell myself that it was because I hadn't been kissed in so long, at least not the way I wanted to be kissed, but that wasn't the truth. The truth was that I had just wanted to feel his lips against mine, to find out how it would feel when his hands cupped my face, whether I would shiver at the contact and move closer.

My mind whirled with thoughts the whole way to

the preschool and by the time I pulled up in the lot, I couldn't even remember how I got there: it was all a blur.

"Did you have a nice day?" I asked Eli once we were on our way back to the apartment.

"Yeah." He looked out the window. "Can we go to the park?"

I checked the time.

"Not today, sweetie, maybe Saturday?"

"Okay."

He looked upset, but I knew if I asked him, he wouldn't tell me. There was no pushing Eli, if I pushed too hard he'd clam up and I'd never know what was wrong so it was best to let him come to me. He'd talk about it when he was ready.

We were both silent the rest of the way. My thoughts wouldn't stop churning around and around in my head. Round and round like a merry-go-round that just wouldn't stop.

Maybe I had imagined the whole thing? I couldn't see what someone like him would see in someone like me. Either way, he didn't know the real me.

The broken me. The *liar*.

How could he think I was incredible? I was far, far from it.

I'd told so many lies over the last couple of years that sometimes I didn't know whether they were lies or actually the truth.

The only thing that made me get up in the

morning was Eli, without him I honestly didn't know what I would have done. I was so far from the person who I used to be, it felt like someone else's life that I would remember. That fun, bubbly, girl was a distant memory. One I feared I'd never get back.

"Mama?"

"Hmm?"

"Why is Dad here?"

I snapped my head to the side as I pulled up outside of our apartment block. "I... I don't know, sweetie," I stammered. My heartbeat picked up as I started to panic, staring wide eyed at him as I turned the car off.

Max stood against his car, one knee bent, his boot on the front bumper as he watched us. His posture was stiff and his eyes narrowed but when they met mine he smiled and pushed up off his car, walking toward us as I turned the engine off.

I slid out of the car and walked around to the back before I undid Eli's belt.

"Hey, baby." He flung his arm around my shoulders after I closed the door and steered me toward the apartment. I held my hand out for Eli, his little hand clutched mine the same way that I clutched his—like we were each other's lifelines.

"Been somewhere nice?"

"Huh?" I looked down and my eyes widened even more. "Oh, no. I... just thought I'd try something new."

I hadn't even thought about him seeing my work clothes.

"Mmmhmm, if I didn't know you better, I'd say you've been somewhere today." My throat went dry as he held the door open and I kept my head down, not daring to make eye contact with him. I walked behind Eli up the stairs, Max following behind us. "But I know you wouldn't do that, would you?" I shook my head as we turned to the next set of stairs. "You're a good girl, and good girls listen."

I held my hands behind Eli as he stumbled. "Careful, sweetie"

"*Don't they*," he murmured in my ear.

"Yes," I croaked.

He stayed silent the rest of the way up and that made me more nervous than him talking.

It was on the tip of my tongue to ask him why he was home because he never came home this early, but I knew better than to question him so I kept my mouth closed and walked up to the apartment.

"Can I watch TV?" Eli asked when I opened the door.

"Yes, of course you can, sweetie." I followed him into the living room and switched it on.

I walked into the kitchen and flitted my gaze to him where he stood against the counter as I opened the fridge to see what I could cook for dinner. Max was never here when I cooked dinner, it felt so wrong for him to be here at this time in the day.

"Let's go out."

"What?" I asked, turning toward him.

"I wanna take you out." He took two steps toward me and wrapped his arms around my waist from behind before he nuzzled his face into my neck.

Flashbacks from a week ago when he pushed me against the fridge assaulted my mind and my muscles tensed. The swelling had gone down but the bruise was still there. Max hadn't even mentioned it, not that I expected him to. I reasoned that he probably didn't even remember doing it in the first place.

"What about a babysitter?" I asked.

"That old bat down the hall can watch him."

"Max." I spun around, a pleading look on my face. "Please don't call her that."

His eyes flashed a warning and I swallowed, cursing myself for talking out of turn again. "Just go and ask her." He stepped back, tapped my butt and walked out of the kitchen.

I heard the pipes groan a couple of seconds later as he turned the shower on and let out a slow breath. *Guess we were going out.*

I STUMBLED TOWARD THE DOOR UNSURE OF whether this was a good thing or not. Max had never hidden the fact that he couldn't stand Miss Maggie watch Eli so had never suggested that she watch him.

Nerves flowed through me as I walked through the small hallway toward her door. I winced, not wanting to think about how he would react if he found out that we didn't just talk to each other in passing. Punishment was sure to take place if he did.

I rapped my knuckles on Miss Maggie's door and opened it. "Miss Maggie?"

"In here, dear."

I shut the door behind me and twisted my fingers around themselves. "You okay?" I asked when I walked in the living room.

"Yes, of course." She narrowed her eyes and tilted her head. "Are you okay?"

"Well, erm... the thing is..." I sat on the edge of the couch, taking a deep breath, trying to work out what was going on tonight and the change in Max. Was it a good thing he was taking me out? If it was then why did I have a sinking feeling in my stomach?

She rolled of her eyes good naturedly. "Spit it out."

"Could you watch Eli for a couple of hours?" I blurted, looking around at anything but her. I spotted Henry as he trotted into the room from the hallway. He stared at me for a beat before he looked at the door, settling down as he sat watching it intently.

"Sure."

"Max wants to take me out and he suggested I ask you to watch Eli," I rambled on, knowing that I didn't need to tell her but wanting to voice it out loud.

"That's nice." She patted my hand and I looked up

at her. Her eyes flashed. "You sure that everything's okay?"

I stared at her, my mouth opening and closing like a fish. I wanted to tell her that everything was changing. That my world no longer revolved around Max and Eli, that since I'd been working nothing felt the same—*nothing looked the same.*

I wanted to confess that the thought of spending time alone with Max terrified me, and that I didn't want to live the way anymore. I wanted to feel like I was doing something good in my life and not just waiting around for Max to correct me when I did something wrong.

I wanted more than the existence I have now.

And Ty... I didn't want to think about the effect he was having on me.

But the fact of the mater remained: he was all I could think about.

I shook my head, closed my mouth with a snap and stood.

There was no way that I would tell her any of that, instead I said, "Everything is fine."

She hesitated, her lips in a grim line. "If you're sure."

"I am." I smiled.

"Do you want to bring Eli over here?"

"Yes, I'll give him some dinner before I bring him over."

I kissed her cheek and let myself out, knowing that

if I stayed any longer I'd let everything out that was swirling inside of me.

Max was sitting next to Eli on the couch when I came back from Miss Maggie's. He waved me off and told me to go and make Eli something to eat. I hesitated but when Eli smiled at me, I left them to it. It was nice to see them spending time together, even if it was just watching TV. *It was normal.*

They didn't get the chance often; more times than not Eli was in bed when Max came home and Max... well, he was normally too drunk to care.

When Eli was a baby, Max had doted on him but as the years went by, something changed. Max barely talked to him now, and as much as I wanted them to have a good relationship, I couldn't help but feel like it was better that Max was distant with him.

There was less of a chance that Eli would do something wrong.

I made Eli his dinner, sat in the kitchen while he ate it, and then took him to get changed.

"Eli?" I pulled out some pajamas as he came into his bedroom.

"Yeah, Mama?"

I sat on the edge of his bed and blew out a breath. The strange feeling in the pit of my stomach became more intense.

"You be good for Miss Maggie, okay?"

"I will, Mama."

He pulled on his pajamas, shoved his feet into his

slippers and waited while I gathered up his blanket off the end of his bed.

"I'm just going to take Eli over," I said to Max as I walked by him in the hallway.

"Okay, baby." He smiled and winked.

I pulled my lips up into a small smile before taking Eli's hand.

Henry was still sat in the same place when we walked in and he jumped straight up onto Eli's lap as soon as he sat down.

"Thanks for doing this, Miss Maggie."

"Hush now, child, you know I love to spend time with Eli." She waved her hand at me.

I loved that Eli had someone that resembled a grandma. Sure, he had Max's parents' but he hardly saw them, and my dad hadn't even met him.

"I'll see you later." I planted a kiss on Eli's head and walked out of the living room.

The door clicked shut behind me, but I didn't have time to make it back to our apartment before Max came out of our door.

His blue polo shirt and jeans told me that we weren't going anywhere fancy—not that I had expected that. His dark hair was still wet from his shower and slicked back.

His eyes held something that had my stomach dipping and my hands shaking—a promise of some kind that I couldn't help but worry about.

Max extended his hand and I placed mine in his

slowly. He held on tight and I was sure that he noticed I was shaking but he didn't mention it, not even when he let go as I opened up the passenger door when we got to the car. I was thankful that he didn't because I wouldn't have been able to explain why my nerves were getting the better of me.

"So, where are we going?" I asked as he started the car.

He turned his head and grinned big and wide. "It's a surprise."

I hated surprises and he knew that.

I turned away as he drove off from the apartment block.

It wasn't until fifteen minutes later that I recognized where we were. I took the same route to work each day, passed the same row of shops and turned at the private road that he just drove past. There was no way that Max could have known that I had a job. I'd been really careful; today had been the only time he had seen me in what I wore for work.

He drove for another couple of minutes after going past the compound before he pulled into the parking lot of a bar called "Barney's."

I kept my mouth shut, but he must have seen the questions on my face because he said, "A buddy told me about this place," as he got out of the car.

I nodded but stayed silent as he led us inside. We walked through the dark wooden doors and the smell of food wafted around me making my stomach grumble.

The right side of the room was set up with pool tables, a bar ran across the back wall and seating spread all around.

People were eating and laughing, the atmosphere alive. The corner of my mouth lifted as a waitress showed us to our seats.

She sat us on the far side, farthest away from the bar and asked, "Can I get you something to drink?"

"Water please," I said as Max grunted, "Beer."

I bit my lip to keep from saying something, held up the menu and scanned what there was.

"Wings are meant to be good here," Max said. "My buddy says they're the best in a fifty-mile radius."

"That's nice," I replied, not quite sure what to say.

The waitress came back with the drinks, placed them on the table and pulled out a small pad.

"Are you ready to order?"

"I'll have the burger, side of wings."

"Burger as well please," I requested before I handed her the menu. Her fingers closed around the edge of it as goose bumps spread along my arms.

I swallowed at feeling like I was being watched, and when she moved, walking toward what I assumed was the kitchen, my eyes scanned the room. I felt him before I saw him, and when my eyes connected with his chocolate brown ones, my breath left my body.

Ty.

Chapter Ten

My shaking hands fluttered up to my throat as his eyes narrowed. I couldn't move; couldn't look away. He stepped forward, and for a second I wanted him to come over to me, to talk to me in the only way he could. He had this way of calming me.

Then I came to my senses. Ty was here... in the same room as Max. I panicked and shot up from the table causing the drinks to topple. I reached for my glass of water at the same time that Max grabbed his beer.

"What the—"

"Just going to the..." I looked around for any excuse. "Bathroom." I walked off before he could reply.

I had to walk past the bar to get to there.

Ty watched every step that I took, his eyes warmed me in a way that wasn't good—I knew that but I couldn't stop myself from basking in the feeling. He smirked, his eyes flashing. I had a feeling that I knew what it meant and I honestly didn't know if I could hold myself back this time.

It was wrong to feel anything for somebody other than Max, but I couldn't help it. I couldn't stop the way my heart had started to beat harder when I was around Ty or the way my lips would lift of their own accord when he was looking at me.

I already felt like I was living two lives: one with Max, and one at work. I wore a mask in front of everyone there—a mask that I had perfected. But Max was the only one who saw the true me: the broken me; the bad me. I wasn't a good person; I knew that and so did Max. He was the only one who told me the truth, who was honest with me, but it didn't stop me wanting to feel like more than I was. Ty would give that to me, he'd make me feel like a good version of myself while I hid the bad.

I tilted my head at Ty as I walked past, hoping he would follow but not talk until we were out of sight. I was halfway down the darkened hallway when his hand gripped my arm and he shoved me through a door.

Mops and cleaning supplies were strewn about, the smell of bleach stinging my nose.

"What are you doing here?" Ty asked, his voice low and throaty.

"Max brought me out." I shrugged, daring to glance up at him.

"No, Kay. What are *we* doing here?" He pointed at the floor.

I couldn't bring myself to tell him what was actually going on—the half of me I kept hidden. I didn't want him to think less of me. If I told him, I didn't know what he would do. I'd only worked with him for two weeks and I hadn't once seen him angry. I hated the thought that I could be on the receiving end of his anger.

"Ty..." I stepped back, my instincts kicking in.

I didn't want him to know I had lied. What would he think if he knew that one lie out of my mouth always turned into another and then another? That was the thing with lying: to cover the first lie you had to lie again and again. It was a vicious circle that had no end in sight.

Having a good memory was a must because if you couldn't remember what you'd lied about in the first place then you would slip up, revealing yourself.

"The thing is..."

Ty smirked, he could see how uncomfortable I was, but it wasn't only because I was about to lie *again*. It was being stuck in such a small space with Ty. He sucked all the air out of the room with his presence, making me feel both hot and cold at the same time—out of control.

"Yeah," he drawled, his feet moving toward me. I couldn't move, mesmerized by his eyes and the gold flecks that flashed as the light hit them.

"The thing..." I gasped as his hand cupped the side of my face.

I couldn't concentrate when he was touching me. My stomach dipped, my skin alight. I felt alive when he touched me, like he'd just brought me back to life with that one single touch.

"You're so beautiful," he whispered.

He moved closer, not one part of his body touched mine only his hand on my face but I was already coming undone. I had to dip my head back to look at him from this close.

"All I've been able to think about is you..." He closed the last bit of space. "And those lips..."

I wanted to tell him that was all I had been able to think about as well. That I couldn't get the image of his lips touching mine out of my head.

Three seconds. That's how long we stood and stared at each other, neither of us moving. It was the longest three seconds of my life.

Then his lips slammed down onto mine.

He was firm but gentle at the same time, kissing me once; twice, before his tongue swept along my bottom lip. It made me dizzy with desire and I couldn't hold back any longer. I needed to do this. Just this once. If I got it out of my system, then maybe I'd be able to move on.

I opened my mouth and swiped my tongue against his, he groaned in response and pulled me tighter against him. His hand slid down my back and gripped my ass. His hand spanning wide, his fingertips grazing me in my most intimate part.

I couldn't stop the moan from slipping between my lips. It spurred him on even more as he spun us around and pushed me against the door, his whole body flush against mine.

I couldn't get enough of him, of his lips, and definitely not his tongue.

He pulled back, his forehead resting against mine as we both panted for breath.

"I had to," he pleaded.

He leaned back, his eyes scanning my face. I didn't know what he was looking for, but when he nodded to himself, he seemed to get the answer.

"What were you saying?" he asked.

I couldn't remember my own name after that and he wanted to know what I was saying?

"About Max?" he prompted.

Shit. Max.

I opened my mouth but the lie wouldn't come out. It had always been easy: they would flow out of my mouth without a second thought.

But now, as Ty stared at me, I couldn't get the

words out. They were stuck in the back of my throat, refusing to come forward.

"It's okay." He pulled back and adjusted his jeans. "I won't come over to you."

I sagged with relief. I couldn't have my two worlds collide. I needed my job for my own sanity but if I had to choose, it would have to be Max. I didn't want to have to make that choice.

I swallowed against the dryness in my throat. "I'm gonna go."

"You don't have—"

"Sweetheart." He cupped my face again, his rough callouses rubbing against my soft cheek. "There's no way I can sit across the room and watch him touch you, not after..."

I nodded, solemnly, causing his hand to drop back down to his side. I didn't understand completely but I was grateful.

"I'll see you tomorrow?"

"Yeah." I didn't look back at him as I walked out. If I did, I wouldn't have been able to leave that room.

I opened the door, looked both ways and went over to the ladies' restroom.

It wasn't until I saw my swollen lips and hair that what was a mess that I realized what I'd done. I stumbled back, my eyes wide and my face paling.

How had I allowed myself to get caught up in Ty with Max only in the next room?

Max was right. I *was* a bad person. This just confirmed it.

But if this was what it felt like to be bad, then I didn't want to be good because right now, I felt more alive than I ever had.

I patted my hair into submission as best as I could, but there was only so much I could do with the frizz ball. The cold water that I splashed on my face helped a little, but I still felt like it was all a dream—like I had imagined it.

My hand touched my swollen lips. They tingled, confirming that it hadn't been a dream, that it had happened. *Ty had kissed me*. His soft, full lips had caressed mine and I swear I could still feel his hand on my ass.

"Are you Kay?" I jumped at the voice. My hand dropped from my face as I stared at the woman in the mirror who was standing behind me.

"Erm..." I looked around the room as I turned around. "Yes."

"Your boyfriend is waiting outside." She pointed back at the door then walked to a stall and closed the door behind her.

I took a deep breath, checked my face one last time in the mirror for any obvious signs of what had just happened before I opened the door.

Max was standing with his back against the closet door that me and Ty had been in. His face was shadowed by the low lights, a muscle in his jaw ticking as he watched me.

"What the fuck took so long?" he gritted out. I swallowed, my mouth dry. "Well?" He pushed off the door.

I stepped back out of instinct. His eyes flashed, a smirk lifting the sides of his mouth. *He fed off my fear of him.*

He wouldn't do anything here, not with all these people about, right?

"You think you can get away from me?" His low tone chilled me to the bone, causing me to rub my hands against my arms.

"I... I'm sorry."

His hand came out lightning fast, his grip bruising as he pushed me against the wall. My back hit it with a thud and I squeezed my eyes closed, not wanting to show him that he was hurting me.

I couldn't help but compare the way he touched me with the way Ty touched me. I felt alive when Ty touched me, but when Max touched me I felt like I was dying a slow but sure death.

His face came within centimeters of mine as he growled, "You think you can just walk away from me?"

"No—"

"Without asking first?"

"I—" His hand moved from my arm and for a brief second, I felt relief but that soon disappeared as his hand wrapped around my throat. A beat passed where his grip was light, loving almost, before his hand tightened, squeezing and cutting off my air supply.

"You need to be corrected." He shook his head. "When will you learn?"

His eyes were almost black; I couldn't see any of the green.

His grip intensified and I grasped his arm, willing him to let go without being able to form any words. The edges of my vision started to turn black. If he didn't let go soon I'd pass out.

"You need to be taught..." He grunted. "How to behave"

"Please—" I managed to croak out.

The sound of a door opening gave me an ounce of hope. He squeezed one last time before he let go. He didn't move other than to let go of my throat, his body still centimeters from mine and blocking me from view.

I coughed and sputtered, rubbing at my throat, aware that from this position, things could be seen in a very different way. We looked like any other normal couple having a moment of passion in a dark corner.

"Everything okay here?"

I knew that voice. I held back my groan and met Ty's eyes from behind Max, my hand dropping from around my throat, but it was too late, he'd seen me trying to relive the burn.

His fists were clenched and his eyes guarded as he stared at me. He flicked his gaze to Max, assessing him before he looked back at me. The knowing flash in his eyes told me that he saw something.

"Mind your own business," Max gritted out.

Ty stood there unmoving, his eyes glued to mine.

"Let's go." Max pulled me off the wall and threw his arm around my shoulders. "Keep your mouth shut," he warned, only low enough for me to hear.

I looked down at the floor as we walked past Ty, keeping my hand planted against my side to stop from reaching out.

"Good girl," Max murmured.

I didn't look back up until we were safely outside.

I PULLED A SCARF AROUND MY NECK THE NEXT morning before I got out of my car. The bruises were faint but I didn't want to risk any questions.

I pulled the metal door open and came face to face with Luke.

"Morning." I smiled.

"Yeah," he grunted back and tried to move around me.

I blocked the way until he looked up at me with narrowed eyes.

"I need to get past."

"Am I really that bad?" I asked, genuinely curious.

I'd been working here for several weeks now and he had hardly spoken to me, only when absolutely necessary. I got that he was the silent broody type, but the fact that it was only me he ignored convinced me that it was something to do with me and not him.

"What's the hold up?" Kitty asked from behind me.

"She won't move." Luke huffed.

"What? Why won't you move?" She rested her chin on my shoulder and I turned to her, our faces centimeters apart.

"He needs to say 'good morning' first."

Kitty laughed, right down my ear. "Oh God! You're hilarious."

I winced at the loudness of her voice before taking a small step to the side. "What? It's something that he should say. I can't understand half of the grunts that he uses!" I waved my hand about in the air.

I saw him smile out of the corner of my eye—he couldn't hide that smile because it lit up his whole face. I whipped my head around, ready to catch him but he frowned as soon as I turned.

"Good morning," he grunted.

I moved to the side and waved my arm wide for him. "That's all I wanted!" I shouted after him.

"Crazy."

"I heard that!"

"Good!" he shouted back.

I stepped into the warehouse with Kitty behind me, walking to the kitchen before I switched on the coffee machine and pulled my coat off.

"You got time for a chat?"

"Sure." I held my coat and bag up as I gestured toward the door to let her know I was going to put my things in the office.

Ty was sitting behind the desk when I walked into the office, his arms crossed as he watched the doorway intently.

My heart thumped erratically in my chest. I wanted to walk back out again, but walk toward him at the same time. I was torn, not knowing for sure what it was I wanted.

"Kay—"

"Not now, Ty…" I paused. "Please." I hung my coat up and put my bag on the couch, all the while keeping my eyes connected to his.

I wanted to avoid the conversation that we needed to have. I wanted to pretend that I didn't see him last night; pretend that I'd had a good night's sleep and not stayed awake most of the night because all I could remember was the way he had held me—the way his lips felt against mine.

I should have been worried about the way Max had been, how pissed he was. I *should* have been thinking of a way to apologize to him. Instead, I had lay there most of the night with my hand pressed against my lips, a smile on my face as I relived it over and over again.

"We need—"

"I can't." I choked out and fled from the room.

I rushed out of the office and to the meeting table where Kitty was waiting with two cups of coffee.

I could feel my cheeks burning as I pulled the chair out before sitting down next to her.

"So..."

"So..." I took a sip of my coffee and raised my brows.

"How do you like working here?"

"I love it." My back straightened. This was something that I had no doubt about. Whatever went on outside didn't matter when I was here. This place had become my sanctuary, somewhere that I didn't have to watch my every step. Where I could be more than just a mom.

I loved Eli more than life itself, but I was eighteen when I had him and I hadn't done much of anything apart from being his mom. I needed time to be *me*. To figure out who I was.

"The best part is when I get to go out. I love to watch people; see how they are when they think no one is looking." She opened her mouth to say something but I beat her to it. "Do you know how many men pick their nose and eat it?" I laughed at the grimace on her face.

"That's so gross." She shook her head.

"I know, right?" I snorted.

"How's it going with boss?" she asked.

"Good." I nodded, trying to keep a straight face

and willing my cheeks not to heat even more. I took a sip of my coffee. "I have a question though"

She raised her brows, tilting her head.

"How old is Ty?"

She frowned, leaning back in her chair. "Twenty-six... why?"

"Just wondered." I shrugged. I was sure that he was older than that—he acted way older. Maybe it was the whole "boss" thing.

We were both silent for a couple of seconds before Kitty spoke again. "You ever done anything like this before?"

I leaned back in my seat and held the coffee on my lap. "No; I had a job in a hotel when I was younger." I shrugged. "But I had to give that up when I had Eli."

"Eli?"

I lifted the cup to my lips. "My son."

"Oh frack! You have a son?" Her eyes widened. "I never knew you had a son."

I pulled my cell out and clicked onto the pictures. I'd seen so many Moms do this in grocery stores or the park, but I hadn't ever been able to do it. It didn't strike me until that moment what a normal thing it was to do: to show someone a picture of my son.

I found my favorite picture of Eli—Spiderman t-shirt and a face covered in chocolate—and handed it over.

"Awwww, he's adorable." She swiped her finger on the screen, smiling or chuckling at each picture.

"Those eyes." She looked at me with wide eyes and I nodded, knowingly. I knew all about those eyes and the effect they could have on you.

"What are we looking at?"

I yelped at the voice near my ear. What was it with these men sneaking around? "Jeez, Evan!"

"Sorry not sorry." He shrugged and walked around to Kitty then looked over her shoulder and back to me.

"Who's lil' dude?"

"Her son, Eli," Kitty said and handed the cell over to Evan

"Wow, how old is he? Like, ten?"

"He's four, Evan." I rolled my eyes and looked away.

It was only then that I realized Ty was sitting at the head of the table with Luke next to him. I swallowed at the look in his eyes as he watched me with an intensity that had me shifting in my seat.

"Didn't know you had a son," Luke said. I tore my eyes from Ty which was a feat in itself and met Luke's gaze.

"Yeah." I nodded.

He smiled. A real genuine smile and held his hand out for the cell.

I'd never have guessed that out of all the things that would make Luke smile at me it would have been finding out I had a son. Evan passed him my cell and sat next to Luke.

"I put our numbers in," Evan said.

"Oh…" I stumbled on my words. "Thanks" I never even thought about having their numbers. I only used the cell to take pictures and in case the preschool needed to get ahold of me.

"You should bring him over sometime," Ty told me.

I bit my lip to keep from saying anything. There was no way I'd bring him here; I wouldn't make Eli lie about me to Max. I'd told enough lies for several lifetimes and I wouldn't subject Eli to that. I didn't want him to become like me.

I looked away and pushed back on my chair.

"I need to—" My pad and pen slid down the table toward me.

I looked back at Ty, this time butterflies swarmed as his lips lifted into a smile. His eyes flicked down to my lips.

Was he thinking the same thing as me? Remembering how my lips felt against his? Could he not forget the way they made him feel either?

Only one thought reverberated in my mind: That one kiss could have possibly turned my whole world upside down.

Chapter Eleven

I TRAINED with Evan almost every day since that first time. It was always the same: me punching the pads, but the only difference now was that I had gloves.

I was getting better. At least I thought I was.

As far as I was aware nobody knew what we did which meant I had an excuse to escape Ty and take my frustrations out on Evan. I was avoiding him, plain and simple.

It had been a week since the "bar incident" as I'd taken to calling it in my own head, and I'd successfully avoided him and all of his attempts to talk to me so far.

I didn't want to face him; I didn't want to listen to what he had to say or the rejection that he was going to give me. So, I avoided him instead.

Evan had arranged for us to do some training

before everyone else came into work. We normally did it during the day when everyone was out on jobs but he said that he wanted to start and do it before everyone came in. I'd asked him why but he gave me a lame excuse that I didn't quite believe but went along with it anyway.

I parked in my normal space and went into the warehouse where the lights were already on.

That should have been my first warning.

I gasped when I lifted my head.

Ty was standing in the middle of the training mats; feet shoulder width apart, arms crossed, and a fierce look on his face. I couldn't stop my eyes flicking down to his arms and the tattoos that mesmerized me.

"Ty"

"Kay."

I moved closer, my brow furrowed, not under-standing what was going on.

"Ready for training?" he asked, unfazed by my confusion.

"What? I don't—"

"You thought I didn't know?" He chuckled. "Sweetheart, I know everything that goes on around here"

My head reeled back. Evan had promised me that no one knew about our training.

"But—" I stumbled at the edge of the mat. How had he known? And more importantly: why was he here instead of Evan?

"Where's Evan?"

"Out," he grunted. I looked around, sure that Evan would come in any second now. I couldn't trust myself around Ty. One touch and I'd melt into a puddle of goo.

"I think I'll... erm..." I felt him move closer and lifted my head up to meet his eyes. "Ty—"

"Ready for training?" he asked, softer this time.

I stared into his eyes: I could get lost in them for hours. He was always so open with me; I could read him like I'd never been able to read anyone else before. I noticed how he would only drop his walls with me, whenever we were around the others I could see the difference in the way that he looked at them.

"Okay," I whispered and opened my bag for my gloves.

"You won't need those," he said and moved back a couple of steps.

"I won't?"

"No." He shook his head. "Self-defense today."

"But we always—"

"You need to know how to protect yourself." His eyes flashed with a meaning behind them. Only this time, he threw his walls up and wouldn't let me see past them. I hated that he had done that.

I frowned down at my bag then looked back up at him. "Right." I cleared my throat. "Okay."

"Come here." He flicked his wrist, motioning me forward.

Moving closer, I breathed him in and enjoyed that freshly showered smell wafting in the air around us.

Great. Now I was thinking about him showering. I shook my head, trying to get rid of the images and concentrated on Ty.

"Try and get out of my hold," he said and wrapped his arms around me from behind.

I struggled for several seconds, using all of my strength but I wasn't getting anywhere.

At least I thought I was using all of my strength.

He let go and huffed out, "You're not trying."

"Sorry, it's a little hard when you're squeezing so tight." I blew a breath out the side of my mouth, frustrated.

"Kay..." He shook his head but I saw the grin that spread across his face. "Let's try again."

"Okay." I straightened up and widened my stance.

"This time, I'm going to try and get you down onto the mat."

His arms wrapped around me from the front this time. I squirmed in his hold, our bodies touching in ways that I'd only imagined.

He pulled me to the side and rocked back, both of us landing on the mat with Ty's arm coming out to cushion the blow.

We both grunted but neither of us moved.

My legs were open and Ty fit perfectly inside them. I sucked in a breath at the contact, my chest rising and falling rapidly.

My eyes closed as his breath flowed across my neck, a shiver rolling through me.

"Sweetheart," he whispered. "What are you doing to me?" I sucked in a breath as he moved closer. His hips sending sparks between my legs at the contact and moaning as he pressed his lips against my neck.

I lifted my hips up to his and moved my head to the side to give him better access. My hands wandered over his arms and up to his shoulders; feeling every dip and curve of his muscles.

"Ty." I groaned. "Don't stop."

"I won't," he growled and grabbed my thigh, bringing it up and over his hip.

I lost myself in his kisses and the rolls of his hips, my head thrown back.

I didn't have a care in the world.

All that mattered right now was the way he was making his way to my lips, and the touch of his hand as it slid further up my thigh.

When our lips finally met, I moaned even louder. He opened his mouth, swallowing the sound and answering me with one of his own as our tongues slid against each other.

I never knew I could feel this way: so out of control but so in control all at the same time.

I never wanted it to stop, but it did as he pulled back. I followed him, not wanting it to end.

"Sweetheart."

"Hmmm."

"Stop," he groaned.

"Why?" I opened my eyes, studying his heaving chest before looking deep into his chocolate eyes.

"Because..." he whispered.

I frowned. Because? That was his answer? He just told me that he wouldn't stop and now he was stopping?

I moved my eyes to his; he told me so much with that one look.

"Fine," I ground out and squirmed from underneath him.

My head spun as I stood up too quickly.

"Kay—"

"No." I lifted my bag off the floor and walked toward the office. "Forget it."

THE NEXT COUPLE OF WEEKS PASSED BY QUICKLY. I didn't go out on another job with Ty; he'd offered but I thought it was best we stayed away from each other for a little while. The temptation was too strong, too enticing.

I often found myself thinking about the kiss or staring at him when he wasn't looking. I would trace his face with my gaze and stare at the tattoos that wrapped around his arms, wondering if each of them had a story behind them.

I went out with Kitty on jobs instead of Ty, using

the excuse that we were getting to know each other better. She had an interesting life and often talked about the all places that she had been and all the people that she had met.

I noticed she didn't talk about any family though. I'd asked her about them one day and she'd clammed up and stuttered for several sentences so I left the subject alone. It wasn't something that she wanted to talk about and I understood completely. After all, I knew how it felt to not want to open up too.

She let me take photos of the people we were watching; I enjoyed it and found that I was getting good at snapping pictures of people. Even Luke said how good they were the other day; I had squealed like a little girl and jumped up and down. Luke didn't give praise often, so when he did I knew he meant it.

The last couple of days I had stayed in the office to catch up on some paperwork. My office duties had slid since I'd been going out on jobs and I had several reports to type up. The excitement I felt was beyond belief when I saw my name at the bottom of a few reports.

Ty had been out most of the day and had only come back five minutes ago. Kitty and Luke were reviewing some footage that they had captured and Evan was writing some computer code or whatever it was he did on that ten computer screen system.

I'd learned not to ask what he was doing. He'd start using all these big words that made my brain hurt.

"Kay," Ty said as he hung his coat up and took his beanie hat off.

I watched his muscles ripple as he lifted his arm to try and tame his hair.

"Yes?" I croaked.

"Let's talk about the job." He sat in the chair opposite me, spread his long legs out in front of him and stared.

Today marked the end of my one-month trial, I knew it had been coming but I hadn't realized how fast it would go by.

"Okay." I gulped.

"You're doing a great job in the office." He paused. I waited for the but part. I knew it was coming. "But..." *Here it is.* "You're good outside of the office as well."

"I am?"

He nodded, brought his knees up and leaned forward.

"I know you don't have the training that we have but I think that's a good thing."

"It is?"

His fingers drummed on his knee. My eyes flicked down to them, they were tapping on a small rip that stretched out where his knee was bent. "I think that you'd be an asset to the team."

"I don't understand." I shook my head and leaned forward, elbows on the desk, hands clutched in front of me.

"What don't you understand?" He smiled.

I gripped my hands harder to keep still. I couldn't concentrate when he smiled like that.

"Will I be working in the office?"

"Yes." I furrowed my brows at his answer and then he continued, "And out on jobs."

"You want me to do both?" I asked with wide eyes.

There was no way that I'd be able to do what they did. They all had these super ninja skills; I'd watched them train in the warehouse and there was no way that I'd be able to do what they did.

Even Evan could do it. You wouldn't have thought that a computer nerd could do half of the things that he did. But believe me, he was a ninja nerd.

I chuckled at that: ninja nerd.

"I've seen the surveillance photos you've taken: you have a natural talent for it." He paused. "But I want you to be able to defend yourself in any situation that you could get caught in which means we're upping your training and you need to take it seriously."

"How would it work?"

"You'd be in the office two days a week and out on surveillance jobs the other three."

"But who will answer the phone?"

"Really? That's all you wanna say?" I stared at the phone and shrugged. "We'll divert the calls to our phones. Besides, how many times have you answered that phone in the last four weeks?"

"I don't know, maybe twice?" I looked up at him.

"Exactly." He leaned back in his seat.

"But that's because they always call you on the cells." I rolled my eyes. "What's the point in having an office phone if you never use it?" I huffed and looked down at my hands. My knuckles were white with how hard I was gripping them.

Could I train the way they did? Did I want to?

Of course, I wanted to.

Max flashed in my mind briefly.

He'd been gone from the apartment for a week now. I didn't know where he was staying but after the third day I had called his work and they said that he was there. Where he was staying didn't matter to me.

It was calmer not having him around: the apartment had a nicer atmosphere. I'd also noticed Eli was much more relaxed at home with him gone.

I wanted to tell myself that Max didn't affect Eli in anyway, but seeing the difference in him was the wake-up call that I needed.

It made me question things.

Was I always in the wrong? Did I need to be corrected when I stepped out of Max's invisible lines? Lines that he had drawn. Lines that I had no idea where began or ended.

I thought about how he had told me that I should hide my bruises because if people saw them they would know how much of a bad person I was.

But was I really bad?

Was it bad to not have dinner ready on the table for when he walked in the apartment?

Was it bad for me to suggest he spend some time with Eli?

Was it bad of me to not ask him if I could be excused from the table?

The one thing that I knew was bad was keeping my job a secret. I'd thought about quitting several times, but as I stared into Ty's eyes, at the sincerity that shined back at me, I knew I wouldn't be able to quit.

"Okay," I said and took a deep breath. "I'd love to do it."

"Great." He clapped his hands once and stood. "Welcome to the team."

There were so many things I wanted to say to him. I wanted to ask if he thought about me half the amount of times that I thought about him. But most importantly: I wanted to ask if he could still feel my lips pressed against his.

Instead, I said, "Thank you."

"You're welcome." He walked to the door and turned back around to face me. "Training starts Monday: bring gym clothes."

My eyes widened. He chuckled and left the office.
Exercise.

I hated exercise.

Chapter Twelve

I was on top of the world when I got home. I couldn't wait to start training the way the other guys did, nothing and nobody could move the smile that stretched across my face.

Then Max came home.

No explanation to where he had been, what he had been doing or where he had been staying. He sat down and waited for me to place his dinner on the table—as usual.

I'd made his dinner every night this week in case he came home, and not once had it been eaten.

I didn't ask him where he had been, aside from not caring, I knew that it wouldn't go over well if I questioned him. Instead, I filled him in on the things that Eli had done this week.

He grunted his answers, stood from the table when he was finished and settled onto the couch.

Me and Eli stayed in the kitchen and made cookies. We laughed and made a heap of mess, but that was the best part about baking. Memories of my mom flashed in my mind throughout the night, but they weren't bad. They were happy.

We were happy.

I couldn't help but think about how different my life could have been if she was still here. Would I have Eli? If I did: would I be in the position I was in now?

I knew that I loved Max, he was the father of my child. But was I *in love* with Max?

I wasn't so sure anymore.

He was the only person who would have me. Not that I would have been able to leave even if I wanted to.

I'd thought about it several times, mainly after he'd just hurt me. But one apology and a promise that he wouldn't do it again, and I forgave him every single time.

Those apologies had started to dwindle into nothing, and now I knew not to expect any acknowledgment afterwards.

This was my life and I had to carry on the best I could—for Eli.

Me and Eli took the warm cookies into his bedroom with our glasses of milk and settled on the bed in our pajamas.

And that was how I woke up the next day: with a sore neck, cookie crumbs all over me, and Eli snoring in my ear.

I looked around at what had startled me awake and closed my eyes when I couldn't hear anything. Just as I was falling back to sleep I heard the phone ringing.

Saturday.

Only one person would call on a Saturday at this time.

I jumped out of bed and ran to the kitchen, listening, trying to find where the sound was coming from. I grabbed my bag; there was so much stuff in there that it took an eternity to find the goddamn thing.

"Hello?" I panted.

"Kay?" I slumped in relief and popped my head into the living room.

Max was still here. I wouldn't be able to talk to Corey inside the apartment.

"Hey, Corey." I smiled. "You okay?"

"Yeah, I'm good." I could hear voices in the background as I crept into the hallway. "How's the job?"

I shoved my feet into my chucks and grabbed my cardigan.

"Good." I put the latch on the apartment door and went out into the hall. "I got offered a permanent position yesterday."

"Yeah?" If I closed my eyes, I could almost see the grin on his face.

"Yeah." I pulled the cardigan over my shoulders.

"Hold on a minute." I balanced my cell on the banister and shoved my arms through the sleeves.

I picked it back up. "I'm back."

"So, do you like it? Everyone treating you good?"

I thought about all the guys. I had never laughed so much; especially when I was around Evan. Kitty was fast becoming the best friend that I'd never had. Luke was still grumpy but he'd gotten a little less frosty with me lately.

And Ty. I didn't even know where to start with Ty.

"Yeah, I love working there," I walked down the hall and watched the apartment door.

"You like working in the office?"

"Yeah, but I love the surveillance jobs too. Ty says—"

"You love what?" he growled down the line.

"The surveillance jobs," I rushed out. "I only take photos."

"I can't believe—"

"There's nothing dangerous; I swear. Ty says that I'm good at it, he wants me to do it more often."

"I don't like the sound of that, Kay."

"What? Why?" I narrowed my eyes. Even from halfway across the world he still wanted to protect me.

"It's too dangerous, Kay. The people that Ty deals with aren't good."

I huffed out a breath. I'd never win this battle with him, but that was beside the point. It wasn't as if he could do anything about it anyway.

"How's things over there?" I asked, trying to change the subject.

There was a beat of silence, then he replied, "Yeah, good. Should be home soon."

"Really?" I smiled wide. I couldn't wait for him to come home.

"Yeah." There was a loud noise in the background. "Fuck!"

"What?" I asked, panicked.

"Gotta go. Love you."

The line went dead before I had the chance to say it back.

"I love you, too," I said into the silence of the hall. I stared at my cell for several minutes, wishing that it would ring again.

I hated not being able to talk to him whenever I wanted: he was my only family and I missed him so much that it hurt.

"Kay? What are you doing?" I jumped at Miss Maggie's voice and spun around.

"Miss Maggie," I blew out a breath.

She stood outside her apartment with her robe wrapped around her. It was so long that it almost hit the floor.

"Are you okay, dear?"

"Yeah," I croaked as I pulled my cardigan tighter around me before holding up my cell. "Corey called."

"Oh." She raised her brows. "How is he?"

"Yeah, he's good."

"And, how are you?"

She moved closer to me, her slippers dragging against the floor with every step she took.

"I'm okay."

"Are you sure." She frowned. "You look a little pale."

I opened my mouth to tell her how worried I was about Corey. I could put things out of my mind when I didn't know he was doing anything for certain. But I knew that sound meant he had to head out into whatever war zone he was in right now.

The possibility of him getting hurt strangled me, the noose becoming tighter. The lump in my throat bigger.

"Kaylee?" Max called from inside the apartment.

"I..." I pointed back to the apartment. "Better go"

I spun around and headed back to the apartment. I was about to open the door when she said, "I'm always here." I turned back to her. "If you need to talk."

"I know." I nodded.

"Oh, and tell Eli the new episode is on today."

"Okay." I went through the door, closed it behind me and leaned back against it.

It wasn't until then that I realized I didn't know what series she was talking about.

"Breakfast," Max grunted from the kitchen.

I took a deep breath then pushed off the door.

Would it really hurt him to make his own?

I batted that thought away as soon as it came. I

needed to get back to my life and that meant doing as Max said. If he wanted breakfast, then he would get breakfast.

———————

EVAN BOUNCED INTO THE OFFICE MONDAY morning, flopped down in the chair opposite me with a big grin spread across his face. "Howzit, Kay?"

"Morning," I huffed.

As mornings went, this one had been one of the worst. First, I had woken up late, which meant that I had to rush to try and make it out the door on time, and the more I rushed, the longer everything took.

We'd left late which meant Eli had missed his morning snack time. He'd cried and moaned that he wouldn't be able to eat until lunch time so I'd stopped off at the shop to get him a snack to eat on the way.

Then he spilled his drink all down him, so we had to go back to the apartment to get him changed, which made us even later.

To top it all off, I got stuck in traffic on the way to the compound.

My first day after my trial period and I was late. *Way to make a good impression.*

I'd missed the morning meeting which meant I had to use Ty's notes to type up the whole meeting, and let me tell you, they were absolutely no help whatsoever. His writing was barely legible.

Four files waited for me on my desk when I finally walked in. The office phone had gone off so many times I was sure everyone knew what a bad day I was having. I wished I'd not said anything about the phone ringing the other day now, it was karma, I was sure of it.

"You look stressed," Evan commented. I flicked my eyes to him and raised my brows.

"Yeah." I snorted. "You could say that."

I picked the finished files up from the desk and opened the filing cabinet. I'd finally caught up: it had taken me most of the day. Now I was counting down the hours until I could go to bed, sleep, and start fresh in the morning.

"You wanna blow off some steam?"

"Huh?" I turned back to him.

"Come on." He stood and held his hand out to me. I stared at him, unsure. What were we going to do? "Come on," he coaxed a second time. I looked back up at him, his face showing his signature Evan cheeky grin, one that told me he was about to do something that he shouldn't.

I moved forward. I could do with a break, I reasoned with myself. Plus, I wanted to see what he was up to.

He grabbed my hand and pulled me out of the office door and into the main warehouse.

"Where are we going?" I laughed, his excitement contagious.

"You'll see." He pulled his brows up and down, his teeth glinting with his wide smile, and I giggled at how comical he looked.

The sound was so foreign that even Evan stumbled a little. There was something about Evan that brought out the child in me.

I'd had to grow up so fast that sometimes I forgot that I was only twenty-two years old.

He pulled me over to his work station and I frowned. That's what he was excited about? I walked past his collection of computer screens every day.

"I know what you're thinking." He nudged me into his chair and pulled out another one. "But you're gonna love this."

He clicked several buttons on the keyboard, then several screens flashed to life and voices came out of the speakers.

"What the—" My eyes widened.

"I know, cool, right?" He could barely stay still he was that excited.

I stared at the screens, seeing an image of Kitty and Luke sitting in one of the SUVs, on a job.

"How are you seeing this?"

"Wouldn't you like to know." He winked.

"Come on," Kitty whined.

"What?"

"If you had to kill one, torture the other, and let another go."

"And who are the options?" Luke asked.

"Me, Evan, and Kay."

I spun around in my chair and stared at Evan with wide eyes. What the hell were they talking about?

"Let's see," Luke said. "I'd kill Evan."

"Why?"

He groaned. "You never said I had to give reasons."

"Well I changed the rules." She shrugged and flipped her hair over her shoulder.

"Fine, I'd kill him because he'd be a squealer."

"I know, right?" She nodded. I looked at Evan to gage his reaction.

"I wouldn't." He shook his head. I smiled at him. "I swear I'd take it like a man." He pulled his arms up and flexed his biceps. I snorted as he kissed them.

"I'd torture you."

"What!"

"Yeah, for making me play these stupid games," he grunted.

"He's right, she's obsessed with games like this." I laughed. Every day I had been out on a job with her, she came up with a new game to play.

"I know." He huffed. "Drives me crazy, she'll text me in the middle of the night expecting me to play." He rolled his eyes.

"And I'd let Kay go."

"You would?"

"Yeah, she's got a kid." He shrugged. "Kids need their moms."

Kitty nodded then but didn't say anything else. I felt like I was intruding on a private moment.

Luke's face looked haunted as he turned away from Kitty. I was sure he didn't let anyone see that look on his face, but I spotted it right away.

I looked away, swallowing. "I think you should turn it off."

Evan's face looked somber as he pressed a few buttons and sat there, his eyes focused on the now blank screens.

"Well," I said and stood. "That was fun." I scanned the warehouse, only just now realizing that Ty could have caught us spying on them.

He looked at me, his eyes shining bright. "Do you think every kid needs a mom?"

My eyes widened. "Erm…" I was startled by the question, not knowing what to say.

"I didn't have a mom, but I turned out okay. Right?" he asked with hopeful eyes.

My heart broke for him: I knew how he felt. Sitting back down, I reached for his hand, squeezing gently.

"My mom died when I was seven," I started and took a deep breath. I hadn't talked about her in so many years—it felt strange.

"She did?"

"Yeah." I shrugged. "Sometimes I wonder if it was a good thing to get seven years with her or whether not knowing her would have been better."

"I never knew my mom." He looked out into the warehouse. "I was adopted as a baby."

I let go of his hand and leaned back.

"So, you had an adoptive mom?"

"No." He shook his head.

"I don't understand." I frowned.

"I have two Dad's." He looked back at me. I tried to keep the shock off my face but his knowing twinkle told me I wasn't successful.

"I don't think you do need to have a mom, but..." I stood and patted his shoulder. "Having two parents who love you are better than one who was there but didn't care." He opened his mouth but I turned and went back to the office before he could say anything else.

I didn't need to think about my own parents. What I needed to do was make sure that I was the best mom I could be to Eli.

That's all that mattered.

I didn't care what happened to me.

Chapter Thirteen

"You NEED to wear it every time you go out on a job."

I stared at the radio Ty handed me with wide eyes. I'd seen them sitting on the charging unit in the office but I hadn't used one before.

"I have to wear it?" I hadn't had to wear one when I went out with Ty or Kitty before.

"Yeah, it doesn't matter who you're with: you need to have it on." He turned and started to walk out of the office but stopped when he saw I wasn't following him.

"Come on." He waved his hand in the air.

"I didn't have to wear one before," I voiced my thoughts to his back as I followed him through the warehouse.

"It's different now." He looked over his shoulder at me "You're part of the team."

He pressed his hand against the palm reader to the safe, a light flashing behind his hand followed by a soft click that echoed throughout the empty warehouse.

"We'll need to get your hand scanned and put into the system too," he said as he pulled the door open.

"O-kay," I stuttered.

I came in early this morning, knowing today was the first day that I was officially going out on surveillance. I'd been nervous all night and I hadn't slept at all. I'd gone to bed early but all I did was toss and turn, not able to settle.

It was different when I went out on surveillance before, I was just there as an extra. Now I had to be able to do it properly, and it made me sick to my stomach to think that I wouldn't do a good enough job.

That I'd let Ty down.

I hadn't known what to wear this morning. I'd gone back and forth so many times that in the end I'd pulled on my black skinny jeans, chucks, and a white tank top, but brought normal office clothes in with me.

I'd told Ty this when he walked into the office a couple of minutes ago and he had laughed, full on throw your head back laughter. He'd told me that I could wear pajamas to work in the office and he wouldn't be bothered as long as the work got done.

His eyes flashed when he looked me up and down, so I'd say he liked the skinny jeans. I'd pretended not to notice and looked through my bag, but I could feel the heat of his gaze on my skin.

Ty pulled open the door and stepped inside the safe. I stood and watched as he brought things out and placed them onto the meeting table. After three trips, he closed the door and scanned his hand on the palm reader again. Two beeps signaled that it was locked.

I followed him to the table and stood, eyes wide at all of the items he had set down.

"Put this on first." He handed me a black t-shirt. I opened the plastic wrap and pulled it over my head. It was the same that they all wore, black with "MAC SECURITY" written on the front in white writing. Evan was the only one who didn't wear them, instead he wore bright colored t-shirts with slogans on the front.

But he rarely left his computer so it didn't matter.

"You'll put everything on this belt." He handed over a black, leather belt, several pockets hanging off it and small flaps that had press studs on them.

I pulled it open and wrapped it around my waist.

"No," he said and moved forward. "Like this."

I sucked in a breath as he took the belt from me and crouched down, his face level with my— "You need to have it at the right height." His long fingers grazed along my stomach, the two layers of fabric didn't stop the shiver that rolled through me. "So that you can grab things easily." He pulled it tight, fastened it together and looked up at me.

It was only then that he realized where his hands were. He glanced at his hands then back up. My heart hammered a drum beat in my chest when I heard his sharp intake of breath.

His brows furrowed as he stood up slowly and moved back a couple of steps. I couldn't move as I watched him pull his beanie hat off his head and rake his hand through his hair.

I'd noticed that he'd only do that when he was stressed.

"What was I—" He pulled his hat back on and picked up another item off the table. "You need a flashlight... baton... spray." He picked them up and turned toward me.

"Where do I put this?" I held up the radio that he'd given me in the office.

"On the left of your belt there's a holster for it." I looked to the left but couldn't see one big enough for it. "Toward the back." I twisted to the side and found it, pulled the flap open and pushed it inside. I felt Ty move to the other side of me and looked up to see what he was doing. "Just gonna put these on the belt." I nodded at him and pulled the wire from the radio up to my neck. "Baton on your right, spray next to it, and cuffs in the back," he listed off.

"Will I need the cuffs?"

"Better safe than sorry," he replied. I agreed, but I had no idea how to use any of this stuff.

"Is that pepper spray?"

"Yeah." He nodded and moved back to the table. "I've got you a bulletproof vest, too."

My eyes widened as he held it up. "Could I get shot?" I gasped.

He looked down and shifted on his feet. I'd never seen him so uncomfortable.

So... nervous.

"Well, it can be dangerous sometimes."

"Corey," I said out loud. The look on Ty's face said it all. "He talked to you, didn't he?"

He shrugged and picked up the last thing on the table, a small notepad with a pen pushed into the spirals at the top. I took it from him and pushed it into the last pocket next to the radio.

"I can't believe he would—"

"He's just looking out for you," he told me in a firm voice. I wanted to tell him how ridiculous it all was, but it was best to keep my mouth shut—I'd learned that over the years.

"I don't even know how to use these." I waved at the belt, its heaviness surprising me.

He pulled his chair out at the head of the meeting table, sitting down. "You'll learn."

"But what's the point if I can't use any of it yet?" Sitting in my usual seat next to him, I shuffled on the seat. The belt stopped me from leaning back fully so I perched on the edge of the chair. It already felt uncomfortable, I didn't know how they wore them all day.

"You need to get used to how it feels."

I guessed that made sense.

We had our usual meeting. All the guys

commented on how I looked. Now that I knew what was on my belt, I noticed the different things that they had on theirs. They each carried a stun gun on their belts and a gun concealed somewhere else. Ty was the only one who had one on his belt, although I suspected that he had another one somewhere else too.

I'd have to remember to ask Ty about that later. Then I thought better of it: I didn't know if I'd have the guts to fire an actual weapon.

Everyone moved when the meeting ended, Ty said he needed to get the case file we would be working on today and headed for the office.

Evan walked toward me, holding out two devices, I took them and raised a brow at him.

"That's a camera." He pointed to the bigger one "It's got loads of internal memory with added external too. It's covert enough that it can be mistaken for a cell."

I smiled at him. "Thanks, Evan."

He shrugged, his cheeks turning pink. "It'll come in handy when you're on surveillance."

I held up the other device. "What's this one?"

"That's a works cell."

"But I've already got a normal one." I tried to pass it to him but he stepped away.

"No, you need one just for work: for meetings and stuff." I opened my mouth to say something just as Ty walked back out the office.

"It's got a tracker on as well, you know, just in case."

I frowned at the just in case comment but when Ty walked past me and said, "Let's go," I didn't say anything about it.

I looked over at Ty who was holding the door open for me as he waited before I told Evan, "Thanks again for these." I pushed the cell into my front pocket of my jeans.

"Welcome," he said as he shuffled off to his computers.

I slid past Ty. Knowing that we'd be going in his monster SUV, I waited at the passenger door for him to unlock the doors.

"Here," he said from behind me.

I jumped when his fingers grazed my neck, the rough callouses making me shiver along with his breath that skirted over my skin. My body reacted to him like a flame to gasoline. I'd never felt this kind of connection with anybody before and it confused me immensely.

Even when Max and I first got together I didn't feel anything close to this.

I felt the earpiece go into my ear. Then he was gone and the lights flashed on the monster. I shook my head and pulled the door open.

What did I think he was going to do?

WE SAT AND WATCHED THE SAME HOUSE FOR AN hour. It's exterior exactly the same as the rest of the houses that lined the street. Each garden was immaculate, the grass a green that could only be achieved with some kind of chemicals. Not one thing was out of place, not even a lone wrapper floating down the street.

It was the epitome of suburbia.

We followed David Rangle all over town; he'd stopped at several different places until he pulled into one of the driveways and went inside.

His file was open on my lap and I studied it: we were watching for any suspicious activity. But so far, I hadn't see anything that would be suspicious. Unless you counted his obnoxious sports car that screamed "midlife crisis."

"What do you think he's doing in there?" I asked.

"Really?"

I looked up at Ty, he smirked at me and raised a brow. I turned my head back to the house and then to Ty and back again, trying to work out what he was saying without words.

"You think..." I gasped.

"Yeah." He pulled out his cell and tapped away at the screen before his body turned toward me.

I huffed and closed the file. I hadn't learned anything that I didn't already know from the five other times I'd read it.

"Oh look," I whispered as he came out of the

house. His hair was mussed and his shirt was sticking out of his pants. I'd say that he had been up to no good for sure. I had a sneaking suspicion that she wasn't his wife.

Would that warrant as suspicious activity?

Ty straightened up and waited for him to pull out onto the road before he followed him at a distance.

"Make sure you write down how long he was in there." I pulled my pad out and wrote the time. I'd had to put down every place that he had stopped, the time he arrived, and the time he departed.

I was just pushing it back in when I felt a vibration from my pocket. I lifted up slightly off the seat and pulled my cell out, not looking at the screen before I'd answered it.

"Hello?"

"Hi, is that Miss Anderson?"

"Yes..." I replied, my eyes wandering over to Ty as he tilted his head a little with his eyes still on the road.

"Oh hi, this is Miss Cooper, from Eli's preschool." My heart hammered in my chest.

"Yes, hi," I croaked.

"Eli isn't very well. Would it be possible for you to come and collect him?" I swallowed past the lump in my throat. I hated it when he was sick, all I wanted to do was wave a magic wand and make it all go away.

"Of course, I'll be there really soon." I pressed the end call button and pushed it back into my pocket, my mind running rampant.

The look on my face must have alerted Ty that something was wrong because he pulled off to the side of the road.

"Can you take me back to the compound?" I asked, my hands clutched together in my lap.

I didn't know what to do: there was nothing worse than not being able to get there right away.

"Why?"

"Eli's sick I need to go and get him."

Ty pulled back out onto the road. "Did she say what was wrong?"

"No." I shook my head. Why hadn't I thought to ask that?

I stayed silent as I stared out of the passenger window, not really seeing anything as we drove past houses and shops.

"Kay?" I turned to face Ty, only now realizing that we were parked outside of the preschool.

I pulled off my vest and belt, not wanting to draw any unwanted attention then jumped out of the car and ran inside, my eyes scanning the reception area for Eli.

He was sitting with a bowl next to him, his face ashen. How had he gotten so sick in the space of a couple of hours?

"Sweetie?" I bent down next to him and held my hand to his forehead. He was burning up.

I picked him up and stood. His head flopped into the space between my neck and shoulder as I held him tight. He mumbled something that sounded like "I don't feel well" and pressed his face into my neck.

"He was fine one minute, then the next..." Miss Cooper grimaced as she stood from the seat. "He vomited... everywhere."

"I'm so sorry. He was fine this morning." I readjusted Eli.

"I know," she said then placed her hand on Eli's back. "Get better soon."

I turned and walked toward the door. Ty was standing on the other side and he opened it as I approached.

"You okay? You need me to take him?" he asked as we walked to the car.

"No, I got it," I said and waited next to the back door. Ty opened it and I placed Eli on the seat then went around to the other side.

"Fuck, he's burning up."

"I know." I slid along the seat and pulled Eli's head onto my lap.

"You need to get medicine?"

"No, I've got some at home." Ty nodded and closed the door.

I directed Ty to the apartment, but I had a suspicion that he already knew where we were going anyway.

Now that I thought about it, I was the only one who didn't live on the compound. They all had their own places, but because I hadn't been inside any of them I had no idea who lived where.

I imagined Kitty living in the cottage, not too sure about Luke and Evan. But I did know that the big house with the wrap around porch was Ty's.

Ty jumped out as soon as we pulled up to the apartment block and picked Eli up from the back seat. He was fast asleep and didn't make a sound as we all went up.

I started to panic then; I couldn't remember if I'd tidied the living room before we'd left that morning.

It was a stupid thing to think of but I couldn't stop it.

"It might be a little messy," I told Ty. He shrugged and walked behind me to the apartment door. "That way." I pointed down the hallway when we were inside the apartment. Eli still fast asleep.

I walked behind and pointed to Eli's room. Ty put him on the bed and I got to work on stripping him down to cool him off.

"Medicine?" he asked from behind me.

"Cupboard in the bathroom."

Ty wandered off and I heard him rummage in the bathroom before he came back with several bottles of medication.

"You've got a whole pharmacy in there." I forced out a laugh and took the bottles from him.

I didn't tell him that I needed all of those things; that my first aid kit was constantly being replenished.

I'd rather he thought I was one of those people who was prepared for anything, but in reality, it was far from the truth.

"Eli?" He rolled over as I poured some medicine on the spoon.

"Sweetie, you need some medicine." He grunted and opened his mouth. I chuckled at him and held the spoon out.

I made sure he was comfortable and fast asleep before I moved. His small body looked so fragile paired with his pale skin.

"Probably just needs to sleep." Ty said as he followed me to the kitchen.

"Yeah." I blew out a breath before my eyes widened. "Oh damn, my car." I spun to face him.

"I'll get Evan to bring it over." He pulled out his cell and tapped the screen. "Where are your keys?"

"In my bag." I pulled open the fridge and grabbed two bottles of water. "Here." I handed him a bottle.

"Thanks." He tapped away at his cell so I sat down at the table.

Neither of us said a word for the next twenty minutes. Ty didn't put his cell down and all I did was stare at his long fingers as they cradled it.

My mind wandered several times, the main thought being: What else could he do with those fingers? I shoved those thoughts back down, deep down, and locked them away for good measure.

His cell buzzed and a couple of minutes later there was a knock on the door.

"I'll leave your keys next to the door, if you let Evan in you'll never get him to leave." He forced a smile onto his face and was out of the door before I had a chance to even say thank you.

I spent the rest of the night going over things in my head. The only explanation was that I'd done something wrong.

It made sense: that's all I seemed to be able to do.

OVER THE NEXT COUPLE OF DAYS, I BARELY HAD A wink of sleep. All I did was clean puke up from various surfaces and wash countless items of bedding and clothes.

To say Max wasn't pleased is an understatement. "I better not catch that or else," he'd warned.

I knew what "or else" meant so I kept Eli away from him, it wasn't that hard as Max stayed on the couch most of the time anyway.

Saturday morning, Eli woke up with some color in his cheeks so I gave him some breakfast and a few hours later he'd managed to keep it down.

He said that he wanted to go and see Henry so I waited to make sure that he was well enough. Once he started to jump around the room like a kangaroo, I was assured that he was back to his usual self.

It amazed me how quickly he could recover.

We went to Miss Maggie's and Henry practically leapt at Eli. They sat on the couch together and didn't move for the next couple of hours while I told Miss Maggie all about my new position and the new tools that I had.

Her eyes lit up when I told her about the bullet-proof vest.

"Is that a possibility? That you could get shot?"

"Ty said that it's better to be safe than sorry."

I lost track of time whilst we were there and I even dozed off for a little while. Lack of sleep was catching up to me.

Rubbing eyes, I searched for the clock. My eyes widened when I saw the time: Max would be home by now.

I rushed us out of there and right back to the apartment. I was greeted by a very unhappy Max sitting at the kitchen table, his jaw clenched and a dangerous glint in his eyes.

I smiled at him tentatively and told him that I was going to start dinner now. But My stomach rolled because I knew what was coming. It didn't make it any easier knowing that I was going to be corrected.

We ate dinner and I could feel his eyes on me the whole time, burning an angry path into the side of my head.

That night I only received a slap to my face. It hadn't even bruised, so I reasoned things were improv-

ing. I'd had worse for smaller things; I held out hope
that maybe things were changing again. He'd held back
this time. It was a sign. I was sure of it.

I kept Eli off preschool on Monday. Ty was fine
with that and I was relieved that he wasn't angry or
upset about me missing work. I didn't like letting the
guys down, but I came to reason that it was better than
being called out of work to pick Eli up again.

I'd set everything out on Monday night ready for
the next morning as he was going back to preschool
and me back to work. Eli dragged his feet, not wanting
to get ready. It took a great amount of effort and even a
bribe to get him out of the apartment.

I was half way to work when I realized I'd
forgotten my belt. I'd hid the belt and shirt away when
Ty had left on Wednesday because there was no way
I'd risk Max finding it.

Pulling a U-turn, I headed back to the apartment.

I'd left it on the bed for me to pick up on my way
out so I hadn't got a clue how I'd managed to forget it.
My morning had been a nightmare, all I wanted to do
was throw myself back into bed, pull the covers over
my head, and forget this day all together.

Double parking right outside the building door, I
didn't notice anything on my way inside. I pulled out
my phone to call Ty and tell him that I'd be late. The
tone came through the speaker as I pushed the apartment door open.

I walked to my bedroom, completely unaware of

my surroundings but frowned when I looked down at the bed. My shirt and belt weren't on the bed; I was sure I had left them there. I spun around and headed toward the kitchen.

"Kay?" Ty asked through the cell. I pulled the phone down and pressed the end call button as I walked into the kitchen, the blood draining from my face as my hands started to shake.

Max was sitting at the table. One hand clenched into a fist, the other clutched onto my MAC Security shirt.

"What the hell is this?" He threw it onto the floor and bought those evil eyes to mine.

"Max—" I croaked, my throat dry.

"Kaylee." He was calm. *Too calm*.

"I can explain." I lifted my hands in the air, the international sign for keep calm, to let me explain.

"Yeah?" He stood, lifting the belt off the table. Everything was in the same place I'd left it, including the radio in one of the pockets. "If this is what I think it is, then you've been a bad girl."

I swallowed, my dry throat scratchy. "Ma—" He dropped the belt, the metal pepper spray bottle clanging loudly on the floor.

"You know what happens to bad girls." He took another step toward me, his almost black eyes boring into me.

"Bad girls have to be corrected," he sneered.

Chapter Fourteen

I THOUGHT I'd be prepared for when this day came. But I wasn't.

The look in his eyes was pure evil—something I'd never seen from him before.

He'd waited for this day; I could see it written all over his face.

Why did he always want to hurt me?

What had I done that made him so angry?

How had I never seen the inexplicable need to exert power over me right at the start? I wish I would have known then what I know now. But it's no use thinking about the past, because as I stared into his eyes the realization slammed through me.

This was about him: not me.

My back straightened and I met his soulless eyes. I wasn't going to keep living like this. I'd had enough.

"What did I ever do to you?" I asked.

He stalled a few feet away, narrowed his eyes and looked me up and down. "What did you ever do?" he sneered.

"Yes." I nodded.

My body was strung tight, but for the first time I felt strong.

Somewhere in the back of my mind a voice said I shouldn't poke the beast, that I should get out of there while I still could.

I pushed that voice away. I wasn't going down without a fight—not this time.

I was sick and tired of the way things were: having to make sure his dinner was done on time, that his socks were paired a certain way, and being careful of what clothes I wore.

He'd established early on what clothes were acceptable and what weren't. At the time, I thought it was sweet. It wasn't until now that I realized how much I'd let him control me. Ty and the guys had opened my eyes to it all. I went from living in black and gray to being graced with full color.

I didn't deserve this.

"You came into my life," he growled and pointed to his chest. "You got pregnant." He turned his finger toward me.

"We got—"

"*You!* It's all your fault! You turned me into *this*." He waved at himself.

My eyes widened: how had I turned him into this?

"No, I didn't—"

I flinched as he flew toward me, his hands wrapping around my throat as I gasped.

"This is your fault," he spat.

He squeezed his hands tighter and pushed me back against the door. I gripped his arms, my nails digging into his clenched muscles.

I could feel myself slipping back into the box that he'd tucked me away in. If that was the only way I could survive right now then that's what I'd have to do. All my earlier bravado slipped away: it was this or nothing.

"Please," I begged while gasping for breath.

"You need to be taught." His lips curled back in disgust.

I scraped my nails down his arms, digging into his flesh. I begged him to let go over and over again, but he edges of my vision blurred. I could feel the fight leaving me, my body was caving in.

Then Eli flashed in my mind. His bright green eyes begging me to stay. To *fight*.

I couldn't give up.

I couldn't leave Eli with *him*.

I lifted my leg and kicked out, the front of my chucks catching his shin.

"Fuck!" He let go and stumbled back rubbing his leg.

I bent forward gasping, but I didn't have time to think because I needed to get out of there quick.

I spun around, fumbling for the door handle. I could see the apartment door from here. My escape.

I'd got the door halfway open and was about to step out when his hand came down on the back of my head and pushed with more force than he ever had before.

My cheek slammed on the edge of the door as I fell. I cried out at the pain as he pulled me up from the floor by my hair.

Wetness trickled down my cheek, flowing down my chin and onto my neck. My throat burned from him choking me, the pain so intense I couldn't concentrate on anything else.

"Where do you think you're going? Huh?" He pulled my hair again then pushed me back into the middle of the kitchen floor.

Landing on my hands and knees, I tried to scramble up but I wasn't quick enough to get away from his boot as he kicked me in the side.

"Please, stop." I groaned, falling and curling into a ball. He crouched down next to me, lifted my head and stared straight through me.

The air stilled. His eyes unmoving. He waited a couple of beats, then pushed me over onto my back.

I saw his foot lift and watched in slow motion as it

came closer, gasping when his boot connected with my ribs again. My body curled into a fetal position, the pain too much to bear.

"I've had enough of your attitude." He shook his head and took a step back. I closed my eyes, wishing for something or someone to make him stop—just this once for someone to know the hell that I lived in, to come and save me.

I heard a drawer open and close, then his footsteps came back toward me.

Opening my eyes, I swallowed. His body blocked the light coming through the kitchen window as he stood over me. His face a mask of a demonic being. His eyes twinkled, a smirk lifting the corners of his mouth.

How had I never seen that before? Or had I seen it but chose to ignore it?

My eyes caught the glint of something in his hand. I gasped when I saw the large knife, wriggling between his feet to try and get away. The white-hot pain in my ribs intensified but I had to get away.

"Now, now," he said in a calm voice and lowered himself, straddling me.

I wriggled and bucked, determined not to get caught underneath him. I didn't care about the pain, all I wanted was to get away from him. From that knife.

He cursed when I smacked against his stomach and answered me with a punch to the face, his fist slamming into my eye two more times—each blow harder than the one before—before he pulled back.

I'd never felt anything like the force of those punches. He'd never hit me as hard as he did then, it was as if he wanted to end this—us, *me*. I struggled to keep my eye open but I had to see him from all angles otherwise I'd be in real trouble.

If I couldn't see what was coming things would be worse.

A lot worse.

"Keep still," he warned, the knife hanging dangerously in the air. I thrashed again, shaking my head back and forth until something lying on the floor a few feet away caught my eyes—my belt.

I stilled.

This could be my way out. If I could just reach it then I could use something out of it against him. I didn't care what it was. I was just desperate to get away from him.

"That's it." He smirked like he'd won. "Be a good girl and keep still."

I stared at the belt as he ran the knife up the middle of my shirt, the fabric splitting in two. He stopped just under my breasts and ran the tip of the knife down my side. The cold metal sending a shiver through me.

He groaned. His eyes flashing as they landed on my side.

I moved my arm out slowly, careful not to alert him.

His fist in my side caught me by surprise, a groan slipping from between my lips. His punch landing in the same place that he'd just kicked me. The pain so intense that I was sure I'd pass out.

"Ahhh..." He groaned, his eyes closing as he tilted his head back, relishing in my pain he was dishing out.

I moved my arm back out, aware that it was one of those now or never moments. I didn't know this man anymore; I was starting to think that I'd never truly known him. How had I not seen how unpredictable and dangerous he was?

The heavy weight of his body made it hard to move, but I managed to crawl my fingers closer to one of the belt loops.

His eyes popped open. I halted my movement.

"You like that don't you?"

I wouldn't win in any verbal match against him so I stayed silent, praying that he didn't notice my arm making its way towards the only things that could help get me out of this situation.

He shuffled down my hips and onto my knees. I had more freedom now: it was a test. I could see the glint in his eyes, he was waiting for me to move.

He lifted his arm and I watched the knife lower to my stomach. I held my gasp in when the metal tip ran down my stomach.

"So, I've come to two conclusions," he murmured

as he glanced up at me. "You're either fuckin' someone or you went ahead and got a job."

I stared right at him, not giving him the slightest bit of emotion, knowing how much he hated when I did that.

"Answer me!" he roared.

"I—"

"Not that anyone would want to fuck you anyway." He threw his head back, his laugh surrounding us. "I mean, look at you."

His arm lifted again and I prepared myself for the knife to plunge into me but it didn't come.

"Either way you disobeyed me." His eyes flashed as my fingertips touched the edge of my belt. Stretching further, I gripped one of the loops slowly, trying not to gain his attention as I inched it closer.

Keeping my eyes connected to him, I tried not to let the panic show as I struggled to open one of the pouches. Finally, a loud pop in the kitchen alerted me that I was one step closer.

I paused, gaging him out of my better eye: I couldn't tell if he had heard it or not. If he had, then he wasn't letting on, he was too focused on the knife he was trailing along my skin. Trying to get ahold of whatever was in the pouch, I realized it was the baton. I could feel the heaviness in my hand, and I knew I wouldn't be able to flip it open but I hoped that the handle would be heavy enough.

His eyes moved to mine as I started to raise my arm, a smirk crossing his face.

"And you need to be taught a lesson."

Then I felt it; the sharp pain as he stuck the knife in my leg. I squealed as he pulled it back out and felt the blood oozing from the wound.

I hesitated with the baton.

He looked down to see his handy work, that was my opportunity so I took it and lifted my arm higher, putting all of my weight behind it.

The chilling sound of metal on bone as it hit his head made me cringe, the vibrations spread up my arm causing me to drop it as I panicked. He stilled, his eyes wide.

Then he fell forward, his weight crushing me. The knife scattered along the floor.

The only thought running through my head?

I'm free.

I LAY THERE FOR A FEW SECONDS, THE ADRENALINE pumping through my body, numbing the pain. I struggled to breath from the weight of Max on me but I needed to get out of here. I tried to push him off several times but he wouldn't move.

My leg throbbed and I could feel the wetness from the blood as it soaked through my jeans. Each time I tried to move and shove him off me, my ribs screamed in agony. My whole body was running high on adrenaline and I knew more pain was sure to come.

I gritted my teeth, counted to three and put all the strength I had behind the next push.

His body finally rolled off me, his head lulled to the side. I stared at his face. With his eyes closed, he was completely defenseless and looked like any other man.

Any *normal* man.

But I knew better than anyone what lurked beneath his fake exterior, behind his handsome face, and the show that he put on in front of people. Nobody knew him like I did, he always wore a mask, only ever taking it off when he corrected me. I'd seen the true evil behind his eyes today and I would never forget it. It would be ingrained in my mind forever.

I reached for my belt and baton and started to crawl toward the door. My work t-shirt lay in a crumpled heap on the floor so I pushed that along with the rest of the stuff.

Sitting against the door to catch my breath, I stared at Max. He lay there in a crumpled heap, looking like he wouldn't hurt a fly. I scoffed at that.

Tearing my gaze away from him, I folded the t-shirt up in a makeshift bandage and tied it around my thigh to stop the blood flow. It would do until I got somewhere safe. The upside was that it was black so the blood wasn't visible.

I took a deep breath and got onto my hands and

knees, my leg throbbing with the pressure and my ribs screaming in agony. I clenched my teeth and pushed up, using the doorknob to help me stand.

My head spun, and for a second I was sure that I'd pass out.

My stomach dipped at the sound of Max's groan. I looked back and saw him starting to stir so I didn't waste any more time, I grabbed my keys, my belt still in my hands, and limped down the hallway and out of the apartment.

It wasn't easy going down the stairs but I threw myself down them as fast as I possibly could, checking behind me to see if he was coming. I said a silent thank you when I was out of the building and headed for my car.

I'd never been more grateful for double parking than I was in that moment.

I pushed the key into the lock, my hands shaking so bad that I missed it a couple of times before I finally got it in. I heard the building door squeak open just as I was pulling the car door open.

My head shot up, I stared into Max's eyes, his smirk told me that he thought he'd just won. But I wasn't going to let him, not this time. I pulled the door open and slumped into the seat, sticking the key in the ignition. I flipped the locks on the doors and started the engine just as Max got to the door.

I didn't look at him or listen to what he was shouting through the window, instead I sped off.

The only thing on my mind was Eli. What if he tried to go and get him?

There was no way that I could turn up at the preschool like this. I could barely breathe or walk. My jeans were soaked with blood, my ribs smarted every time I moved. I shouldn't have been driving with only being able to see out of one eye but I didn't have a choice—I had to get away.

I pulled my phone out and found the number for the preschool. Not even thinking about what I was doing.

"Hello, this is—"

"Hi, I need to talk to Miss Cooper." I sounded like I had the worst sore throat and it burned when I spoke, but this conversation needed to happen, I didn't care if it made my throat worse.

"Miss Cooper isn't—"

Holding in my grunt of pain as I stopped at the lights, I said, "It's an emergency."

I needed to speak to her. I needed her to keep Eli safe.

"I... I'll go and see. Erm... who shall I say is calling?"

"Eli's mom." I hissed from the pain in my throat.

The light turned green and I drove forward. I'd automatically headed toward the compound because I knew that I'd be safe there, but ultimately it didn't matter if I was safe and Eli wasn't: he was all that mattered.

"Hello? This is Miss Cooper."

"Hi." I took a steadying breath. "This is Eli's mom."

"How can I help?"

"If Eli's dad comes there to pick him up, don't let Eli go with him."

There was a pause. It was a strange request, I knew that. I could almost hear the wheels turning in her head.

"I'm sorry, Miss Anderson, I don't understand."

I pulled onto the private road that led to the compound and checked in my mirror. Max hadn't followed me; it could only mean he was still at the apartment or on his way to get Eli.

It was something that he would do just to hurt me. He'd threatened me plenty of times with Eli but nothing ever came of it. If he got ahold of Eli, there'd be no stopping him.

I couldn't let that happen.

"He's not to be released to his dad," I gritted out. The more I talked the more my throat burned. I needed this conversation to be over.

"Has something happened that I'm not aware of?" She sounded concerned and although I really didn't want to tell her what had just happened, I felt like I may have to.

I pushed the button to open the gates to the compound and drove through them.

"I really don't want to discuss it over the phone

right now." I pulled up into my usual spot and turned the car off. "I really need you to do this, Miss Cooper."

"As I've never met his father, I wouldn't release him anyway," she replied in a gentle voice.

"Okay." I blew out a breath that I didn't realize I was holding. My whole body sagged now that I was behind the gates.

"Is everything okay?" she asked quietly.

I watched as Luke walked across the compound, stopping when he saw me staring.

"It will be," I said. "I'll be in touch within the next hour to let you know who will pick Eli up."

"It has to be someone I've met, Miss Anderson."

"Okay," I replied and ended the call just as Luke started to walk over to my car. I took another deep breath, wincing at the sensation in the back of my throat before I pushed my door open.

"You can't phone Boss then end the call—" His eyes widened as I fell out of the car.

"Luke," I croaked. My voice was beyond hoarse now, it felt like it was on fire.

"What the—"

Luke stared at me in shock. His eyes wandered over my body and down to my leg. That seemed to bring him out of his trance because he shook his head then scooped me up.

I groaned at the pain in my ribs and rested my head against his shoulder. All I wanted was to go back to sleep: I was so tired. My eye was now swollen shut and it was taking great effort to keep the other one open.

"Open up!" Luke shouted when we got to the metal door, he turned and kicked it with the bottom of his boot a couple of times. The vibrations causing me to whimper.

A minute later, Evan opened the door with a cheeky grin on his face. "Your muscles too big to even open a door now?"

"Move." Luke grunted.

Evan looked up, his eyes wide when he saw me.

"Shit." I could hear the panic in Evan's voice.

"Get Boss," Luke ordered as he carried me into the warehouse.

He placed me down onto the table we use for meetings and crouched down next to me.

"What happened, darlin'?" His voice was soft and not at all like the Luke that I knew. "Where are you hurt?" he asked when I didn't answer.

"Everywhere," I croaked.

He stood and moved down to where I had tied the t-shirt around my leg, I winced as he pulled it off and turned my head toward the office just as Ty and Evan were coming out.

"Kay?"

"Ty," I whispered.

He rushed forward, his eyes scanning my whole body as if he could see all my injuries with just one look.

"What happened?" Ty asked as he took my hand. I groaned. I really didn't want to get into this right now. I didn't want him to find out who I really was.

"Evan get the first aid kit," Luke barked out. He pushed my t-shirt aside and Ty moved to see.

I could see the anger burning behind his eyes. This time I knew that the anger wasn't directed at me but *for* me.

"Sweetheart," he murmured. "What the fuck happened to you?"

I kept my eyes on his, I didn't want to look away.

"I'm gonna have to stitch up your leg," Luke said as he prodded at my ribs. I yelped each time he touched them.

"I don't think any are broken." He moved to the bottom of the table where Evan placed the bag.

"What do you mean, stitch up her leg?"

"Looks like a stab wound," Luke replied.

"You were stabbed?" Ty growled.

My mind was elsewhere; I'd have to answer his questions at some point but all I could think was that I was free and out of that apartment.

I didn't have to go home and worry about what I would do wrong. I didn't have to worry about hiding my bruises because I wouldn't have any to hide.

It was a relief; a weight had been lifted off my shoulders and I wondered why I hadn't left earlier.

Why *had* I stayed?

I knew that I loved Max at some point. I even liked

him, but I couldn't understand how we'd got to the point that we had ended up at.

Things used to be so good, and I think I'd held out hope for things to get better.

"Kay? Kay!" I looked at Ty, my eyes starting to feel heavy. "Tell me what the hell is going on."

I stared at him. Through him. Did I trust him enough to tell him?

I didn't know what to think but his eyes begged me to trust him.

"Doesn't look too deep," Luke murmured. "Gonna have to cut your jeans though." I nodded, even though he probably couldn't see me.

"Max," I croaked.

Ty stared at me a second, his eyes flicked from confused, to understanding, then to outrage. I could see the flames practically leaping out of his eyes.

"Your boyfriend Max?"

I nodded and turned away.

Shame covered me in a sticky film. I didn't want them to know what a bad person I was but now I didn't have a choice. My breaths came in pants, my head spun, and my skin broke out in goose bumps.

I turned my head back to Ty, about to open my mouth to tell him that I didn't feel too good, when everything went black.

Chapter Fifteen

It was the thumping in my head that woke me, then the burning pain in my leg followed closely behind. Groaning, I tried to open my eyes but my left eye wouldn't open.

For those first couple of seconds I was blissfully unaware of what had happened, then the memories flashed in my mind. They came thick and fast, flashing through my mind on a constant reel. I didn't want to remember what Max had done. I tried my hardest to push them away but they wouldn't stop.

I startled when I heard footsteps come toward me and a soft voice saying, "Sweetheart, it's just me."

I opened my eye and stared into chocolate brown ones. Not evil green ones. And the memories fell away.

The longer I looked into his eyes, the more grounded I felt.

"Ty?" I shivered at the look in his eyes, I hated the anger that flashed in them.

"Hey there, sleepy head," he said softly with a lopsided smile.

"Hey," I croaked back and tried to sit up.

I winced at the pain and laid back down on the couch in the office. Gritting my teeth, I was ready to try again when Ty's hands came under my arms and lifted me up. His touch gentle.

"How you feeling?" he asked when I was up against the arm of the couch.

"I don't know," I answered honestly.

And I didn't.

I felt like I was wading through a fog that was very slow to lift. I was so tired, all I wanted to do was sleep but something was nagging at me. I just couldn't think what it was.

"Luke stitched up your leg," Ty told me as he crouched down beside me. I lifted the blanket that covered my legs, my jeans were cut all the way to the top of my thigh. "He doesn't think anything is broken but you need to take it easy."

I looked back at Ty and blew out a breath. I hated that he was seeing me like this, I felt exposed—raw.

"The bruising on your face and neck will take a couple of days to come out," he continued. I shifted a little, trying to get comfortable with the arm of the couch digging into my back. Ty watched me with narrowed eyes then stood up, walking across the office and wheeling the big office chair over. "Come on," he said and bent down to pick me up.

"I'm fine." He ignored me and lifted me up. Placing my arms around his neck I whimpered at the movement.

"You're okay, sweetheart," he whispered in my ear. I nodded as he sat me down, holding in the sob that desperately wanted to break free.

He turned and picked up the blanket off the floor, placing it over my lap. I felt like I could breathe a little easier now that I was sitting up properly. *I loved this chair.*

"Where is everyone?" I asked, trying to distract myself. The place was silent. The door to the office was open and I couldn't hear a thing coming from the warehouse.

Ty shuffled his feet and looked away.

"Ty?"

"I sent them to see if they could find Max."

"Why would you do that?" I croaked.

He narrowed his eyes at me and gritted out, "Did you really just ask that?" I gulped at the fierce look in his eyes. I didn't want them to find Max, I just wanted to forget all about him. "It doesn't matter anyway." He shrugged. "He's gone"

"Gone?"

"Yeah." He nodded. I clutched my hands in my lap and looked down. "Sweetheart."

I sucked in a breath when Ty's hand landed on my knee, his thumb rubbing back and forth.

"Yes?" I croaked.

"What happened?" I stared into his eyes, tears forming in mine and opened my mouth. "No lies," he said in a firm voice.

I gulped and looked away. The lies came so easily; I was so used to them slipping out that I had to make a conscious effort to keep them inside. He didn't need someone like me in his life.

"I can see those wheels turning. I just want the truth, Kay."

"I'm not ready," I whispered.

"Okay, sweetheart." I looked back at him, prepared to see the disappointment in his eyes.

"Sorry," I choked out.

He shook his head. "Don't be sorry. When you're ready, I want you to come to me, yeah?" I nodded. "I mean it, Kay. I won't see you any differently. You can talk to me, sweetheart."

We locked eyes, neither of us looking away, caught in that space where nothing else existed and nothing else mattered. Not me, not him, not even El—.

"Eli!" I tried to shout, but my voice broke on the first letter.

"Huh?"

"Someone needs to pick up Eli." I looked around

the office for my cell but couldn't see it. I couldn't remember if I brought it in from my car.

"I'll get Kitty and Luke to pick him up," Ty said as he pulled his phone out of his pocket.

"No." I tried to reach out but stopped when a sharp pain shot up my side. "Crap."

"What?"

"They can't pick him up, Ty. Miss Cooper said it has to be someone she's met." He looked over my head, his brows furrowed in thought.

I needed to get some things from my apartment but the thought of stepping back into that place had me breaking out into a sweat. I certainly couldn't pick Eli up with my jeans cut up my leg, flapping out at the sides.

"I'll go, I can get—" I stopped.

It occurred to me then that I didn't have anywhere to stay, I didn't have family members that I could turn to. The only place I had was my apartment.

I'd have to find a motel: it would do for now. Hopefully Max wouldn't find us, and I was earning my own money now so I could actually afford it. With money came freedom. Maybe that was why Max didn't want me to work in the first place? He didn't want me to rely on anyone but him, that way he had all the control.

"Kay?"

"Hmmm?"

"What were you about to say?"

"Oh, right." I cleared my throat. "I need to go back

to my apartment and get some things."

"What sort of things?" Ty asked as he pulled his jacket on, shoving his beanie hat on his head.

"Clothes, toiletries. Then I need to find a motel." I just needed to do a simple search to find out where the closest one was. I didn't want to be too far away from the compound.

"Motel?" Ty moved back toward me.

"I can't go back there," I said in a small voice.

He crouched down again, this time both hands came down on my knees.

"You're not going back there, sweetheart, you're staying with me." I opened my mouth to say something but he cut me off, "No arguments."

I stared at him, shocked that he would open up his home to me. I didn't want his pity; I didn't want to feel like a burden to anyone.

The fact of the matter was that I had lied to him. I'd lied to everyone.

I wanted to say all of this to him, but the look on his face told me that there was no point. Once Ty made up his mind there was no changing it, that was something that I'd learned quickly.

"I'll go and get Eli, then go to the apartment and pack you some things."

"You're going on your own?"

He stood up, his hands sliding from my knees and I stared at where they'd been, missing the feel of them.

"I'll get Luke and Kitty to meet me, Evan will be

here in a minute." He tapped away on his phone.

"I need to call the preschool."

"Why?"

"To let Miss Cooper know that you're picking Eli up."

He handed me the office phone and stood in front of me.

"I'll help you back onto the couch."

"No, I want to stay sitting up." I attempted to smile but I knew it was more of a grimace.

He smiled back, his eyes lighting up. "You're much stronger than you give yourself credit for, sweetheart. You gonna be okay here for a little while?" I nodded at him, not being able to form a coherent thought. He'd never know how much those words meant to me. "Okay, I'll be back in a while. You need anything then you use the radio." He picked up two radios and gave one to me.

"Ty?"

"Yeah?" He turned to face me in the doorway.

"Don't let Eli in the apartment, Ty... please." His eyes flashed again with anger and frustration. "Take my keys," I said, even though I had no idea where they were. He gave me a jerky nod and turned out the door.

I listened until the metal door shut, then I was all alone. *I was always alone.*

I stared at the radio and told myself over and over again that I was safe now. He couldn't get me here. He couldn't get into the compound.

But that didn't stop me from jumping out of my skin when Evan walked in the warehouse.

EVAN HAD TRIED TO KEEP ME OCCUPIED WHILE TY went to get Eli. He told jokes and spoke about all the software that he'd just installed and it worked for a little bit, until all I could think about was Eli.

How had he reacted when I wasn't there to pick him up?

Did Ty make sure Eli hadn't gone into the apartment and stayed with Luke or Kitty?

My mind was on a constant whirl of what ifs. I hated sitting still and not doing anything. The more time that passed, the more thoughts I had.

My whole body ached and each time I tried to move it only got worse.

I shifted in the chair and held in a groan as I tried to concentrate on Evan, but it was hard when I could only open one of my eyes.

"Kay?"

My head was spinning, my throat dry and sore. I closed my good eye and took a deep breath—in and out —it helped for a second, until I felt movement next to me.

My eye sprung open, my breathing picked up as Evan walked toward me.

"Kay?" he asked again, only this time his hand

landed on my shoulder.

I tried my hardest not to flinch at the contact but I couldn't help it. In the back of my mind I knew that Evan wouldn't hurt me, but that didn't stop my body's reaction: I didn't want to be touched.

I opened my mouth to try and tell him to take his hand off me, but nothing would come out.

"You okay?" He didn't move his hand and it felt like I had a ton of bricks weighing down on me even though his touch was feather light.

The edges of my vision darkened, the walls closing in on me. I clutched my hands in my lap, squeezing them to try and get the shaking under control.

I could feel myself retreating to that happy place that I went to so often when Max would hurt me.

"Evan!"

Everything sounded like I was in a tunnel, but that voice called to me in a way that nothing and nobody else ever had. My vision started to clear, my breathing becoming a little easier as it rattled through my chest.

"Move your hand," he growled.

I gasped as the weight of his hand lifted off me and Ty crouched down in front of me, cupping the side of my face gently. I stared at his brown eyes as they willed me to come back to him, to escape out of my own head.

"Just breathe." I took a shaky breath in and blew it out. "In and out. That's it." I could feel people behind him, but I didn't take my eyes from Ty's. He grounded me, kept me here in the present instead of me retreating into my memories.

It was a dangerous place to be—inside my own head.

"Eli?" I croaked.

"He's here, sweetheart."

He stood and moved to the side and there stood in the doorway was Eli, Luke and Kitty on either side of him. I could see the hesitation in his wide eyes as he looked at Ty before moving back to me.

"It's okay, bud," he told him.

"Mama?" his small voice rang out in the silence as he walked toward me.

"Hey, sweetie." I opened my arms and gritted my teeth against the pain that flowed through me at the movement.

He stepped into them and I encircled him in my arms, relishing in knowing that he was fully safe now. He stayed still, almost as if he knew not to make any sudden movements.

However much I liked to tell myself that he didn't know what was going on, I knew deep down that he knew more. I think we both liked to pretend that we didn't—to not acknowledge it.

I closed my eye and breathed him in, relaxing the longer that I held him.

"We staying here, Mama?" I pulled back, staring at him, searching his confused eyes. It broke my heart to see him like that.

I turned my head toward Ty. He smiled at me, one of those huge full teeth smiles that told me everything would be okay. It would take time, but things would work out—I hoped.

"Yes, sweetie." I turned back to face Eli. "Is that okay?"

"Can I still watch cartoons?" he asked with a completely serious face. I laughed at that. I didn't care about the pain I was feeling, it felt good to forget about everything else and concentrate on the most important person in my life.

"Depends," Luke said from the doorway.

"On what?" Eli turned toward him.

"If I can watch them too." Luke lifted his lips into a smile, his eyes sparkling. It was strange to see Luke like this. Nice, but strange.

Eli looked back at me and raised his brows. "Can I watch them now, Mama?"

"You can if you want to, sweetie." He nodded and went to move away from me before stalling and whispering, "Love you, Mama," before he walked off toward Luke.

"I love you, too, sweetie," I choked out.

"Want to go now?" Luke asked him.

"Yeah, my favorite starts soon!"

Luke looked over at me, a silent question in his eyes.

"Bring him over to mine in a couple of hours," Ty told him.

I watched as they walked out of the room, Eli's small hand wrapped in Luke's large one.

"Will he be okay?" I asked Ty

"Yeah." He looked over my head; I knew that Evan was still standing there but I couldn't bring myself to look over at him.

"I'm sorry, Kay," Evan whispered. I nodded. "I didn't mean—"

"Evan." Ty tilted his head toward the door.

They both moved over to it and Ty whispered something to Evan. He didn't look happy and I wanted to say that it wasn't Evan's fault. He didn't know that just by touching me I would freak out. But I couldn't bring myself to open my mouth.

"How you feeling?" Kitty asked.

I moved my eyes from Ty and Evan to her. I tried to smile. "Like I got ran over by a truck."

"Ha!" She moved over to the couch and held something out to me. "Take these. They'll help with the pain." She winked as I took the box of pills and bottle of water out of her hand before she turned and followed Evan out of the room.

Ty turned back to face me before he leaned against the door frame. His big body intimidating, but to me it just screamed protection.

"Let's get you back to the house and into something more comfortable," he said as he sauntered toward me.

Chapter Sixteen

I'D IMAGINED what Ty's house looked like many times, the wrap around porch with the swinging chair screamed family home. If it wasn't for the location, I would have thought a family lived there.

You know the type, happily married with two children, one boy, one girl. Dad who goes out to work while the mom stays home.

I expected to find a lone couch and pizza boxes all over the place. A typical bachelor pad. I should have known better. I'd worked with Ty now for well over a month and in that time I'd gotten to know him pretty well. He was organized down to a T and never had anything out of place and always knew where everyone was at any given time.

Opening up the front door with his free hand, he

carried me inside. I looked around, noting the polished hardwood floors that led to a staircase lined with photos much like those in his office. It was all open floor plan with the living room to the right and a door at the back of the room.

A large corner sofa sat in the middle facing an open fire and above that, the biggest TV that I had ever seen. He walked us through the living room to the door I'd noticed as I stared at the paintings that hung off the light gray walls.

Pushing through the door, my breath caught in my throat, I'd never seen anything like it. I'd only ever seen photos in magazines of these sort of kitchens, I'd never imagined I'd be inside of one.

The whole back wall was covered in floor to ceiling glass doors, the sun shone through them, making the counters sparkle.

Helping me sit in a chair, Ty walked over to the glossy white cupboards and pulled two glasses out. I stared in amazement out of the glass doors, the backyard backed straight into the woods. It was breathtaking.

My gaze wandered around the room, a large stove sat in the middle of the counter. Everything shined and sparkled in only the way an unused kitchen would. My fingers itched to make a mess in here, the kind of mess that only Eli and I could make while we made cookies.

"Don't get taking those tablets until you've had

something to eat," Ty interrupted my thoughts as he opened the fridge.

"Okay." I wasn't hungry but there was no point in me voicing that right now.

I closed my eyes and breathed in deep; this place somehow settled all the rampant thoughts that swirled in my mind. I didn't know whether it was this house or Ty. Maybe it was a combination of both?

Ty had just pulled out some food and a bottle of water when the front door opened.

"Bro? You home?" a deep voice shouted.

My good eye sprung open and I gasped, looking over at Ty, my face full of panic. He hadn't told me anyone would be coming over and the thought of someone new being in the same place as me had my heart racing uncontrollably.

"It's okay, sweetheart." Ty rushed over to me, the water and food forgotten about.

"I... who..." I stuttered, staring at the door we had come through as the footsteps became louder.

"It's only my brother, Charlie." He crouched down in front of me.

"Bro!" I flinched at the voice: I felt so out of control. All I wanted to do was disappear.

"In here," Ty answered back. I could feel his gaze on me before his hand came up to my face, cupping my cheek gently as he moved me it toward him. "I'm here," he said. "I got you."

"What's so urgent?" Charlie asked as he pushed through the kitchen door.

I closed my eye and tried to control my breathing. Nothing bad would happen to me—not with Ty here.

"Erm... Hey?" the voice said. I opened my eye and looked up at him.

He stood at the same height as Ty, but where Ty was all sharp lines and broody this guy screamed cocky. He had a badge clipped to his belt and what looked like a gun holster. He looked from me to Ty and I could see the questions in his eyes.

"Hey." Ty stood but stayed standing beside me, his hand grasping my shoulder softly. "Want a drink?" Ty asked and went to move away from me.

I moved to clutch his hand and groaned, my side screaming in pain. However much I really wanted to tell Ty that he was out of order for calling his brother, I couldn't bear for him to be away from me. Not right now.

"Nah, I'm good," Charlie said and moved closer to the table, I squeezed Ty's hand in response. "So..." He pulled out a chair opposite me. "Am I here as your brother or..."

Ty looked at me and I shook my head. There was no way that I would make an official statement. I knew what happened to women who reported these things: there was never enough evidence and then they were worse off than they were if they would have kept their mouths shut.

"My brother." Ty pulled the chair out next to me and kept my hand in his. My entire hand was encased in his long fingers, his calluses rough against the softness of my skin.

"Well?"

"I needed you to see Kaylee."

"Ty?" I whispered.

"Sweetheart," he started as he turned to face me. "If you want to make an official statement then Charlie can do that." I was already shaking my head no. "You don't want to press charges?"

"No," I said with more force than I meant to.

His eyes flashed as they scanned me from head to toe. I still had the blanket wrapped around me and I knew from the look in his eyes that he didn't agree with me.

"If you don't want to make a statement..." He raised his brows, as if I'd change my mind if he repeated it. He huffed. "Then at least let Charlie take something unofficial." He scraped his hand down his face. "Just in case."

It was only now that I noticed the dark circles under his eyes. I hadn't thought about what everyone else must be feeling. I felt bad now that I thought about it. I'd turned up like this and just expected them to help me.

"I'm sorry," I whispered.

"What?" Ty pulled back.

"I know your Corey's friend and I just expected

you to help me automatically." I looked down. "I shouldn't have done that."

"Hey." His voice was soft. "I'm not doing this because of who your brother is." I looked back at him, unsure. But those eyes told me all what I needed to know without any words being said. "I'm doing this because I care for you."

"Corey?" Charlie asked.

Ty ignored him. "Can you take some kind of unofficial statement?"

"Yeah," he drawled. "But now might not be a good time." Ty stared at me, his eyes doing that thing that they did: assessing the situation. "Why don't you rest for a couple of days and then we can talk?" Charlie directed at me.

I nodded slightly, the more time I had to think things through, the better.

"I don't—"

"Corey?" Charlie interrupted.

"Yeah." Ty ran his hand down his face.

"What's he got to do with this?"

Ty looked out of the windows, his jaw clenched. "Kay is his little sister."

Charlie's eyes widened, his body slumping down in the chair as he looked from me to Ty.

"Are you two—"

"No." Ty growled.

"Cause you know he wouldn't—"

"Yeah, I got it."

"Well just—"

"I said." Ty stood. "*I got it.*" He tilted his head to the door. "A word." He didn't move until Charlie was by the door, which I was grateful for. "I'll be back in a minute," he directed at me before he leaned down and planted a soft kiss on my head. "Then you need to get some food down you before you go to bed and rest."

"Okay." I nodded and watched him leave.

THE FOLLOWING COUPLE OF DAYS WENT BY quickly. I wasn't apart from Eli for long, and each night I fell asleep beside him. I couldn't bear to be apart from him: I had to know that he was safe.

Ty had given us each a guest room but I hadn't stayed in mine yet. Every time I would close my eyes I would see Max standing beside me with a knife glinting off the moonlight, so instead of sleeping, I watched Eli.

The evil look on Max's face was burned into my brain and nothing I did would ever make that go away.

We'd made it to Thursday night before Eli asked to go back to preschool. I hated the thought of not being able to see him all day: to make sure he was safe. Just thinking of him not being behind the compound gates gave me chills.

But when he asked me with those sad, green eyes, I

couldn't say no. He had this way of wrapping me around his little finger.

We'd settled into a routine over the last couple of days. But now, as I sat watching Eli eat his breakfast, I couldn't help but notice how relaxed he was in this environment. He was only ever like this around me, at preschool, or when we were at Miss Maggie's.

Never around a man.

But with Luke and Ty he'd been his animated self and I knew that he would be the same around Evan, but he hadn't been around since I freaked out on him.

I'd told Ty to tell him that he should come over to the house but he still hadn't shown up.

My eye had turned a dark shade of purple and the swelling had gone down: I could open it a little now. I could bear more weight on my leg now too, although it still hurt to walk. My side was covered with dark green and purple bruises, along with my neck, and my voice was still croaky.

Luke had been around every day checking up on me, but each time I had managed to avoid him. I didn't want to be the center of attention, I wanted them to forget what had happened.

I wanted to forget what had happened.

I didn't want Max to have any control over me anymore.

"Mama?"

I startled at Eli's voice. I'd gone inside my head

again, that had happened a lot over the last couple of days.

"Yes, sweetie?"

"I finished," he said with a giant grin and a milk mustache.

"Come on then." I placed my now cold coffee down and pushed off my seat. It was slow going as the pain was still there, but I tried my best not to let it show in front of Eli.

Jumping down off the chair, he placed his small hand inside mine. "Can I choose my clothes today, Mama?"

I gasped when I went to push open the door and it swung toward me. My eyes widening when I saw that it was Ty.

I'd barely seen him. Not for his lack of trying; he'd come to check on me and Eli to make sure that I was coping okay and that we had everything we needed. I'd caught him watching us a few times but I didn't say anything. I just needed time so that I could figure my own head out. I had this need to be by Ty, I'd never felt anything like it before and I knew that it was a bad thing.

I couldn't rely on Ty, it wasn't fair on him to take all of this on, he had his own life and didn't need all of the baggage that I came with.

He had this pull on me though, and I didn't know how much longer I could resist it.

"Ty!" Eli shouted and let go of my hand.

"Hey, bud." He held his hand up for a high five and Eli jumped up to slap it. He turned toward me, "Hey."

His eyes were full of questions like that first day, but this time they were louder than before. I knew that it was natural for someone like Ty to want to know the ins and outs of the whole situation, but I couldn't tell him everything.

"Hey," I whispered back.

We stood there with Eli between us, neither of us saying anything out loud, but so many things being said silently with our eyes. I tried my best to not show him how much pain I was in as he watched me, but the bruise on my face didn't help. His whole body would tense every time he looked at me.

A small voice inside said that he was angry with me for bringing this to him. However much I tried to shut that voice up, it always came back.

"Mama?"

Eli's voice brought me out of the trance and I grabbed his hand to shuffle past Ty without another word or looking back at him. Whenever he was around I had this inexplicable need to be near him. The itch I felt to touch him was becoming too much.

I shouldn't be thinking like this.

Not after what I'd escaped from, but I couldn't get him out of my head. I hadn't been able to since the first day that I met him.

I shook my head and tried my best to concentrate

on the task at hand: getting up the stairs. It had gotten easier each time I did it but it still didn't stop my leg from burning or the throbbing in my ribs.

It took us twice as long to get ready and once I was back down the stairs and pushing my feet into my chucks I felt like I could sleep for a week.

Eli was beside me on the couch as I caught my breath and jumped up when Ty came down the stairs, his boots banging loudly on each step.

"You ready, bud?"

"Yeah." Eli stood and tried to put his coat on.

I went to move to help him but Ty was faster. Then I noticed he was ready for work: belt clipped around his waist with a radio attached.

"Ty?"

"Hmm?"

"What are you doing?"

"Putting Eli's coat on." His face was as innocent as Eli's when he swore that he didn't have any chocolate before dinner. Only I knew what that face meant: he was up to something.

"No." I shook my head, wincing as I pushed up off the couch. Ty offered me his hand but I ignored it. I had to do this on my own.

"What?" He raised a brow at me, the side of his mouth lifting in a knowing smile. He knew exactly what he was doing and I wasn't in the mood to play games.

"What are you doing?"

He shrugged and pulled his beanie hat on his head. "Taking Eli to preschool."

"I'm taking him." I pointed at my chest.

"No," he said in a firm voice as he pushed his ear piece in.

The door opened just as I was about to answer him back.

"Mornin'!"

"Luke!" Eli ran at him with so much force that Luke actually stumbled but the grin that spread across his face said he didn't mind.

"Could you take Eli to the car?" I asked Luke, keeping my eyes on Ty, the sound of my blood pumping in my ears beating an erratic rhythm.

"Erm... Sure."

They shuffled out of the house. I didn't move until the door had shut and I heard them go down the steps.

"You can't tell me what to do," I seethed as I shuffled closer.

"Kay—"

"No," I choked out, my emotions getting the better of me. "I can't do this again."

"Sweetheart." He took two giant steps and was in my space. "Do what again?" I shook my head and looked down; I'd said too much already. "You need to rest. You're not going to heal properly if you don't," he said softly.

There was no way that I was going to let someone else take Eli, that was my job.

"Ty—"

"No, you listen now." He placed his finger and thumb on my chin and tilted my face back. "I'm only looking out for you. I'll take Eli today and then we can see how you are on Monday."

"But—"

"Your face resembles a punching bag and you can hardly move." He raised his brows, challenging me. I guess that it might not have been a good idea for me to take Eli, not in the state I was in anyway.

"It's only ever been me," I mumbled.

"What has?" he asked, his hand cupping the side of my face. I leaned into it without even realizing.

"That's taken him to preschool, I did everything. I'm not used to all of this." I waved my hand around.

"All of what?"

"This... this help." I huffed.

He smiled. "Well get used to it, sweetheart."

I searched his eyes; what I was looking for I didn't know. But there was something there that told me to trust him.

"Okay." I slumped into him and his arms came around me. I leaned my head on his chest, listening to the steady beat of his heart.

"I'm here now," he whispered. "You're safe."

Safe.

One simple word, but it meant so much to me.

A warm feeling settled into the pit of my stomach as he held me. I didn't want to think about what it meant, but I felt safe in the knowledge that Max couldn't get us here.

"Luke will check you over when we get back," he told me when he pulled away.

"What about Eli?" I panicked. "What if—"

"Kitty's stayin' there," he interrupted as he walked toward the door. With a wink, he pulled the door open and left.

Chapter Seventeen

"IT'S HEALING NICELY," Luke said as he covered my leg up the next day.

I'd slept most of yesterday; I'd obviously needed it because I felt much better today. Feeling some semblance of normal, I even put on some makeup to try and cover the bruising. It helped a little but didn't cover it completely and you could still tell I had a black eye, but it made me feel better when I looked in the mirror.

"How long until the stitches can be removed?" I asked as he helped me sit up on the bed.

"Soon," he said, not giving me an exact time frame.

He gave me an amused look when I groaned. The difference between the Luke that I first met to the Luke that I know now was astounding. There was still a darkness to him that I could identify with but I couldn't put my finger on it.

His eyes were haunted.

"Luke?"

"Yeah?" He packed up his kit, not looking at me.

I waited. Chewing on my lip while debating whether I should say anything. Stopping what he was doing he flicked his eyes to mine.

"Do you think Eli will be okay?"

Zipping up his bag he narrowed eyes at me, the same look that he used to give me, only now I knew that he was assessing me. His gaze causing me to squirm.

Seeing what he must have been searching for he slumped onto the edge of the bed.

"Yeah, he'll be fine." He dipped his head.

I shifted on the bed and couldn't stop the next words that came out.

"Are you speaking from experience?" I whispered.

He took an unsteady breath and looked up at me.

I stared into his ice-blue eyes, not daring to move an inch. I waited for him and saw his shields as they lowered, letting me see all of his pain.

"Yeah," he croaked.

I blinked, I hadn't expected him to answer.

"My dad," he said and looked at the half open door. Whether to see if anyone was listening or because he couldn't look at me I didn't know.

"You don't have to tell me," I whispered.

Shaking his head, he continued, "Every night he'd come home and find some excuse to hurt her," he said in a haunted voice.

Not knowing what to say, I kept my mouth shut and let him carry on: he was somewhere else so I doubted he'd hear me anyway.

"Nothin' she did was ever right." He turned, his eyes full of sadness and anger. "I couldn't help her," he choked out.

I moved closer, placing my hand on his arm I squeezed reassuringly. There was nothing that I could say that would make a difference, but sometimes all you needed was to get it out into the open—to get it out of your system. It was funny because even though I knew this, I still hadn't told anyone what had happened that night. Maybe that would help my nightmares?

"I can still hear her screams. Every night she'd beg him to stop."

"Luke—"

"I had to stop him," he said hauntingly. "He wouldn't stop." His arm was so tense; it was like touching a rock. "I—"

"It's okay," I whispered.

He startled as if he didn't realize that I was still there and then flung himself up off the bed and stood frozen to the spot.

"He never saw anything," I whispered.

"What—"

"Eli." I met his eyes. "I made sure he never saw anything."

He laughed, his whole body shaking from the force. "Kay." He smirked. "If you think that he didn't know what was going on then—"

"He didn't." I gritted my teeth. Sure, he saw some bruises but I could have gotten them from anywhere.

"Darlin', he saw your black eye and didn't even question it. He hasn't even asked about his dad."

"But—"

"You did the right thing." I narrowed my eyes at him. "Leavin' him."

"Did I?"

I couldn't look at him. Knowing he had been in the same position as Eli: he knew what went on in a home like ours which freaked me out.

Max's face flashed through my mind, it was always the same image: him standing above me with that knife.

Did I do the right thing? I'd caused this in the first place, had I not wanted to get a job he never would have flipped out like that. At least, that's what I told myself.

Maybe it would have been better to stay and live like that if it kept Eli safe. We were protected here but we couldn't stay in the compound forever, I'd have to go back out of those gates at some stage and the thought terrified me.

"Yeah." Luke sat back down. "You did."

I searched his eyes. His swirled with so many emotions that it was hard to pinpoint one.

"Mama!" Eli shouted as he came through the front door. I watched as Luke put his walls back up: it amazed me how well he could do that.

"I'm up here, sweetie." We listened as they stomped up the stairs, neither of us saying another word.

"We went to the woods!" Eli bounded into the room with a face covered in mud.

"Really?"

"Yeah! It was so much fun." His face was taken over by his toothy grin. "We played hide and seek!"

I smiled at him. "Did you find Ty?"

"Yeah!" He snorted. "Of course, I did!"

Ty stood against the door watching me, his bulging arms crossed and his beanie on his head.

"He cheated." Ty shook his head.

"Did not!" Eli put his hands on his hips and spun around.

"Ye—"

"Right." Luke clapped his hands and stood. "Who wants to watch a movie?"

"I do!" Eli jumped up and down.

"Come on then." Luke waved his arm and walked toward the door. "You good?" he asked when he met my eyes.

"Sure." I nodded and moved my eyes to Ty who

was frowning at him. "Thanks, Luke." He left the room with Eli on his tail.

I pushed up off the bed. I made it halfway off the bed before Ty's hands gripped my hips to help me up.

"I can—"

"I know," he whispered, his breath fanning across my neck making me shiver. "How is everything looking?"

"Yeah. Good." I cleared my throat; his hands burned through my clothing. Closing my eyes, I could almost feel his hands on my bare skin.

"Sweetheart," he murmured. I opened my eyes and tipped my head back, his hooded eyes calling to me. I leaned into him.

"Ty—"

"Come on, Mama!" Eli shouted from downstairs.

Ty's eyes widened as he shot away from me, his head whipping to the door and back. I patted him on the shoulder as I walked past, laughing at the awkwardness on his face.

"It's not funny." He followed me out.

"Sure." I laughed and started down the stairs. He groaned, which only made me laugh harder.

"I'll be out all day," Ty said as he pulled his coat on. "Luke will be with Eli."

"Okay." I nodded and kissed Eli's cheek. He'd

been back at preschool for a few days now and I still hadn't taken him. My eye wasn't healed yet and although I could cover most of it with makeup, I couldn't bring myself to go out of the gates. The more time I spent inside the compound the more I didn't want to leave.

"Love you, sweetie."

"Love you." Eli ran out of the door and straight to Luke who was waiting by the car.

"Kitty and Evan will be over later." He pulled his beanie on and took Eli's bag from me.

"Okay." I swallowed.

Ty hesitated, opening and closing his mouth several times. He finally closed it, shook his head, and leaned forward as he placed a kiss on the top of my head: it had become his thing to do before he left. Leaning against the door frame, I watched him get into the car and waved as they drove toward the gates.

I'd grown comfortable in this bubble: no one could get in or out without any of us knowing. The compound had become my crutch. I was terrified of going outside those gates but I didn't think anyone knew that. I hoped they just thought that I needed time to heal—physically and mentally.

This place felt like home. I kept reminding myself not to get too comfortable because we wouldn't be able to stay here forever—I'd need to leave at some point.

But staring at those big gates and imagining walking through them sent chills down my spine.

I leaned against the open door and yawned. Last night was the first night that I had slept alone, although not much sleeping had taken place. Ty thought that I slept with Eli because he didn't want to be alone, but it was me who didn't want to be on my own.

I couldn't bear to see those images when I closed my eyes so instead I stayed awake and stared at the walls.

Nobody had mentioned Max, not even Eli. I was sure that he would have asked what was going on but he just got on with things like nothing had changed. In fact, he was happier than I had ever seen him. Ty hadn't pushed for any more information since Charlie had left last week. I could still see the questions in his eyes every time he looked at me, but not once did he ask and I was grateful for that.

I jumped, a noise startling me and turned to where it came from. I gasped and rushed back into the house when I saw Evan leaving his cabin.

I hadn't seen him since I freaked out on him last week. I couldn't stay away from him much longer, I mean, we worked together and right now we lived on the same compound so I had to face him eventually.

It wasn't that I was afraid of him: I was embarrassed about what had happened. Evan was one of the gentlest people that I knew and yet I hadn't been able to stop my body's reaction to him that day.

I peeked out of the window in the door. He was stood in the middle of the compound staring at the house. I watched him turn his head toward the warehouse and then swivel back around to face the house.

My hands started to sweat as he started walking toward the house. I wasn't ready to see him: I didn't know what to do or say to him. My breathing started coming in pants the closer he got and by the time he knocked on the door I felt like I had an elephant sitting on my chest.

"Kay?" He brought his face closer to the window and I ducked to the side. The fast movement caused my side to twitch in pain as I held my breath waiting for him to go.

"I know you're in there." I could tell by his voice that he was smiling. My breaths slowed the more he talked. I found it ironic that he was the reason I felt like this yet he was also the reason that I was calming down.

"Come on, Kay." He groaned. "I miss you."

I peeked up at the door, his face smashed up against the window trying to see inside. He must have seen me because he pulled back and smiled wide.

"Will you be my friend?" He pouted.

My hand clutched the door handle "Depends."

"On what?"

I pulled the door open. "If you'll forgive me," I said in a small voice and looked down.

"Forgive you?" He gasped with wide eyes.

"Yes, I'm so sorry I freaked out, Evan. I... I..."

"Hey." He moved forward, his arms outstretched,

though this time he didn't touch me. He waited until I moved forward.

"I'm sorry, too," he said when I moved into his arms and lay my head on his chest. "Let's just forget about it, yeah?"

"Yeah," I said to his chest. Why did they all have to be so tall? I let out a deep breath, relieved that we were back on good terms.

"Hey!" Kitty shouted and we both turned to her. "What's going on?"

"Oh, man, I have some gossip for you," Evan whispered in my ear.

"You do?"

"Uh-huh." He nodded and pulled away. Grinning as he walked backwards with his brows dancing up and down. He jogged down the steps and toward the warehouse.

"Later, alligator!" he shouted as he walked past Kitty.

"What was all that about?" She frowned, not taking her eyes off Evan.

"Nothing." I shrugged walking into the house.

Huffing, she followed me inside and threw herself on the couch.

"So..."

"So, what?" She rolled her eyes at me.

"What's been going on?"

She ignored me and pulled her cell out tapping away at the screen. I leaned over trying to see who she was texting but she covered her cell. I'd never seen her so secretive.

"Cookies?"

"Huh?"

"Eli said you bake the best cookies." Jumping up she pushed her cell into her pocket.

"Okaaay..." I blinked.

"Teach me?"

So, I found out that Kitty's teach me is: you bake while I watch and eat them as they come out of the oven. That's where we stayed for most of the day, me baking, Kitty eating, and us talking about nothing but everything at the same time.

She told me about her sisters and her parents. How she came from a good family but had to escape from their suffocating rules. She had this far-off look to her eyes when she talked about them.

They were all opening up to me now. Why couldn't I do the same?

I managed to bake seven batches of cookies and by the time everyone had finished there wasn't one cookie left. Eli and Evan had a cookie eating contest while I watched them all laugh and have fun.

Just watching them all took my mind off the fact that it would only be a couple of hours until bedtime.

Until I closed my eyes and saw him again.

Chapter Eighteen

I'D NEVER SUFFERED from any kind of nightmares. Not when my mother died, not when Max had hit me for the first time or any time after that. I'd had dreams and then woke up and promptly forgot them.

But this time was different; each time I would close my eyes, he'd be standing there. An evil grin on his face and a knife in his hand, but we'd never be in the apartment.

We'd always be wherever I fell asleep.

This made the nightmares so much worse. If it was me reliving the memories then I could separate that, but when he was here—in Ty's house, on the compound—it made them that much worse.

Each nightmare lasted longer than the one before

and every time he would get a little bit closer to me. This time he actually touched me.

I shot up in bed and whipped my head back and forth, expecting him to be standing next to the bed.

Groaning from the pain of sitting up so fast, I narrowed my eyes at the dark corner of the room. My chest heaved up and down, all that I could hear in the room were my heavy pants and my breaths becoming louder the more I stared at the space.

I covered my mouth to hold the scream in when someone knocked on the door.

"Sweetheart?" Ty's gruff voice whispered. "You okay?"

He was the last person that I wanted to know about the nightmares. He'd want to know what was in them and then that would lead to what had happened that day.

I still wasn't ready to tell him.

"Uh-huh," I said when I pulled my hand from my mouth, all the while not taking my eyes from the dark corner.

A crack of light came into the room when he opened the door, I could see now that there was nothing there. Breathing a sigh of relief, I looked over at him.

"Kay?" He stepped into the room, leaving the door open halfway.

His hair was sticking up in different directions and my gaze traveled down his chest widening at the sight.

The tattoos on his arms continued way up and over his broad shoulders, I couldn't see his back but I imagined they continued there.

"What?" I shook my head. His mouth was moving but I couldn't hear him over being distracted by his bare chest. It was chiseled to perfection, I shouldn't be thinking about his perfect chest like that but when it was screaming at me from across the room it was hard to not stare.

"I said: Is everything okay?"

His muscles moved with each step he took closer, the tattoos dancing on his arms. I smiled and nodded my head. He was so close now that if I reached out I could touch him.

"I'm okay."

"I heard screaming." He frowned down at me.

I shook my head and lay back down. "I'm fine."

"Don't lie to me, Kay." His gruff voice warned.

"I... I..."

Ty tilted his head, those eyes assessing me in that frustrating way. He huffed as he sat on the edge of the bed.

"Nightmare?"

The words were stuck in my throat so I nodded instead. I held my breath as he moved closer, his hand stretching out. I closed my eyes, not knowing what he was about to do and when his hand touched my arm lightly I shivered. My eyes sprang open and watched as his thumb rubbed back and forth.

"You're safe here," he whispered. "

"I know."

The rough pad of his thumb was nearly as distracting as his bare chest. I needed to stop seeing him like this: to stop thinking about him. I was broken. I wasn't good enough for him: I wasn't good enough for anyone.

Maybe I was meant to be with Max, he always said that I needed to be taught how to behave. At least I stayed in line with him. At least, I had *tried* to stay in line.

"You want to talk about it?"

"Not really." I looked away.

"It's just me, Kay."

If I told him what I dreamed about, what actually happened that day, then he wouldn't look at me the same.

I've told so many lies that sometimes I couldn't tell the difference between the truth and the lies that I told. How were you supposed to tell someone that you were so far gone that nothing would be able to bring you back from the brink?

"I see him." I hadn't meant to say it but it came out anyway.

"Max?" His hand stilled, I moved my eyes back to his, watching as they flashed in anger.

"Yes."

"When have you seen him?" he gritted out.

I looked down at my arm, concentrating on his hand.

"Every time I close my eyes." I followed the path that his veins made all the way up his arm and to his neck. Silence weighed heavy in the room.

Shifting in the bed, I cleared my throat.

"But you—"

I shouldn't have said anything. The one time I try and tell the truth and he doesn't believe me. "Just forget it." I lay down and pulled the covers up to my neck.

"I thought you were sleeping. You did when—" I rolled over and squeezed my eyes shut. I couldn't look at him anymore. "That's why you slept with Eli? Have you been getting any sleep?"

I stayed silent, maybe if I was silent long enough he'd think I'd fallen back to sleep.

He was quiet for so long that I almost did fall asleep. My eyes felt like sandpaper and I didn't think I could keep them open much longer, and with Ty in the room I could finally relax.

Even though he had me on edge for completely different reasons, the image of his bare chest was scorched into my brain. But knowing that he was in the room with me made me feel protected, as if Max couldn't get to me if he was here.

The bed shifted and my eyes opened: he was about to leave. Looked like I wouldn't be getting anymore sleep tonight.

"Mind if I stay?" he asked and lay down next to me.

I turned my head, raising my brows. He was laid on his back above the covers, hands behind his head.

I swallowed shaking my head.

"Good." He smiled and I closed my eyes. "Now go to sleep." His mouth was still kicked up in a grin and my own lips spread to match his.

I rolled over and closed my eyes. The only person I dreamed of this time was Ty and his bare chest.

***

It had been four days since Ty had come into my room. Each night that followed, I'd wake up screaming and he'd come in and lie on top of the covers so I could get some sleep. He wouldn't say a word, just smile, close his eyes, and settle down. Then I'd sleep like a baby for the rest of the night.

I liked that he wouldn't ask what had happened, but I started to want to tell him. It would bubble up in my throat and try to slip out. Only every time I opened my mouth, nothing would come out.

I wanted to tell him how lost I was feeling. That I didn't know who I was anymore.

I found myself wanting to tell Ty what Max had done to me, what he had said to me and the names he used to call me.

Nothing would come out though so I'd end up thinking it all but never saying it.

It was funny how much sleep helped me heal. Something as simple as letting your body rest made such a huge impact: I couldn't remember the last time I slept so well. Maybe it had been when I lived at home with Corey?

Either way, it was a long time ago.

I woke up late Monday morning, rushing to get out of bed; it was the first time since the incident I felt more like myself.

The house was silent which meant that Ty had taken Eli to preschool. I shook my head at the time, Ty had let me sleep in again, he had to stop helping me like this. When we moved out and got our own place it would be so much harder to get used to being on our own again.

Not only that but I feared that Eli was getting too close to everyone. When we moved off the compound it would be such a big change.

I peeked through the bedroom window, all of the cars were outside of the warehouse. A quick check of the time told me that the daily meeting would start in fifteen minutes.

My hair was greasy and there was no way I could get away without washing it so I used those fifteen minutes to my full advantage. I took a quick shower, plaited my hair and dressed in my black jeans and MAC Security t-shirt.

I couldn't bring myself to put my belt on so I left that and shoved my feet into my chucks.

It felt good to be going back to work. I wanted to start my training again and get back to normal; I was looking forward to having something to do with my days again.

All I had done the last two weeks was sit here and think about Max. I needed to keep my mind busy and getting back to work would do that.

The bruising on my eye and throat was almost gone and easily covered with makeup. My ribs still screamed if I moved too quickly but I felt almost back to normal, at least, *my* version of normal.

I relished in the sound of the gravel crunching under my feet when I walked over to the warehouse, pulling the metal door open without a struggle. I breathed in deeply: it had its own distinctive smell, a mixture of coffee and man, something that put my body at ease.

Everyone was at the table and all conversation stopped as I walked in. They all turned around, each with varying degrees of shock on their faces. I ignored them and walked to my chair, still with a slight limp but smiling.

Though my leg was better it still wasn't fully healed, I could walk on it which to me was all that mattered. It was better than sitting around at home.

Home.

I had to stop thinking about Ty's place as home.

"Morning." I smiled and sat down.

I pulled the pad and paper from next to Ty and read what they had already covered, all that was on there was today's date. They were all still staring at me when I looked up.

"Kay?"

"Yes?" I turned to face Ty.

"What are you doing?"

I scanned the warehouse, everything still looked the same but I couldn't bring myself to look down at the table. I was sure that there would still be blood on it.

"Writing the meeting notes." I rolled my eyes, picking up the pen I drew a line underneath the date.

"You don't have—"

"No," I interrupted and shook my head. "I do."

Ty leaned over and whispered, "Are you sure you're ready?"

I turned toward him again and stared into his eyes. They told me that everything was okay, that everything would be okay. He'd never know how much confidence he instilled in me.

"Yes." I nodded. "I'm ready."

His eyes flitted back and forth between mine and after several seconds he nodded, clearing his throat.

"Where were we?" he asked, turning to face the others.

They were silent for a beat and then Luke said, "You were saying about Charlie?"

"Right." Ty pushed the open folder closer to me and I scooted my chair closer to his.

"There's been some suspicious activity at the country club." I held my hand on the paper and tapped my finger.

"What kind?" Kitty asked.

"He thinks there's some kind of underground ring being run from there."

"Underground ring?" I asked.

"Yeah, there's been several girls that have disappeared. All aged between thirteen and sixteen."

"What do they want with the girls?"

"Well—"

"So, what does the country club have to do with it?" Luke asked.

"That's where they're being taken from."

Ty went on to tell us that they have a suspect but the police couldn't get anything on him and now he has some kind of injunction against them.

I couldn't believe that young girls were being taken. What did they want with them? Why the country club?

"What about the girls?" I interrupted.

"What about them?"

"Have they been found?"

"No," Evan said from behind his laptop. "There have been nine so far."

"Nine?" I choked.

"Charlie said that he thinks it's some kind of sex ring."

Sex ring?

"This is now a priority." Ty slammed the folder down on the table. "We need to find these bastards and those girls."

I hadn't been involved in a case like this, I didn't even know that a case like this existed. I could see the burning rage in everyone's eyes.

I didn't know if I was ready for this case, but just thinking about what those girls would be going through made my mind up for me.

If anything, it would occupy me.

I might not be able to do what everyone else could do, I wasn't trained the same but I'd put my all into finding those girls.

"Where do we start?" I asked, turning my face toward Ty.

"Luke, Kitty: you set up surveillance at the country club. I want cameras everywhere."

Kitty pushed up from her chair. "We got a contact?"

"No, we don't know who's involved. You're on your own with this one."

"Got it," she said and clipped her belt on.

"Evan: I want everything you can find on this guy."

"Who's the guy?" I asked

"Hugo Daley." Ty turned and stuck a photo on the whiteboard behind him.

"Looks loaded," Luke said as he moved closer.

He looked like a model: perfect blond hair swept back off his face and dark-blue eyes. His pearly white teeth glinted through the camera along with the dimple in his chin.

"Yeah." Ty stood and tilted his head at me then to the office. "I need to see you," he said and walked off.

"Glad your back, Kay," Luke said when he walked past me. Squeezing my shoulder, he placed something in front of me.

"Thanks." I smiled up at him.

"Eli's safe, by the way." He pulled the metal door open.

It was then that I realized: if we were all here then who was with Eli?

"Wait—"

"Check out the tablet." Luke smiled.

I picked up the tablet and swiped my finger on the screen, my eyes widening at what I saw. Several video feeds of the preschool played, all with a little red button in the corner and the word "live."

"What—"

"Live camera feed."

I looked at Evan; there was only me and him left at the table now. "I—"

"I know." He patted his chest. "I'm the man."

I snorted and looked back at the tablet. I could see Eli painting and playing with his friends. This was so much better than having someone watching him. It meant that I could check on him at any time of the day.

"Boss will fill you in," Evan said and moved from the table.

Right, I'm sure he would.

Chapter Nineteen

"She hasn't said anything," I heard Ty say as I was about to open the door to the office.

"Fuck," a muffled voice replied, I gasped. I'd know that voice anywhere.

Corey.

"She needs time," Ty said.

I'd been back at work for a couple of days and things were going well. Apart from the fact that I had been put on light duties: Ty's version of light duties was sitting at the desk all day.

I wanted to be out there with the others, trying to find the missing girls and the person who was taking them. But instead, I was stuck in the warehouse staring at the computer screen and making coffee.

"I want to see her."

"Corey—"

"Now," he growled. I swallowed at the anger in his voice. I hated disappointing Corey, he was the one person that mattered the most after Eli. He was also a pro at pulling off the disappointed dad look.

"If you think I'm gonna let you talk to her like that then you're fuckin' delusional."

"The fuck? She's *my* sister!"

"I don't give a shit, Corey, you get control of your-self before you talk to her." I carried on listening, not being able to hear much now that their voices weren't raised.

"I'll see where she is," I heard Ty say and then I heard the telltale squeak of his chair, warning me that he'd gotten up. My heart beating fast, I stepped back from the door. Not seeing Corey's face for so many years and now only seeing him because of what had happened didn't sit well with me.

"Kay?" Ty opened the door and frowned at me. Looking behind him he closed the door and moved closer to me. "Corey—"

"I know," I whispered.

"He only wants to know what's going on." I nodded, my eyes stayed glued to the office door. He was on the other side of that door—his face was anyway.

"You don't have to tell him anything," Ty continued.

"Okay," I whispered. Ty held his arms open and I

didn't hesitate as I walked right into them, laying my head on his chest. His soft t-shirt rubbed against my cheek as I breathed him in. Closing my eyes I took a deep breath after a beat and then stepped back.

"Come on," he whispered, holding his hand out to me.

I placed my hand in his and followed as he pushed through the door, waving to the office chair. I stared at the back of the computer screen, knowing that I'd see Corey on the other side.

Letting go of Ty's hand, I stepped towards the desk, my blood pumping louder in my ears as I ventured closer.

"Corey?" I said when I saw his face on the screen.

"Hey, lil' sis." He smiled and a lump formed in my throat at the combination of seeing his face and hearing his voice at the same time.

"You've grown." He laughed.

"Yeah, you too," I croaked. I could still see the Corey that I remembered only this one was different. His wide shoulders barely fit in the screen and I watched as his muscles rippled when he ran his hand over his short, black hair.

That was another thing that had changed, he always used to have longer hair which was great for me to practice my braiding on.

"I haven't got long." Corey shifted, moving closer to the camera. "What's going on, sis?"

"What do you mean?" I looked over the top of

the screen at Ty, I'd expected him to leave but judging by his face and the way that he sat on the chair opposite me, I guessed that wasn't going to happen.

"Fuck, Kay. Don't start that shit." He held his head in his hands.

"What?" I smiled. He got stressed so easily when it came to me.

"What has that asshole being doing to you?" he gritted out, causing the smile to fall off my face.

"Nothing." I gulped and twisted my fingers in my lap, diverting my eyes from Corey all the while trying not to look at Ty either.

"Bullshit!" he swore. "I saw the goddamn photos."

"Watch it," Ty warned.

"Photos?" I gasped, swinging my head to Ty.

"He's lucky I'm over here. What I want to do to that bastard."

"Cor—"

"How long?"

Furrowing my brows, I looked down. I didn't want to lie to Corey but I didn't want to tell him the truth either. I could lie to most people easily about Max but I didn't want to keep deceiving them, not the people who meant the most to me.

"I don't know," I whispered.

"Kaylee Anderson," he warned. I looked down at my lap again and then back at the grainy picture. "How long, Kaylee?"

Trying my best to swallow past my dry throat I said, "The first time was when I was pregnant."

"Motherfucker!" He stood and all I could see was his legs. I flitted my eyes to Ty, his hands gripped onto the side of the chair.

"When I was still there?" Corey asked, still not moving his face back into the frame.

"Yes. But it got better. It was only a couple of times."

"A couple of times?" he asked, sitting back down with a clenched jaw.

"It was only when I did something wrong and needed to be corrected."

"Corrected?" Corey gritted out. "And what would you need correcting for?"

"I don't know." I shrugged. "Not having his dinner ready for him when he came home." I saw Ty move closer out the corner of my eye.

"What else?"

I gulped, afraid that I was saying too much. "Answering him back. I shouldn't have done that," I whispered.

It felt good to tell Corey this. He'd understand once I explained it to him. Once he knew that Max was doing it to keep me in line, everything would be better.

"And what happened the last time you answered him back?"

"Erm..." Looking at Ty, I saw his face turned down

to the floor, fists clenched so tight that I could see the whites of his knuckles.

"He... erm..." I gulped. "Slammed my face into the fridge."

"He—"

"When?" Ty interrupted, his head coming up, piercing me with his eyes.

"A few weeks ago?"

"The black eye?" he asked, nostrils flaring. I nodded and looked away. "Fuck!" He stood up, his eyes scanning the room.

"Ty?" Corey said through the screen.

"Yeah?" He moved around the desk and leaned down, his arms coming down on either side of me.

"Calm the fuck down." He grinned. "Listen, lil' sis. You don't need correcting. You're fuckin' perfect just the way you are."

I shook my head but stopped when I felt Ty move closer. "He's right," he whispered.

I gasped as his lips feathered across my ear. "So fuckin perfect."

"That bastard is nothing but a wimp," Corey continued, spinning around he spoke to someone out of view and said that he had to go.

"I want to know everything," Ty whispered. I turned, our lips centimeters apart.

"Listen, I'll be back in a couple of months, I want a video call with you at least once a week," Corey said with raised brows.

"Done," Ty said.

"Love you, lil—" The video cut off, I turned back to face the screen but he was gone.

Ty surrounded me. His breaths coming faster and harder, matching my own. Closing my eyes I breathed in his musky scent.

"I'll show you how you should be treated."

He kissed that sensitive spot under my ear. His lips trailed down my neck stopping at the curve where my neck met my shoulder.

"Hey!" I pulled back from Ty staring wide eyed as Evan came into the office. "Who was on the video feed?"

Ty moved across the room, pushing Evan out of the door before turning and giving me a wink then closing the office door.

Closing my eyes, I could still feel his arms around me. I shivered.

It was going to be a long day.

WHEN I WOKE UP SATURDAY MORNING, MY EYES were drawn to the window. Looking out, I could see the woods that surrounded the compound. Memories running rampant of when my dad would take me out on adventures.

I remembered setting up camp one of those times and staying awake most of the night just gazing at the stars and finding all of the constellations. That was back before he drank: when we were all happy. When we would make memories as a family that we'd want to remember instead of all the ones that followed that I wished I could forget.

Shaking them from my head, I made my way downstairs, determined to provide Eli with those memories: the good ones. He'd had enough bad ones and that was my fault, but all of that was changing from here on out.

I wanted him to run through the woods and get lost in the trees while we played hide and seek knowing that he'd be fine because I would always find him.

Pulling out a bag from one of the many cupboards in Ty's kitchen, I started to put food inside. Making sandwiches, I added them to the bag along with some bottles of water and a bag of chips.

I was determined to make today as special as I could and to spend some proper family time with him. Everything had been so crazy over the last few weeks that I'd barely spent any time with Eli.

"What are you doing?" I jumped out of my skin, spinning around my hand flew to my chest as I came face to chest with Ty.

"You scared me," I breathed out.

Smiling, he leaned against the kitchen counter, my eyes slid down his body, taking him all in. Messy hair, with a couple of day's scruff and sweatpants that rested precariously on his hips. A dangerous combination.

"Kay?"

I blinked staring at him with wide eyes. "Huh?"

"What are you doing?"

"Oh." I turned, zipping up the bag. "Going on a picnic."

His head tilted to the side with narrowed eyes.

"We are?" Eli shouted as he came into the kitchen, the door swinging shut behind him.

"Yep." I pulled a bowl out of the cupboard and poured him some cereal. "Breakfast first though." I smiled.

"Where are we going?" He jumped up onto one of the seats, his smile uncontrollable.

"The woods," I said and placed the bowl down in front of him.

"Yeah!" He punched the air with his small fist as he scooped up a bite of cereal.

"Coffee?" Ty asked.

"Please." I sat down next to Eli, watching him eat.

"Is Ty coming?" he asked, a mouthful of cereal and milk dripping down his chin.

I laughed and looked at Ty as he held out a napkin. Smiling, I took it from him, my stomach flipping as his fingers grazed mine.

These feelings had to stop, I couldn't even be in the same room as him without staring at him or thinking of him in ways that I really shouldn't.

"I—"

"I'd love to," Ty interrupted, handing me my coffee.

I guess that was settled: we'd all be going out on a picnic.

"So where are we going then, little man?"

"The place we went before," he said clutching onto Ty's beanie hat. He'd been on Ty's shoulders since we left the house saying that he had the best view from up there.

Ty nodded, moving ahead of me with the picnic bag slung over his shoulder.

"You're gonna love it, Mama!"

"Really?" I moved closer to them. "What is it?"

I stepped over some branches and marveled at the trees, calm washing over me. It was something that I only experienced when I was in the woods. It'd been such a long time that I'd forgotten the feeling it gave me: how much I loved being there.

"Not telling!" Eli taunted.

Ty laughed so hard that he had to stop to catch his breath. "This kid." He shook his head, straightened and started walking again.

We walked for another ten minutes before the trees cleared a path.

"Just up here," Ty told me and bent down so that Eli could get down.

We went through a worn path and in between two big trees, I gasped as I saw where we were. The clearing lined with wild flowers and grass so green that it almost looked like someone had painted it. I'd never seen anything like it. Various wooden equipment sat in the middle, there were ropes and something that resembled a climbing frame, but for adults.

"Training equipment," Ty said as he watched me stare wide eyed.

"You train up here?" I followed him to a picnic bench keeping my eye on Eli who was currently trying to climb the rope but was having no luck.

"Yeah." Ty nodded and put the bag down.

"Ty, come play wiv me!" Eli shouted.

Ty smiled wide at me, his teeth showing then spun around and ran for Eli.

They spent the next hour using the different equipment. They walked across the wooden beams, climbed the rope wall, ducked under the rope that was low to the ground, all the while laughing. It was just as much fun to watch them.

Halfway through, they tried to get me to have a go on the equipment but there was no way that I was going to try. I'd end up breaking something, when I said this to Ty he laughed and ran across one of the beams.

"Come on, sweetheart, have a go." Ty nodded to the climbing wall.

"Yeah, please, Mama!" Eli smiled sweetly, his hands coming together in a pleading motion as he fluttered his eyes at me.

I really didn't want to fall flat on my face but I also wanted to join in on the fun. Biting my lip, I contemplated it. They looked like they were having so much fun and the whole point of today was to make some new memories.

"Come on then." I dusted my hands on my jeans and hooked my leg over the bench. Eli squealed and ran ahead of me.

They both waited at the bottom of the rope for me. Taking a deep breath, I planted my foot on the bottom rung, squealing as it swung with my weight. I gripped onto one of the squares like my life depended on it.

I waited for the rope to stop moving then scaled it as fast as I could, slow and steady as my leg started to burn. Considering I still wasn't fully healed I'd say I did it quite well. I swung my leg over the top and sat on the wooden frame to give my body a rest.

Grinning down at them, I said, "Bet you couldn't do it that fast."

Ty tilted his head, his shoulders back. He backed away from the rope and ran at it, making it up to me within a couple of seconds. He swung his leg over the top bar, pointed at me and said, "Oh yeah?"

I rolled my eyes, swinging my other leg over to

climb down. I was doing okay until Ty started to climb down at the same time as me. The rope started to move in all directions causing my foot to slip. I closed my eyes tight and braced for the fall.

It never came, instead a hand grabbed onto me. I hugged the ropes and breathed a sigh of relief. That was until I realized that Ty had grabbed my ass to stop me from falling. I opened my eyes watching as his were fixated on his where his hands were.

"Ty?" I croaked.

He looked up at me, his eyes full of hunger. My tongue came out to wet my bottom lip and his eyes tracked the motion.

"Mama!"

We both pulled back, eyes wide. How had I forgotten that Eli was there?

I didn't know how much longer I could be around Ty without something happening. It was getting harder and harder to be around him and not want to kiss his soft looking lips.

And now I was thinking about his lips. *Again.*

Chapter Twenty

THE BIG GATES loomed over me like a dark cloud, reminding me that I still hadn't stepped foot outside of the compound. Every day when I walked past them they reminded me that the outside world was still there—waiting for me.

Max was still out there.

I'd gotten so comfortable with my surroundings that I started to wonder what was so great about being out there. In my world all that existed beyond those gates was pain. I didn't want was what was behind those gates, I wanted what was inside them—protection and safety.

My hands would sweat and my breathing would come faster and harder each time I got closer to them.

It was becoming harder to keep it a secret; it would only be a matter of time before someone noticed.

I was sure that Luke suspected something when he asked me if I wanted to pick Eli up and I said I was busy. The raised brow told me he knew something was up, but I just smiled and got on with my imaginary work.

I desperately wanted to pick Eli up. I'd been all he had known for such a long time but now there were other people in his life and I found myself relying on them more and more.

It couldn't last forever, I had to go outside those gates at some point. Miss Maggie hadn't heard from me for almost three weeks; I didn't doubt that she knew what had happened, or at least a version of it.

But if the thought of going outside the compound terrified me then going back to that apartment block was even catastrophic.

I leaned back in the chair, blowing out a huge breath and not being able to stop the whirring thoughts in my head. It was tiring keeping up a front all of the time.

"Ugh!" My eyes sprang open. "What a week," Evan said as he slumped down on the couch and grinned at me.

I smiled, standing from the desk. "Hey Evan."

"So..."

Bending down, I grabbed my jacket and bag from the cupboard and looked up at Evan. "So?"

"You're Corey's little sister?" he asked, a mischievous smirk on his face.

I stared in shock at Evan. I'd asked Ty to keep it a secret but I guess that with everything that had happened it wouldn't stay like that for much longer.

"Yes," I said, making my way over to him on the couch. Sitting on the edge, I rolled my eyes as he moved forward, his eyes scanning my face.

"I thought you looked familiar."

"Huh? I didn't know you had been in the forces."

"I wasn't," he said resting his arms on his legs.

"Then how do you know Corey?" I asked frowning.

"We met when he last came to visit."

"Last came to visit?"

"Yeah, about ten months ag—" I stood and nearly tripped over my own feet trying to make it to the door. "Kay?" I ignored Evan and practically ran out of the warehouse, my jacket and bag forgotten.

I couldn't believe that Corey had visited, he'd been twenty minutes away from me and hadn't even bothered to come and see me, or his nephew. I was angry—no, I was *furious*.

The gravel crunched as I stomped over to the house, Evan on my heels. Flinging the door open I went straight up the stairs knowing exactly where Ty was.

"Ty!" I shouted, pushing his home office door open.

Sat behind his desk with the phone to his ear, his eyes widened when he saw me.

"Kay, I'm—"

"I need to talk to you." I looked behind me at Evan. "Now," I gritted out.

"I'll call you back," he said into the phone.

"Boss—"

"Corey came to visit ten months ago?" I seethed.

He huffed, sitting back in his chair. "Yeah."

"I can't believe this." I started to pace the small office and mumbled curses at Corey. If only he was here to hear them.

"Wait, what's the problem?"

"The problem?" I laughed, turning to face Ty. "Do you know when the last time I saw Corey was?"

"Ten—"

"Four years ago!" I threw my hands up in the air and watched as understanding passed over his face. I paced the room back and forth, not taking in any of my surroundings. My jaw was clenched tight, I hadn't felt this kind of anger in... well, never.

"I got this, Evan."

The door clicked shut, then it was just me and Ty.

"Sweetheart." Standing up, he sauntered toward me. "I didn't know."

"I can't believe he was this close and didn't come to see me or his nephew," I choked out.

Corey was my only family and he'd just left me behind. I'd heard the phrase out of sight out of mind, but for him to take it literally really hurt. How could he have come this close and not come to see me or Eli?

Without Miss Maggie, I would have had no one to talk to. She'd been my family these last four years, and I hadn't even let her know that I was okay. That thought weighed heavy on me.

"I'm sorry, sweetheart." I stopped pacing and stood in the middle of his office.

I hadn't yet been in here. It looked much like the rest of his house, light walls covered in windows to let the sun stream through. It didn't matter what room in the house you were in, the view was always spectacular.

A sleek black desk was sitting in the middle of the room facing the windows, behind it was a wall full of books.

"If I had known—"

"You didn't." I pointed out as he stood in front of me.

My eyes started to fill with tears as he rubbed his hands up and down my arms.

"Don't cry, sweetheart," he said as a tear escaped and rolled down my cheek. Moving closer, he wrapped his arms around me.

I buried my head in his chest, breathing him in.

"Miss Maggie." I gasped through my tears.

"Miss Maggie?" He pulled back just enough to look down at me.

"Yeah." I nodded and wiped my face. "I haven't

spoken to her since..." His gaze roamed over my face, searching. I felt the heat rising in my cheeks as he assessed me. "She's been there for me and Eli and I... I..."

"Invite her over." He shrugged.

"Here?" I frowned.

I didn't want to get my hopes up but the thought of seeing Miss Maggie changed my mood slightly. That didn't mean I wasn't still pissed at Corey, I was, I *so* was, and I'd be sure to tell him just how pissed I was.

"Unless you want to go to her place?"

"No," I choked out.

"Then invite her over for dinner"

I didn't know how it would all work but I wanted to spend some time with her, I missed her. I'm sure that Eli did too.

"Okay." I sniffed, backing away a little.

Ty pulled me back into his embrace, his breath tickling my neck. I stiffened at first but after a couple of seconds, I started to relax.

"Corey's not getting away with this," I warned.

He chuckled. "I didn't expect him to."

Corey wouldn't. He was in the doghouse for doing that and I started to wonder if that was the only time he came back and didn't see me.

Was that the reason he didn't want any of his friends to know he had a sister? Why he kept me in the dark about his friends?

He had some serious explaining to do.

"Time for some training," Ty said when the meeting ended.

It had been a couple of days since I found out about Corey. I refused to talk to him when he rang choosing to ignore him in the same way that he had done to me all these years. It may have been a little childish but I wanted him to feel what I felt. I still couldn't believe he'd been so close and not even told me.

"Training?" I croaked. "Now?"

"Yeah." Ty nodded

He stood up and walked over to the mats, the others following him.

Now? He wanted me to train right *now* in front of everyone?

Luke pulled my chair out, spinning me around.

"Just some simple self-defense again," Ty said from the edge of the mats.

"Erm... okay?" I shuffled closer.

Ty tilted his head at the mats. "Luke?"

Luke moved onto the mats and crooked his finger at me.

"Wait? I've got to—"

"You need to practice," Ty said.

"Can't I do it with Evan?"

"No." He shook his head. "You're too used to him."

Ty moved onto the mats standing a few feet away

from us. Widening his stance, he looked between me and Luke.

"Luke: grab her wrist." He grabbed my wrist, not too hard but enough that I felt like I couldn't move.

"Kay? Try and get out of it."

Pulling my arm back toward me didn't make his grip loosen at all. I tried several more times but all that it was doing was making my wrist burn from the friction and I ended up frustrated.

"I can't do I." I groaned in frustration.

"You can't get out of it by pulling. You need to turn your wrist so that your thumb is pointing to the ceiling." I moved my wrist. "Now, jerk your arm by bending at your elbow."

I put all my weight behind it, not expecting it to work. It did and I stumbled back as his hand let go, only just managing not to fall onto my ass. It worked. I couldn't believe it actually worked. I stared in amazement at my hand, my arm and then at Luke.

"It worked!" I squealed.

Ty grinned at me. I'd just got out of that big hulk's grip!

I was on a high, nothing would bring me down—

Arms wrapped around me from behind. Squealing, I thrashed about but it was no use and I was brought down within seconds. The air whooshed out of me as I landed on my back.

Guess I could be brought down after all.

"How—"

"Always be aware of your surroundings," Ty said holding his hand out to me. Taking it, I let him pull me up. "We tell you this all the time." He huffed.

"But he came from behind me," I groaned.

"An attacker isn't going to wait for you to turn to face them, Kay," Luke said, shaking his head.

"Once you're aware of your surroundings, you'll be able to feel them coming. You need to spin and incapacitate them."

Feel them coming?

I nodded, trying to take in all of the information. But it felt like I was back at school trying to learn math.

"A hit to the solar plexus will give you the upper hand or time to get away."

"Where's the solar plexus?" I frowned.

"Here." Ty pointed to the top of his ribs, right in the middle.

"Okay." I nodded.

"You could target their nose with an upwards palm strike." He did the action on Luke, not actually touching his nose but showing me how to do it.

"What will that do?" I asked.

"You'll break their nose."

I grimaced, I didn't like the thought of breaking someone's nose.

"Won't that make them bleed?" I squeaked.

"Probably." He shrugged. "Your aim is to be able to get away."

"So, I'm just trying to hurt them to give me time to run?"

"Yep." He nodded. "You're still in training, Kay."

"I know—"

"I want you to be able to get away if you're coming on jobs. The rest will come with time."

"Okay." I nodded, but couldn't see a situation where I'd have to do this. I was always with one of the guys anyway.

"Remember that anything you have on you can be used as a weapon," Luke said as he stepped forward.

"Like the baton and pepper spray?" I asked.

I still hadn't been shown how to use those properly, maybe I'd be shown now.

"No." Ty shook his head. "Imagine that you don't have your belt on."

He rummaged through his pockets and pulled out a comb. I frowned, what was he going to do with that?

"If you hold it like this." He held it with his hand around the top of the comb, the teeth pointing out. "Press it as hard as you can above their upper lip."

"Does that even hurt?" I snickered.

"Hell, yeah it does," Evan said from the side of the mats.

"Really?" I asked, skeptical.

"Try pressing it on yours, you'll see." I plucked the comb from Ty's hand, pressing it onto my upper lip.

"Ow! That hurts." I frowned at the comb and

looked at Luke. I'd get him back for attacking me from behind.

"Don't even think about it," he warned. My lips lifted into a sneaky smile. I raised my brows and took a step forward. "Kay. No," he warned as he stepped back.

I laughed and made a grab for him. Obviously, he was a lot quicker than me but that didn't mean I didn't try to catch him.

After what felt like hours, but was most probably minutes, I bent over gasping for breath. Running wasn't my thing, in fact, no sort of exercise was.

I was so unfit. He didn't even look like he had run at all.

"And that right there means you need to start exercising."

"Exercising?" I gasped

"Yep." Ty nodded as he moved toward the gym equipment. "Get on." He nodded to the treadmill.

"I'm not getting on that thing." I shook my head.

"You can either do the treadmill or we can go running in the woods and up to clearing."

I growled under my breath. This was so unfair.

"Fine." I stomped over to him and stood on the belt.

"We'll go slow at first, just be careful of your leg." He pressed the on button, the belt starting to move.

It wasn't so bad; I could probably keep up with this pace.

"I'm gonna put you on level 3."

"What level is this? This feels good"

He chuckled. "This isn't a level: it's just starting up."

"Ugh." I rolled my eyes, trying to keep up with the belt as it whirled faster.

"What level do you do?" I panted

"The highest one." He smirked. "Fifteen."

I managed five minutes on that machine. Five. Minutes.

It was a death trap. I was *never* going on it again. Hobbling off it, I bent over panting while I tried to catch my breath.

"That's a good starting point, each day you need to up it by thirty seconds," Ty said as he walked back to the house with me, sweat dripping down my face.

"I'm not getting on that thing again."

"You—"

"I'll run around the compound but not on that killing machine," I said as we went through the front door. "My legs are burning."

"You should have a cold bath," Ty said as I stumbled up the stairs. "It helps."

"Yeah, okay, whatever," I spluttered.

Cold bath. There was no way I would be doing that. What was today? Torture Kaylee day?

Chapter Twenty-One

I ROLLED out of bed the next morning with a moan, hoping that I wouldn't be put through that again. My body ached in places that I didn't think it could ache and my leg was feeling a little tender.

I jumped in the shower, braided my hair to the side and got dressed in my black jeans and t-shirt. Ty had given me a pair of combat boots "better for the job" he had said, so I pushed my feet inside them and took a few steps to test them out. They were comfortable and in better condition than my poor chucks.

After getting dressed I woke Eli up and gave him his breakfast before getting him ready for preschool. Luke and Kitty were waiting for him outside the house by the car. Strapping him in, I gave him a kiss and watched as they drove through the gates.

Ty met me on the porch and we walked over to the warehouse together; me having to jog to keep up with his long strides. My heart beat a little faster at the grin he flashed me when he saw me trying to keep up.

"How you feeling this morning?" He pulled open the warehouse door and waved me inside.

"Sore." I moaned as I walked toward the office.

"You should have had that cold bath like I told you." He snickered.

"Hey!" I spun and pointed. "Don't laugh at me." Crossing my arms, I looked away.

"Sweetheart," he whispered, taking a step closer.

"It's not nice," I whispered back.

"I wasn't laughing at you."

My eyes moved back to his and they begged me to believe him. They pulled me in until I couldn't breathe, the depths promising me things that I could only dream of.

He moved closer until we were almost touching. So close but so far away; if I moved a fraction, I would be touching him. I watched his chest rise and fall with a quick breath, I knew that this was affecting him as much as it was me—whatever *this* was.

"Ty," I whispered.

His gaze flicked to my lips, my tongue coming out to wet my own on impulse. My gaze flitted up to his, I could almost feel the way his scruff would scratch against my face and the way his hands would feel on my skin.

If his lips touched mine I knew that I wouldn't be able to move on from him. There would be no going back.

His hand moved to the small of my back, pulling me closer and my hands landed on his firm chest. I lifted onto my toes and met his lips halfway.

They were gentle at first, testing, teasing.

His other hand clutched the back of my neck while mine wandered to places that I never thought I'd be able to. *Screw going back.*

I swiped my tongue along the seam of his lips, begging for entrance. His answering groan sent sparks flying through me, my belly dipped as he opened up his mouth and swept his tongue along mine.

He swallowed my moan, his hand moving down to my ass and squeezing. I was sure to have a bruise, but this was the kind that I didn't mind having.

I could feel his hardness press against my stomach as he backed me up against the wall. We were a frenzied mix of arms, lips, and tongues, until I heard voices. I tried to push him back but he was a wall of muscle.

"Ty." I pulled my face away and he followed, dipping his lips down to mine again. "Wait." I held up my hand.

He tilted his head, just now hearing the voices.

"Office—" he said with a voice that was deeper than usual as he stole another kiss.

"Ty..." If I went into that office, I didn't know if I'd

be able to walk out the same person. I needed to keep my guard up, the last time I let my guard down it had disastrous effects.

I couldn't go through that again.

He must have sensed my hesitation because he said, "I'll be out in a minute," and stepped back, his eyes tracking me all the way down to my toes and back up before he turned and jogged into the office.

I didn't have time to think about what we had just done because the door opened and the guys came into the warehouse.

Had we really been doing that for so long?

I joined them at the table as we all waited for Ty and when he came out a few minutes later, his lips looked swollen. That was the only thing that would indicate that we had done anything. He didn't look at me any differently.

He'd just tipped my world upside down. I was freaking out while he sat there cool as a cucumber.

"I'm gonna follow him today," Ty said at the end of the meeting. I couldn't help but breathe a sigh of relief at having him out of the office for the day. Until he said, "Kay's with me," and my respite disappeared.

I opened and closed my mouth several times before it registered that they had all moved from the table. I scrambled to the office, shutting the door behind me.

"Ty." I leaned against the door.

"Hmm?" He clipped his radio to his belt and hung the earpiece over his shoulder.

"I... I... can't—"

"You can't what?" He held out a radio to me but I just stared at it. There was no way I was going out of those gates. I wasn't ready.

What if Max was there, waiting for me to come outside of the gates? He was unpredictable when he was angry, and this time he'd had time to think about what he was going to do to me. There was no telling to what he had planned for me now.

For the first time, I genuinely feared for my own safety.

"I've got stuff to—"

"Is this because of what just happened?"

"What? No—"

"If it's all too soon then—"

"Ty, it's not that," I said, twisting my fingers.

"What is it then?"

"The gates," I mumbled.

He widened his stance, crossing his arms; arms that had been around me not long ago. I stared at the way his muscles tensed, at the veins that popped and the tattoos that always mesmerized me. When my eyes made it back up to his I saw the realization cross his face.

"You haven't been outside those gates since—"

"I'm not ready," I whispered.

He raised his brows. "You need to do it now, or you never will."

I shook my head. I need time. Just a little more time.

"Eli." One word: that was all it took for me to take a deep breath and push up off the door. "He wants you to take him to preschool, Kay."

"I know." I nodded and chewed on my bottom lip. Could I do this?

"I'll be there with you, sweetheart." His voice softened.

I never doubted that he would be there, but that didn't stop the images that flew through my head. Shaking them away, I held my hand out for the radio and clipped it onto my belt. The belt that I had reached for when Max—

"Good girl."

My breath stalled, goose bumps spreading over my skin as I felt the blood drain from my face. I scrunched my eyes shut and choked out, "Don't... call me that."

"Kay?"

I couldn't look at him. If I did and it wasn't his face staring back at me then I wouldn't be able to look at him the same again.

"Sweetheart?"

I shook my head and turned to the door. "Just don't ever call me that again, please," I begged.

"I—"

"Let's go," I said pulling the door open and

pushing the earpiece into my ear, trying to push past my fears.

If I focused on something else, then I wouldn't freak out. Who the hell was I kidding?

I was totally freaking out.

Turns out it wasn't as bad as I thought it would be. Nothing bad happened when the gates opened: Max didn't jump out at me. Nobody followed us or tried to run us off the road.

The sun shined through the windshield, the trees looking extra green today. I relaxed back into my seat, closed my eyes, and took a calming breath.

We spent most of the day following Hugo Daley around.

His expensive suit was the kind that you had to have made especially for you and certainly wasn't off the rack. He screamed money, his clothes, his car, and even the way he carried himself.

His white-blond hair was slicked back with his sunglasses covering most of his face. I snickered at his bright-blue loafers, they were ridiculous and if that was fashion then I was glad I had no fashion sense whatsoever.

After hours of following him around the city, his driver finally dropped him off at the country club.

Buttoning up his suit jacket, he scanned the parking lot before ducking into the back entrance.

"The cameras can take it from here," Ty said as he turned the car around.

"Cameras?"

"Yeah, Kitty installed them. Although we might have to go into the country club at some stage."

"Into the country club?"

Ty turned and flashed me a smile.

"What?"

"You just gonna keep repeating what I say?"

"I am?" I frowned.

He chuckled and pushed a button on his radio. "Evan, pick up the country club cameras."

I sat back and watched Ty's hands drumming on the steering wheel to the beat of the song that played on the radio.

He was a sexy driver.

Was there such a thing as a sexy driver? If there was then he was definitely one of them.

"Want to go and pick Eli up?"

I startled. Had he saw me watching him?

"Huh?"

"Want to go and pick Eli up?"

My heart hammered in my chest. I'd been fine staying in the car, but the thought of having to get out had me hyperventilating.

"Hey." His hand covered mine, reassuring me with a gentle squeeze. "You'll be fine."

I nodded. There was nothing else I could do. I had to get back to normal, for Eli's sake as well as my own.

I kept my eyes glued to Ty's hand the whole way there, the rough pad of his thumb scratching against the top of my hand as he rubbed it back and forth. I closed my eyes and relished in the sensation.

Before I knew it, Ty was parking in front of the preschool and it was time for me to pull up my big girl panties and get out of the car.

"It's okay, sweetheart, I'm here." I took three deep breaths, gripped the door handle and pushed it open. Ty was out of the car and coming around to my side before I even put my feet on the floor.

"Hey." I smiled.

"Hey." He grinned back and held his hand out. I took it and let him lead me inside while searching the parking lot for any signs of Max. All that I could see were relatively normal people going about their days, pushing carts to their cars and ducking in and out of the shops.

Eli did a double take when he came through the security door and saw us standing there.

"Mama! You came!" He ran at me full force. I bent slightly at the knees and braced myself for his weight.

"Umph." Wrapping my arms around him I picked him up as best as I could. His legs wrapped around me as he squeezed me with all his might.

"Hey, sweetie," I mumbled. My eyes burned with

unshed tears, I didn't want him to see me cry so I buried my face in his neck and breathed him in.

Ty winked when I looked up at him and tilted his head at the door to signal that it was time to go.

"So, what did you do today?" I asked, putting him down and holding my hand out for him.

"Painted." He shrugged and gave Ty a high five as we walked through the door.

"Hey, bud." He clicked the fob to open the car.

"So," Ty said when we were all in the car and on the way back to the compound.

"So?" I turned toward him.

"Wasn't so bad, huh?"

"Meh." I leaned my back against the headrest. "I guess it wasn't".

"So maybe you could phone Miss Maggie now?"

I blinked. After the day I had, I forgot that I was meant to invite Miss Maggie around for a dinner.

"I suppose." I nodded and sat up. "When shall I say for?"

"Friday?" Ty shrugged.

"Okay." I nodded. "I'll do it when we get back to the office," I said, twisting my hands in my lap.

"Mama?"

"Yes, sweetie?" I turned in my seat and looked at Eli, glad that he could distract me from my wandering thoughts.

"Miss Maggie coming here?" He frowned.

"Hopefully." I smiled. Pursing his lips, he

turned his head and looked out of the window. "What's the matter, sweetie?" I shifted closer to him.

"How will she get here?"

"Well... erm..." I flicked my eyes to Ty who had just pulled up at the gates.

"I'll pick her up," Ty told him.

"Can I come with you?"

"Ty's wide eyes shot to mine, not knowing how to answer him.

"Who will help me cook if you go with Ty?" I smiled at Eli; it took all my strength not to shout *no*.

"Oh." Eli nodded. "Okay, I'll help you, Mama."

"Great." I clapped my hands together and turned back around in my seat.

"But what about Henry?"

"What about him, sweetie?"

"Won't he be lonely on his own?" he asked, his face screwed up.

"Who's Henry?" Ty asked.

"Miss Maggie's cat."

I turned back to Eli. "Maybe we can ask Miss Maggie to bring him next time?"

"Really?" He smiled, his whole face lighting up.

"Sure."

Ty pulled into his usual spot outside the warehouse and as soon as he turned the engine off, Eli shouted, "Luke!"

There he was, waiting outside the warehouse for

us. Luke's face split into a wide grin and he made a beeline for Eli's door.

"You did good." He winked at me and undid Eli. "Want to go watch cartoons?"

"Yeah!" Eli punched the air and let Luke help him down.

"That okay, Ma?" Luke pouted.

"Yeah, go on." I rolled my eyes and jumped down from my seat. "Dinner will be ready at six!" I shouted across the compound to them.

They both shouted back, "Okay!" and went into Luke's house.

Moving my eyes to Ty's, I said, "Thanks for today," and moved closer to him.

His gaze flicked down to my lips. "Which part?" He grinned.

"Oh jeez." I flung my hands up in the air and walked ahead of him.

His deep throaty laughed following me into the warehouse.

I couldn't contain the grin on my face either, and I was definitely most thankful for the kiss.

Chapter
Twenty-Two

I FINISHED work early on Friday to get a head start on cooking. We'd told all the guys the day before and they all wanted to come and meet Miss Maggie so that meant cooking for six and a half. The half being Eli.

Miss Maggie had practically squealed when she heard me on the phone and readily agreed to come to dinner. Ty had promised to pick Miss Maggie up and then they were going to go and get Eli from preschool together.

I cooked meatballs and spaghetti, as requested by all the guys, and as always, Evan had a special request for cookies.

"Need some help?" I jumped at Kitty's voice.

"You scared me," I gasped, clutching my chest.

"Sorry." She shrugged, moving closer.

"Can you mix the sauce?"

"This?" She pointed at the pan and frowned. "How do I mix?" I looked over at her: she was staring at the mixture like it was an alien.

"Get the spoon." She picked it up. "Then just go around in circles."

She started to mix and looked at me from under her lashes. I nodded to confirm that she was doing it right and got on with the meatballs.

It was a relief to have someone helping. She set the table when she finished mixing and before I knew it they were all coming in the front door like a herd of elephants.

"Where's my girl?" Miss Maggie shouted.

Butterflies took flight in my stomach. I wiped my hands on a hand towel and went into the hall.

"I'm here." My eyes filled with tears when I saw her. I'd missed her more than I realized. I went straight into her open arms and breathed her in. "How are you?" I asked when I pulled back.

"I'm good, dear." She held onto my hand. "The question is: how are you?"

I looked at all the people that were surrounding us, each one had welcomed me and looked after me and Eli. I couldn't have asked for a better family, and that's exactly what they were to us now: family.

"I'm doing okay." I smiled at Ty and led Miss Maggie into the living room. "Do you want something to drink?"

"I'll have some tea please, dear." Of course, she would.

Ty followed me into the kitchen and leaned against the kitchen counter.

"She's a little crazy."

I chuckled. "I know."

"All she talked about with Eli were cartoons and superheroes."

"She tends to do that." I put the pasta in the pot of boiling water.

"Smells great." Ty moaned, leaning down and waving his hand over the pan and back towards his face. His eyes were closed and he had a look of absolute pleasure on his face.

My mind immediately went back to the kiss the other day. Shaking my head, I concentrated on the food.

There was another good thing about having men in my life that liked to help out: they carried the food to the table. I know it isn't an obvious thing, but have you ever tried to carry a big bowl full of spaghetti? Heavy. *Really heavy.*

We all sat and ate with Miss Maggie in between Eli and Evan. They had their own conversation going on and it was nice to see Miss Maggie enjoying herself and fitting right in. Most chatter stopped when they were all eating, something I found hilarious. These men talked nonstop but put food in front of them and they went completely silent.

Once I had finished eating, I leaned back and watched them all. It was amazing that I had found these people. Luke and Evan were like brothers to me and Uncles to Eli.

Kitty had taken a little longer to get to know and I honestly didn't know if I knew her fully. I had a feeling she kept a lot of secrets, but I understood that. I had lots of those too.

My gaze moved to Ty. I didn't know what he was yet. A friend?

I knew that I didn't look at him like a brother, and if that kiss was anything to go by then I knew he didn't look at me like that either.

Was I ready for something with Ty?

I'd just got out of an abusive relationship, and if I was honest, I knew deep down that I hadn't heard the last from Max. He wasn't the type of guy to go down without a fight.

"Dear?" I jumped when a hand touched mine.

"I'm sorry. What did you say?" I shifted in my seat and turned toward Miss Maggie.

"Would you like to go and sit on that lovely porch swing with me?"

I nodded my head, pushed back in my chair and started picking up plates.

"I got it," Ty answered taking the plates out my hand and nodding towards the door for me to go and join Miss Maggie.

Opening the front door, I stepped out onto the porch with her.

"Such a lovely house," she remarked as she sat down on the swing.

"Yeah." I blew out a big breath and looked over at the woods.

It was so nice to sit out here at night, there was nothing like the sounds of the woods when it was dark or the soft breeze that whistled through the trees bringing the scent with it.

"How are you?"

"Fi—"

"Don't fill me with that bullshit," she said softly. Such a contradiction from the words that she had spoken.

"Have you seen him?" I asked instead.

"No." She shook her head. "Not since that day."

I nodded and looked up at the stars, the clear sky letting them shine bright.

"I tried to get help," she whispered. "I tried to phone the police but I was shaking so much that I couldn't seem to dial the right numbers."

"That's okay," I said gently.

"No, no it's not." I turned to her again and watched as her eyes filled with tears. "I saw you getting away."

She reached out and held my hand squeezing gently.

"You did?"

"Yeah." She blew out a breath and continued, "I was so glad when I saw you drive away."

"Me too." I chuckled.

"Then I saw that man." She pointed back to the house "Ty?"

"Yes."

"He told me that he'd look after you. Looks like he kept his word." She smiled.

"He has. They all have."

"You look happy."

I breathed deep. "I am. For the first time, I feel free. I don't have to worry about—" I pinched my lips together. I didn't want to start that train of thought.

"So..." She raised her brows, her lips lifting into a smile as she changed the subject. "Tell me all about him."

I WAS SLEEPING SOUNDLY WHEN SOMETHING shook me awake. Rolling over, I mumbled something and clutched onto my pillow. I didn't want to wake up, I was having a dream which made a change because normally it would be a nightmare.

"Kay."

"Go away," I groaned.

"Kay, I need you to come with me."

"I'm sleeping," I whined, and I was answered with a chuckle.

Ty had slept in here every night since my night-mares began, he only ever came in when he heard me shout. But tonight, I hadn't shouted out at all. This was a good thing, right?

So why did I feel sad that Ty hadn't gotten into bed with me?

The bed dipped with his weight, his hand cupped the side of my face and turned it towards him.

"It's for a job."

I cracked my eyes open. "Now?"

"Yeah." His hand moved from my face as he stood. It was then that I noticed he was still dressed in his work gear. He held his hand out and I frowned at what he held.

"Your clothes." He placed them on the bed and walked toward the door. "Be ready in five." He wrapped his knuckles on the door frame twice and left the room.

I stared at the dark empty space he left behind, I couldn't believe he was dragging me out of bed just when I was having some undisturbed sleep.

If Eli hadn't of been staying with Luke for the night then I would have had the perfect excuse to not be able to go. He'd stayed over a couple of times now and I knew that he would be looked after there so I didn't need to worry.

Didn't mean that I didn't worry, just that I had no reason to.

"Kay!"

"Jeez! Okay!" I shouted back and rolled out of bed.

I pulled on the jeans and shirt I took off a few hours ago and shuffled down the stairs to throw on my chucks. Ty was waiting at the open front door for me.

"What's going on?" I mumbled.

"Need to do some surveillance." He pulled the door closed behind us.

"Where?"

"Daley," he said, jogging down the steps.

It was only then that I noticed the car sitting outside the house. I frowned at the shadow in the back. "Who—"

"Hey, Kay!"

"Ugh, Evan." I held my hands over my ears. "Too loud."

He leaned forward in his seat as soon as I was sitting in the front seat.

"Ready for an adventure?"

I yawned and leaned back in the seat, turning the heater up to full. "Yay," I grumbled sarcastically.

We drove for about half an hour. I was just dozing off when Ty pulled up and turned the engine off. I peeked around him and saw that it was one of the houses that Hugo had been to the other day when we were following him.

"What are we doing here?" I whispered.

The house was dark; the only sign of life was a light in the security booth.

"You'll see," Ty whispered back.

I turned around to face Evan. He had his laptop open on his lap and was tapping away at the keyboard. A frown marred across his brow with his tongue sticking out of the corner of his mouth.

I wished that I had grabbed a jacket or even a blanket because now that the heating was turned off I could feel the chill in the air. I rubbed my hands up and down my arms for warmth, looking out the window in the same direction as Ty.

His gaze kept moving from the security booth to his cell. The house wasn't just a house: it was a mansion. Gated all the way around complete with those fancy balconies. A giant fountain sat in the middle of the circular driveway. I was awed when I saw it in daylight, but somehow it looked so much grander in the dark.

"Why do they have a security guard anyway? It's not like they're in a bad area—"

"Now," Ty said and opened his door.

I looked back at Evan confused but he just held his hand out.

"What's—"

"Put it in your ear." He didn't look up from the screen, just kept on typing.

"Come on." Ty waved.

I took the small ear piece and put it in my ear as I opened up the door.

"I need someone small to get over the fence without being noticed," Ty said and pulled something out of his pocket. I followed him to the edge of the fence and dipped low when he did.

"There's a computer in there," he whispered, pointing at the security box. "You'll have three minutes to put this in and download whatever files are on there." He held his hand out; I took what he held and realized that it was a USB stick.

"You want me to climb that fence?" I squeaked. He raised his brows in answer so I took that as a yes.

"Kay?" Evan's voice rang through the earpiece.

"Dammit, Evan, you scared me," I whispered and rested my hand on my chest, catching my breath.

He chuckled. "Sorry."

Ty made a come here motion with his hand and I went to him. He gripped my hand and together we went up to a part of the fence that was covered with trees.

Movement in the booth grabbed my attention and I watched as a man dressed in a black suit came out, speaking over a radio.

Ty started to make loads of different gestures with his hands. Tilting my head to the side, I wondered for a second what he was trying to say. The more he moved his hands in the air the funnier he looked.

I grinned and stifled my laughter. "I don't know what that means."

He rolled his eyes and widened his stance. "I'll help you jump over." He hoisted me up and literally threw me in the air, I grabbed hold of the breaks in the fence and shuffled my way up.

"You could have warned me," I whisper shouted, then I heard a beep. I froze.

"Setting the time," Ty whispered.

Right, that made sense.

I was better at climbing than I thought and was at the top in no time.

"Soft landing and roll." What the hell did that mean? I took a leap and landed square on my feet, pins and needles shooting up my legs. Crouching low as a bright light shone, I waited for it to pass by me.

"Go," Ty urged me. I made a run for it, heading straight for the booth.

"Put the USB in the side of the computer." Damn, I forgot that Evan was in my head.

I did as he said and waited, constantly checking over my shoulder. I was sure that someone would come back and I'd be caught and kidnapped or maybe worse.

The laptop pinged and a box popped up with a password to enter.

"It wants a password."

"Shit. Okay, wait a minute let me try and figure this out," Evan said in my ear. My hands started to shake as I watched.

Why would Evan assume that we wouldn't need a password? This whole thing didn't feel so organized. The longer I stood here, the more I was sure I would get caught.

My hands were numb from the cold, I shook them out and tried to get some feeling back in them.

"Okay type this: 6nefj78bdg65." I did and then the box disappeared, replaced by a line with a loading bar.

"It worked." I jumped up and did a little dance nearly knocking over the lamp. I scrambled to save it before it crashed to the floor, straightening it and scanning outside the booth.

"Kay? You good?"

"Yeah, sorry." I cleared my throat and watched the bar load.

"Sixty seconds," Ty's voice said in my head.

It said fifty percent loaded and then slowed right down.

"Forty-five seconds." Oh God, it wasn't going to load in time.

"Thirty seconds." It was up to ninety-five percent now.

"Ten seconds." The laptop pinged and I pulled the USB out. I scanned the area and saw nothing, so made a mad dash for the fence where I thought Ty was.

The only problem was that Ty had given me a hand up.

How was I meant to get back over the fence?

"Ty?" I croaked.

"I got you." His hands came through the fence and interlocked making a step for me to haul myself up from.

I placed my foot on it then hoisted myself up. I

scaled the fence again, jumping right into Ty's arms. He caught me with ease and didn't bother to put me down, instead, he ran back to the car.

He let me down by his door and I scooted over as soon as I was in the car. He climbed in after me and started the engine but left the lights off. I could see two security guards sat in the booth as we drove past.

"You did good," Ty said.

I turned my head and saw the smile on his face. What I would do to see that smile. "I love your smile." I sighed, then grimaced when I realized what I had said and who I'd said it in front of.

Ty's hand wandered onto my leg and gave a gentle squeeze before pulling back.

He switched the lights on, the only sound all the way back to the compound was the clicking of the keys coming from Evan's laptop.

Evan had gone right back to his cabin as soon as we got back to the compound, where he then spent the rest of the weekend cooped up, going through all of the information that we had found.

I was so full of adrenaline that there was no way that I was going to get back to sleep anytime soon so I curled up on the couch and watched a film. I expected Ty to go to bed or to his upstairs office but instead he sat on the couch with me.

That's how I woke up the next morning, me laying down with my feet in Ty's lap and his head leaning against the back of the couch.

Chapter Twenty-Three

Monday morning came around and in walked Evan with a face full of stubble and bloodshot eyes. He sat down, his eyes still glued to his laptop and his fingers flying across the keyboard.

"Coffee." I placed my cup down in front of him and went back to pour another.

"Thanks," he said when I joined him at the meeting table.

"You're welcome."

I closed my eyes, breathing in deeply while we waited for the rest of the guys. It was a rare moment, one where I felt completely at peace. My life had been turned upside down, only now was it feeling like everything was settling down again.

I'd come to the realization that I couldn't change

anything that had happened but what I *could* do was not let it control my life. This was my life and I had to deal with what had been handed to me in my own way.

"Mornin'." I cracked one eye open and watched Kitty slump down in the chair opposite me. Her hair was tied on the top of her head in a messy bun and she wore her glasses. I hated to say it but she looked a hot mess.

"Morning." I lifted my cup, about to take a sip of coffee when she reached over and snatched it out of my hand.

"Hey!"

"Mmmm, I needed that."

"That was mine." I moaned and got back up.

What was it with people and my coffee? I needed that to feel remotely normal. I was just pouring another cup when Ty walked past the kitchen, he stepped back and tilted his head at the table signaling the start of the meeting.

I followed him out, sitting in my usual seat. Luke was now next to Kitty, grinning at me when I smiled.

He'd been a Godsend these last few weeks with Eli. The other guys were great with him but Luke was able to relate with Eli so much more. I loved the bond they had. Eli needed good male role models and now he had three.

"What have we found?" Ty asked Evan who was

still clicking away on his laptop, the tapping of the keys loud in the otherwise silent warehouse.

"One sec." He held up a finger.

The warehouse door opened a crack and they all jumped up, Ty's hand resting on his belt signaling that he was about to grab his gun. My eyes widened as I watched Luke rush to the other side of the door.

Charlie's face peeked through. "Hey." He grinned.

"What the fuck?" Ty let his hand drop

"I called him," Evan said and turned the laptop around.

"Could have said something," Luke grumbled as he went back to his chair.

"Can I?" Charlie asked pointing to the chair next to me.

My back straightened, I didn't think he'd do anything to me but that didn't stop the feeling of slight panic that spread through me.

He either didn't see my reaction or he didn't care because he sat down and grinned at me. On instinct, I moved closer to Ty, my hands clutched in my lap and my knee bobbing up and down.

Ty's hand gripped my knee, stopping the movement. I moved my eyes to him and he nodded, telling me that he was here.

He *knew*. He always knew. He could read me so well.

"First thing." Evan pointed to the screen. "He's not working alone."

"Who's he working with?" Kitty leaned forward.

"I don't know that yet." Kitty rolled her eyes at Evan and sat back.

"How do you know he's not working alone?" Ty asked.

"Because I found entries that name Daley."

"So?" Kitty sneered.

"If he was working alone he wouldn't have put his own name in," I interrupted.

Evan snapped his fingers and pointed to me. "Exactly."

So, this meant we were looking for more than one person. This job just got a whole lot harder.

"How does Daley fit in?"

"I don't know." Evan shook his head at Ty.

Charlie frowned. "All the information we had said that he was at the top."

"And where did you get that information?" Kitty sneered in a way that I hadn't heard before.

My eyes moved from Kitty to Charlie. They were staring at each other, having some kind of silent conversation.

"Put your claws away, Kitty Kat." He rolled his eyes and turned to face Ty. "Bro, we were told he was working alone."

Ty nodded, drumming his fingers on my knee. I bit my lip as I tried to concentrate but the sensation was distracting.

"I managed to get into the encrypted files but

nothing makes much sense," Evan huffed. "But I know that they took another girl Friday night."

"Fuck," Ty spluttered.

They took another girl? While we were out trying to get this information they were taking another girl away from her family?

I felt sick. Physically sick.

"We haven't had any missing person's reports." Charlie pulled out his phone.

"She was taken from the road leading up to the country club."

"How do you know that?" I asked.

Charlie tapped away on his phone and looked back up to Evan and then Ty.

"No reports."

"All the girls are named after the location they were taken from," Evan answered me.

I couldn't bear to think about what was happening to her right now, how her parents must be feeling. It made me want to lock Eli away and never let him out again.

"Do you know who she is?"

"No." Evan shook his head. "It's got everything but her real name."

Everyone was silent.

Ty leaned back, his fingers dragging up my leg with the motion. I shivered. "We need to scout out the country club."

"How you going to do that?" Charlie asked.

"Go on a date."

I didn't want to admit the jealousy that I was feeling at that moment. The small ember expanded until I felt like my entire insides were on fire.

"Kitty: you check the cameras, see if you can get an ID on the girl."

She nodded. "On it."

"Luke: you're on Daley. Charlie, Evan: my office."

I stayed silent, afraid that if I opened my mouth I'd say something that I might regret. They all scattered leaving just me and Ty at the table.

His hand squeezed my thigh once before he stood. "Need to see you after." Winking at me, he strolled into the office.

Well damn.

I spent the rest of the day helping Evan sort through all the information that he hadn't managed to get through. Kitty had gotten a hold of the recording of the girl being taken but we couldn't see who took her.

She wasn't taken how I imagined she would have been. I was thinking that someone would have knocked her out and thrown her into the back of a van. But she has been standing on the edge of the road that led up to the country club when a car pulled up beside her, she got in. It almost looked like she was waiting for them. The only odd thing was that the door opened and her leg came out before the car sped off with the door still open.

The day went so fast and we still hadn't got anywhere by the time I had to go and pick Eli up with Luke.

I still hadn't braved taking and picking Eli up on my own and I honestly didn't know when I would be ready for that. But it was a step in the right direction to be going outside those gates.

Me and Eli spent the evening sitting on the couch watching TV.

It was nice to have some time just me and him, it felt like I didn't get to do it that often now and I missed having that time alone—just the two of us.

His small snores sounded just before bedtime. I watched him sleep, relishing in the peaceful look on his face. I couldn't comprehend how anyone couldn't love him to pieces. Max flashed in my mind briefly at that thought—he was missing out on all of this.

It was his loss. Eli wouldn't be this small forever: he was already growing so fast. It felt like only yesterday that I held him as a baby.

The front door opened just as I was dropping off to sleep myself.

"Ty?"

"It's me," his deep voice responded.

"Oh, hey." I cleared my throat. "I'm just going to put Eli to bed then I'll clean the kitchen." I shuffled to the edge of the couch.

"I've got him." He lifted Eli with ease and went up the stairs.

I watched him all the way up. How had I managed to find someone like him? Max would never have done that. He would have complained about us being on the couch and then shouted abuse at me which in turn would have woken Eli and disturbed him for the whole night.

It was a stark reminder how much my life had changed.

This is what it was like to be normal: to live with someone who cared.

Pushing up off the couch, I walked to the kitchen and started to clean up the mess I'd left after dinner. My hands were in the bowl of water, washing the dishes, when Ty came in.

"You know we've got a dishwasher, right?" Ty chuckled.

"I know." I rolled my eyes at him and washed a spoon. "But I like to do it by hand."

I put the spoon on the drying rack just before Ty leaned against it. He crossed his arms over his chest and my gaze wandered there before they met his eyes.

I swallowed at the look he gave me.

"So, this date."

"Mmmm." I looked away. He was so intense sometimes.

"How does Friday sound?"

"Yeah, sounds good." I nodded and willed my

voice to stay normal. I scrubbed the plate and placed it next to the spoon.

"Good." He leaned forward and planted a kiss on my cheek. "Be ready at eight." My eyes widened: he'd just kissed my cheek. I was so used to the peck he'd give me on my head that him kissing my cheek startled me. It was such a normal couple thing to do, but we weren't a couple, right?

It was probably all in my head.

Wait—Ready at eight? What did I need to be ready for?

"What for?" I turned, water dripping from my hands, down my arms, and onto the floor. I'd have to clean that up as well.

"Our date." He grinned and pushed open the door.

"Huh?" I frowned.

"Sweetheart." He smiled, his eyes alight. "I just asked you out on a date. You didn't think I'd be taking anyone else, did you?"

"I... I... just assumed?"

"Be ready at eight." He winked and walked out. I stared at the door expecting him to come back and say that he was joking.

This was for work though, so did that mean this was a work date or a date date?

Turning back to the sink I was more confused than ever.

I hadn't got a clue what was happening but I knew I didn't want it to end.

Chapter Twenty-Four

I KNOCKED on Kitty's door and waited for her to answer. I'd wanted to ask her all day what all of this meant: what she thought Ty was thinking. But I didn't want to say anything in front of the others so I'd waited until Eli was in bed and told Ty that Kitty needed to talk to me.

He frowned at me and asked me why I was telling him. When I told him that I thought I should ask him if I could go he opened and closed his mouth like a fish, clearly not knowing what to say to me. Shaking his head, I could see the anger building up behind his eyes, and for a split second I wondered if that anger was aimed at me.

"Go," he had said and practically shoved me out the door. "You don't need permission to do anything."

So now here I was, standing at Kitty's door, waiting for her to answer while I had a mini meltdown.

"Oh... hey," she said once she opened the door.

"Hey, can we talk?" I whispered.

"Sure." She pulled the door open wide and waved me in.

I'd never been inside Kitty's house. It was a small cottage with plants climbing up the walls and a garden path that was lined with potted plants.

The inside was just as small as the outside. Four doors led off the tiny hallway and I followed Kitty through the second that lead into the kitchen.

"Want something to drink?" she asked, opening the fridge and pulling out a couple of beers.

"No, thanks." I shook my head and looked around the kitchen. It was tiny but it suited Kitty. The window over the sink looked out into the woods, much like in Ty's.

"So, what's up?"

"Uhh..." I swallowed and gripped my hands.

Now that I'd come here I couldn't get what I wanted to ask her out of my mouth. I tried to clear my throat several times but each time I did and opened my mouth, nothing would come out.

"You need to calm down, chica." She nodded down at my hands noticing how I was wringing them. I took a deep breath and released them. "Come on." She pushed through the door and I followed her into the living room, trying my hardest to get a hold of myself.

This room was almost as small as the kitchen; I couldn't imagine all of the guys being able to get in here at the same time. The image of all of them squeezed in this tiny room relieved some of the tension I was feeling.

The walls were covered with black and white striped wallpaper, all of the furniture mismatched but had that retro kind of look.

Quirky. Just like Kitty.

"Tell me what's going on." She sat cross legged in her wing backed leather chair.

"Well..." I sat down on the couch opposite her. "Ty asked me out on a date."

"Really?" She grinned.

"But it's only to check out the country club so it's not really a date. I mean it's like a fake date right?"

"Kay—"

"I mean, he wouldn't be interested in me." I rolled my eyes. "We might have kissed but it was—"

"Wait, wait, wait." She held her hand up. "You kissed?" Her eyes were as wide as saucers.

"Erm... yes?"

"Start from the beginning." She leaned back and waited for me to talk. "And don't miss a thing out." She pointed with a mock glare.

How much did I tell her? What if Ty didn't want everybody to know?

I looked around and stared at Kitty; I trusted her— it was a gut feeling and I'd learned to listen to my gut so I told her everything. I told her about the kisses, him getting into bed with me after I had nightmares. I even told her about Corey.

"So, Corey is your brother?"

"Yes." I nodded.

"Wow." She stared at me.

I waited. All I could think about was if this was a real date or not. If it was: I didn't know if I was ready. What if it went wrong? What if I did something wrong? Then I'd have nobody. He'd become such a big part of our lives that I didn't know what I'd do without him.

"So, he said: 'I just asked you out on a date', those were his exact words?"

"Yes," I mumbled. She leaned back in her chair, a smile growing on her face.

"Chica, that means he asked you out on a date."

"Really?"

"Uh-huh." She leaned forward. "Wow, this is big."

"It is?"

"Oh yeah, he hasn't dated since—" She shook her head and stood. "You need something to wear."

"I do?" She grabbed my hand and lifted me off the couch.

"Yeah, you do. It's the country club. When did you say you're going?"

"Friday," I answered as she led me into her bedroom.

"We've got two days to get you ready."

"I need two days?" I frowned.

She opened her wardrobe and started to look through all of her clothes. "Yeah." She pulled out a dress and laid it on her bed. "You need to shave, sort those caterpillars for brows out and—"

"My brows?" I asked and covered them with my hand.

"Yeah, those things need to be sorted ASAP." She pulled out a couple of pairs of pumps and put them down next to the dress. "Don't worry. I'll help." She went back to the wardrobe and picked out several more dresses and tops and even a few skirts. By the time she was finished, she had almost her entire wardrobe out.

"You sure this is enough?" I raised my "caterpillars" and grinned.

"Hmmm, you're right." She pulled open a few drawers and started to empty those as well. I rolled my eyes; I'd never been good at sarcasm but I'm sure that was pretty obvious.

Sitting down, I realized this was going to be a long night. All I can do is wait until she was finished, wandering whether I should have asked for her help.

"Okay, let's try these on."

"What? Now?"

"Yeah." She pulled me up off the bed and handed me the first dress.

Yep: this was going to be a long night.

The light glints off the knife as he holds it by his waist. "You deserve this," he sneers. My body won't move: it's stuck to the floor. I try to shout, but nothing comes out, panic washing through me.

He throws his head back and laughs, his eyes darkening as he gets closer.

"You'll never escape me, baby." He leans over me. "I'll always be there... watching... waiting."

I watch as his arm lifts up and comes back down in slow motion. I try one last time to call for help. Opening my mouth—

"KAY? KAY!"

"No, please don't!"

"It's me: Ty." My eyes sprang open, Ty stood over me, a frown marred on his face.

"I... I..." I tried to catch my breath, my throat burning with each inhale.

"You're okay, sweetheart." He caressed my face as he sat down on the bed.

"No." I shook my head. "It's not okay: he's right."

"Who's right?"

I looked around, sure that he would be in the room with us. "Max," I croaked. "He'll always be there: I'll never escape him."

I held back a sob, knowing that if I let it come out I wasn't sure if I'd be able to stop. It was always the knife, he never used his fists in my nightmares, only ever *that* knife.

"I won't let him touch you Kay," Ty said in a soft voice.

"You don't understand." I shook my head and turned to face him. "He'll always be here." I tapped my head and met his gaze. "Right here. I'll never forget what he did to me."

I tried to keep calm, but the more I concentrated the less I could breath. My fingers started to tingle, my head spinning.

"Breathe, Kay."

I shook my head, trying to tell him that I couldn't. I was having a heart attack. I slapped my chest trying to tell him without words.

"It's a panic attack." Ty cupped my face in his hands and breathed with me. "We're gonna count, okay?" I nodded and listened to him count, not moving my eyes from his.

"One, Two, Three, Four—" By the time he got to twenty I felt like I could breathe again.

I was so tired and mentally drained because I couldn't get the rest that I needed. Sleep wasn't helping, in fact, it made it worse.

I lay back in the bed and turned on my side to face Ty.

"You want to talk about it?" he asked cupping the side of my face.

This is where I would always say no, but tonight something felt different. I wanted to tell him about Max, about all the things that happened. None of them knew what happened that day, and for the first time, I felt like I wanted to tell someone—for them to know more.

"Yes," I whispered.

His eyes widened. "Really?"

"I don't want to talk about everything yet." I cleared my throat. "But maybe I can tell you what happened in my nightmare?"

"Whatever you want to do, sweetheart." He lay down on his side, mimicking the way I was lying, only a couple of inches between us.

I took a deep breath. My eyes stayed glued to his, they grounded me, kept me in the here and now. If I looked away, I was afraid I'd get lost in the memories.

"He's always standing over me with the knife." Ty bought his hand to mine and held it. "I can never move, every time I try and scream nothing comes out. It feels so real." I shivered. "I can hear his voice so clear, even when I'm awake. It's like he's standing behind me and whispering into my ear."

"What does he say?" Ty asked in a throaty voice.

"'You'll never escape me, baby.'" I closed my eyes and took a deep breath. "'I'll always be here, watching, waiting.'"

The first tear slid down my face, another one following close behind in a silent stream. I felt Ty's thumb wipe it away.

"I'll never let him hurt you again, Kaylee. I promise."

"But—" I opened my eyes and took in the fierce look reflected back at me.

"No," he gritted out. "From the moment you walked into my office you were mine."

"Ty—"

"I don't mean that in a sinister sort of way, I mean that there was that instant connection. I know you felt it, too."

I couldn't say anything: it was all so fast. How could I move on with Ty if Max was still in my brain and haunting me at every opportunity, making sure that I never forgot what he could do to me?

"He just won't go away." I sobbed.

"Come're." Ty opened his arms. I didn't hesitate, I burrowed into him and lay my head on his chest.

"It'll be alright: I'll make sure it is."

Chapter Twenty-Five

I woke up in the same position that I went to sleep: my head on Ty's chest with his arms wrapped around me. I felt safe and wanted. Two feelings that only a couple of months ago I hadn't felt before. Max had never held me like this and I found that I liked it—I liked it a lot.

I had this amazing man ready and willing to stand up for me and it felt great to know that I could tell him things that I'd never told anyone else. I didn't want this feeling to end and when I moved out of his arms I didn't expect to miss them so much.

I had butterflies in my stomach knowing that tonight was our "date." Whether it was real or not didn't seem to matter as much now, I was just happy that we got to spend time together without it involving work or Max.

Okay, so it was kind of related to work, but it wasn't like we were in the car following someone or sitting in the office.

I couldn't face Ty knowing what I had told him last night and the way he had held me throughout the night. I wimped out and took Eli to school with Luke and went back to the warehouse where I stayed in the office all day avoiding him. If he knew what I was doing, he didn't say anything.

By the time Kitty came in the office I was a nervous wreck and I'd almost certainly decided that I wasn't going out tonight.

"Hey, chica."

"I can't do this Kitty," I whispered.

"Can't do what?" She sat on the edge of the desk.

"Tonight," I said through clenched teeth as I watched the door in case he came through it.

She huffed and slid off the desk. "Come on." She grabbed my hand and pulled me up.

"What? Where are we going?

She didn't answer me as she dragged me out of the warehouse and towards her house.

The next four hours were full of primping and priming; Kitty did my makeup and curled my hair into soft waves. All I had to do was sit there while she told me how great this was going to be, all the while my mind wandered in all kinds of directions.

Finally, after literally hours, she handed me a nude colored dress, dark-purple pumps, and told me to get changed. I opened my mouth to tell her that I couldn't wear something like this but she shook her head and shoved me into the bathroom.

I hardly recognized the person staring back at me in the mirror, she had perfect shiny hair and flawless skin. How Kitty had managed to make me look like this I had no idea.

The dress clung to my waist, a sweetheart neckline covered with lace up to my neck made me feel not so exposed. I moved from side to side in the mirror and was about to open the door and tell Kitty that there was no way I was wearing this dress when the door knocked.

I froze.

"Ty's here!" Kitty shouted through the bathroom door.

Butterflies swarmed my stomach, my hands started to shake and I was sure that I'd throw up any second now.

I could hear them talking but couldn't make out what they were saying. Should I try to listen to what they were saying or just go out there?

I slipped my feet into the pumps and reached out for the door handle with shaking hands. Taking a deep breath, I pulled the door open.

My breath stilled: Ty was in a pair of slacks and a dress shirt and tie. He looked so different without his beanie hat, his hair slicked back and his stubble trimmed.

"Hey." I cleared my throat to remove the husky sound that came out as I stood frozen to the spot.

"Wow," he said with wide eyes.

"Erm..." I looked at Kitty silently asking her what to do. She waved me forward so I took a wobbly step, totally not used to the height of the shoes.

Ty's gaze roamed my whole body; I could almost feel his touch. I watched as he blew out an audible breath, his eyes clashing with mine, I knew then without a doubt that I had affected him.

"Boss," Kitty whispered out the side of her mouth.

"You look... beautiful," he said, his voice deep.

"Thank you." Kitty pointed to Ty, I frowned and tried to work out what was she was mouthing.

"You ready?" Ty asked.

"Yeah." I took another wobbly step, got my balance and met him at the door.

I hated wearing anything but my chucks or boots, why I had to wear these things I didn't know.

I followed Ty outside and to the waiting car out front; I'd seen this car by the warehouse but nobody ever used it.

"Nice car." I smiled. I hadn't got a clue what kind of car it was but I knew that it was the sporty kind.

"Thanks, I figured we'd use this one tonight." He grinned and opened the door. For a second I was confused, he was driving, right? Then I realized that he had opened the door *for* me.

The inside smelled like a mixture of leather and Ty: I couldn't get enough of that smell. Ty started the car, the gravel kicking up as he spun around and pressed the button to open the gates.

"Was Eli okay?" I asked when we were on the main road.

"Yeah, he's getting pizza with Luke and Evan."

"Awesome."

When he turned the radio on I relaxed a little. My eyes kept moving to him of their own accord, fascinated with the way his shirt was rolled up to his elbows and his tattoos danced each time he moved his hands on the wheel. I remembered the way they felt on my body when he held me last night and how his thumb stroked my stomach.

Closing my eyes, I shivered at the memory.

"You cold?"

"No, I was just..." I stammered.

"Just what?" He lifted his brow, his eyes dipping down to my chest.

They flicked back to my eyes then back to the road.

The air shifted; if we didn't get out of this car soon I wasn't sure I would be able to stop my hands from reaching over to touch him.

My stomach rolled when we pulled up at the country club. I'd never been anywhere like this. What if they knew that I didn't belong here? Could they tell just by looking at you?

"Kay?" I turned in my seat to where Ty held open my door. "Come on, sweetheart." He extended his hand to me so I lifted my shaky hand and let him pull me out of the car.

"You good?" he asked. I couldn't formulate an answer so I nodded instead as I tried to function in these stupid pumps.

We climbed up the steps and through large wooden doors. I'd never seen anything like it: marble floors so shiny I could see my reflection in them when I looked down, and open fire places with leather chairs and couches placed around them filled the room, along with men in suits and women half their age dressed in gowns.

Ty led us to the shiny white desk off to the right, behind it stood a man dressed in a suit, only this one had the country club logo on the front breast pocket.

"Mr. Mackenzie." He nodded and tapped away at his keyboard.

"Troy." He nodded back.

"Table for two?"

"Yeah."

"You know where it is?" Troy stepped back as if to lead us wherever it was we were going.

"I got it." Ty waved him away and led me to the stairs.

"They know you here?" I whispered.

"Yeah," Ty whispered back and led me to the stairs.

"But I thought..."

"You thought what?" He turned and grinned.

My breath stuttered; one grin and my head was spinning. How could he affect me so much? I held on tighter to his hand, afraid that if I let go I would fall.

The restaurant was just as grand as the rest of the place. Chandeliers hung from the ceiling and the light danced and glinted off each of the crystals. A wall of windows looked out onto the golf course and it looked beautiful with lights dotted along the green and the main road.

"Your table is ready, Mr. Mackenzie," the man said from behind his podium.

We followed him to a table at the back of the room.

"Do you see that?" I asked when we were sitting down and leaned closer to Ty.

"What?"

"All of those lights?" He turned and looked out of the window.

"Yeah?"

"Those weren't on the video footage," I whispered. "They were turned off."

His eyes moved back and forth. From up here you could see nearly the whole course and the main road that led into the country club.

"What can I get you to drink, sir?"

"I'll have a whiskey."

My heart stuttered, the thought of Ty drinking that made me feel sick.

"Madam?"

"Water, please," I croaked.

"Be right with you," he answered and walked away.

I looked down, opening and refolding my napkin several times.

"Kay?"

"Hmmm?"

"You okay?"

"Yeah." I shifted my gaze to his. "It's just... *whiskey.*"

"What about it?" He reached out and took my hand, his thumb doing that stroking thing again.

"That's what Max always smelled like when..."

"Ah fuck," he spat. Several people looked our way, brows raised and sneers on their faces, but Ty didn't pay them any attention.

"It doesn't matter." I shook my head, watching as the waiter brought us our drinks. I didn't want to stop him drinking.

"I'll have water instead." Ty waved his whiskey off and turned back to face me.

"But, sir, I'll still have to charge—"

"That's fine." I took a sip of my water, relieved that my throat wasn't as dry. I tried to tell him that it was fine but he wasn't having any of it and waved the waiter away again.

"Is there a menu?" I asked to change the subject.

Ty chuckled, the sound so deep and hearty. "Sweetheart." He leaned back, smirking at me. "It's a set menu."

"Oh."

Four courses. Lots of food later and I could barely move I was that stuffed.

"I can't eat anymore," I moaned when they put desserts in front of us.

Ty's chuckle sent a warmth through me, I smiled wide and rested my chin on my hand.

"I love your laugh."

"You do?" he leaned forward.

"Yeah."

"I love your smile," he said in a throaty voice.

It was on the tip of my tongue to tell him that I just loved all of him. Everything about him. Then someone walked into the restaurant, gaining the attention of several people. I'd recognize that face anywhere.

After all, I looked at it every day on the board.

"Daley just walked in," I whispered.

"So, what happened?" Evan asked the next day.

After Daley had walked in we had watched him, taken note of who he spoke to and who he didn't.

Eventually, Ty joined him at the bar and an hour

later we were all sitting around a table talking. If I didn't know what this man was doing, I would have probably liked him.

Apart from the obvious fact that he has lots of money and didn't mind showing it off, he was quite funny.

We'd left without any solid leads but we'd made head way with Daley.

"He's throwing a charity function next Saturday," Ty grinned.

"Wait... who is?" Kitty leaned forward.

"Daley." Ty entwined his hands on the table. "He walked in and we got to know him a little better." He grinned at me knowingly.

I smiled back, caught up in how much fun we had last night.

"Yeah?" Luke raised his brow.

"What's the charity?" Evan asked and opened his laptop.

"Fund The Children." Ty snorted.

Eli looked up at me. "Can I have a drink, Mama?" He'd been playing with his cars quietly since we came in here.

"Sure, sweetie." I pushed back my chair and went into the kitchen.

I couldn't stop thinking about last night. After we got back to the compound, I felt shy and awkward, this was the point where on a normal date we'd go our separate ways. But we were going into the same house instead.

I expected him to leave me at the bedroom but he didn't. He lay on top of the bed fully clothed and we talked. We talked for hours, getting to know each other more.

He told me about his family, how they were quite well off which is why they knew who he was in the country club. He spoke about his brothers and how they were all in jobs that helped people, the forces, fire service and police force. The only exception being his youngest brother who was currently at college.

When I went back to the table, they were discussing where to go from here.

"I think I can get close to him," Ty said.

Evan typed away on his laptop. "You've got the perfect in."

"This is what I'm thinking: Kay and I go to the charity function and see if we can find anything else out. If this is his front then we're guaranteed to run into someone there."

Eli climbed up onto my lap and laid his head on my shoulder. I didn't want to ask what they had been doing all night because from the looks of it they had all been up.

"It's gonna need all of us." Ty turned to face me. "Maybe you could ask Miss Maggie to watch Eli?"

"Sure."

"We'll pick her up during the day." I nodded and wrapped my arms tighter around Eli.

"You're going to need a penguin suit for the function." Kitty laughed.

Ty pushed back on his chair. "Shut it."

"Where you going?" Eli sprung his head up.

"Going to play ball at my parents." Ty came around to Eli. "You want to come?"

"Can I, Mama?"

"If Ty says you can, then yes." I raised my brow at Ty in silent question.

"You want to come too?" he asked me, and my breath stuttered. I wasn't ready to meet his parents.

"No!" Kitty shouted. "She's got to give me all the gossip."

Ugh. I didn't know what was worse: going with Ty or staying with Kitty.

Chapter
Twenty-Six

THE NIGHT before the charity function, Ty invited everyone over for a pizza and movie night. We'd spent the whole week preparing for tomorrow night. Ty had gone over what we needed to say several times. I'd been given the task to try and get more information from Daley while Ty was networking. We'd gone over all of the possible outcomes and came up with a solution for all of them.

Evan had made some special listening devices that could record any information that we gathered and so we could listen to it back afterward. Mine was embedded into a necklace while Ty's was in his bow tie.

Miss Maggie was so pleased to be able to watch Eli

and literally shouted yes at me down the line before I had got the whole question out of my mouth.

Everything was in place and we were determined that nothing could or would go wrong.

"Come and sit down, Kay!" Evan shouted through to the kitchen.

"Coming!" I put the leftover pizza in the fridge and walked into the living room.

Eli had chosen the movie, so yep, you guessed it, an action movie complete with Superhero and villain combo was his choice. I sat down in between Ty and Luke and tried to get comfy between the two hulks.

My eyes were closing before I knew it: movies always did that to me, it was like a light switched as soon as one came on.

I woke up to a dark room, my head on Ty's chest and my leg thrown over his.

"Eli's in bed," he mumbled, my head bobbing as he talked.

Lifting my head, I looked up at him, noticing that he'd been asleep as well.

"Hey," I whispered, aware of where my leg was.

"Hey." He smiled.

My breath caught. His eyes moved from my lips back to my eyes. There were a couple of seconds where neither of us moved then Ty was closing the gap between us. I didn't hesitate to meet him halfway. A moan escaped as his lips softly caressed mine.

His tongue swiped along my lips, opening up to him, a shiver ran all the way to my toes.

I felt his hands grip my leg, pulling me on top of him. I went willingly, feeling his hardness pressed against me, I moved my hips and was answered with a satisfying groan.

Gripping my ass with both hands he pulled me forward and thrust his hips up to mine.

"I want you so bad," he murmured and peppered kisses down my neck.

I tilted my head to give him better access while grinding my hips against his. I could feel my chest rising and falling rapidly with every breath that I took.

"Sweetheart." He pulled back. "If you don't stop, I won't be able to."

Did I want to stop? No. No, I didn't. I was sure of this. Sure of him.

"I don't want to stop," I whispered against his lips.

He pulled back, his eyes flitting between mine. "Kay—"

"Shhh..." I placed my finger over his lips. Running my hand across his cheek and down his arm, I followed the lines of his tattoo, goose bumps rising wherever I touched. I dipped my hand under the arm of his t-shirt and spread my fingers over his bicep.

"I don't want to think about what ifs." I shook my head and met his eyes again. "I just need you," I whispered.

"If we do this." His Adam's apple bobbed as he swallowed. "There'd be no going back."

I didn't want to go back. My life had changed so much: I wasn't scared at the thought of someone coming home. I didn't have to worry if I did something wrong.

The most important thing was that I didn't have to lie. Keeping secrets was so tiring.

I felt free with Ty, he made me feel like a woman. His eyes would follow me in a room and he could read me better than anyone else ever could. *He knew me.* I didn't have to second guess myself, because with Ty what you see is what you get.

"I don't want to go back." I shook my head.

He blinked, wrapped his arms around my waist and stood up. I held on to his shoulders as he walked us up the stairs, our eyes locked the entire time.

My heart beat out of my chest, my stomach dipping as he pushed through his bedroom door.

"Are you sure?" he asked one more time.

"Yes," I breathed.

He shut the door, walked us to the bed and sat on the edge. A large bay window took up the space to the left that looked out onto the woods. I was fascinated at the view he had from up here. The chair was placed next to it told me that he sat there often. I could picture sitting there with a blanket covering me as I curled up next to Ty.

He cupped the side of my face and brought me

closer to him. His soft lips pressed against mine, the scruff on his face scratching against my skin.

My hands wandered up his t-shirt, his muscles rigid. Moaning, I pulled back then he flipped us over, yanked his t-shirt over his head as I wrapped my legs around his waist.

"You're so beautiful," he whispered into my ear, his breath sending goose bumps flying across my skin.

We were going fast, caught up in the moment, but I was glad because if I gave myself time to think then I would chicken out.

He thrust, only our clothes separating us: I wanted them off now.

I reached down, frenzied, and undid his button; if I didn't feel him now then I'd go insane. I pushed down his jeans as far as they would go, eager to get them off him.

"Slow down." He pulled back and chuckled.

"Sorry." I looked away.

"Hey." He gripped my chin softly and turned me back to look at him. "We've gone over this: you don't need to apologize to me."

I nodded. "Okay."

"We're gonna take this slow, sweetheart." He stood, kicking off his boots and pulled his jeans down. "I'm gonna make you feel things you never knew you could feel."

I shivered.

He moved back onto the bed, his hand going

straight for my jeans. The only sound in the room was my zipper being pulled down and my heart beating erratically.

"Look at that." He grinned. "Pink panties."

I covered my face, I couldn't believe I'd worn my bright pink ones. If I'd known this was going to happen I would have tried to wear something sexier.

I jumped when I felt his lips touch my thigh, soft and wet. He pulled my jeans down and threw them across the room.

"I hope you're prepared, sweetheart." He gripped the sides of my panties and pulled. I squeezed my eyes shut at his sharp intake of breath. "Perfect," he whispered. "Just... perfect."

Chapter Twenty-Seven

WHEN I WOKE up the next morning the bed was empty. I was confused for a second as to where I was then it all came hurling back to me.

Me, Ty, his hands, his tongue. *God, his tongue.* I felt the heat rising in my cheeks just thinking about it.

The door to what I assumed was the bathroom was cracked open, steam billowing out. I was glad that he was in the shower because I needed a couple of minutes to gather my thoughts.

I hadn't got a clue where I stood with Ty now. I desperately wanted to ask him, but what if that was the wrong thing to do?

I had no idea and I felt utterly lost and confused.

Sitting up, I scanned the floor for my clothes. My t-shirt was over on one side and my jeans right next to the bathroom door. Rolling off the bed, I tiptoed over to my t-shirt and pulled it over my head. I'd just got to the bathroom door and was about to pull my jeans on when the door opened.

I squealed and tried to shove my leg in the jeans.

"Sorry, I'll get—"

"Sweetheart," Ty pulled me to him, his hands burning through the thin material of my top. My t-shirt soaking up all the wetness off his chest. "What have I told you about apologizing?" He shook his head.

I looked up at him, trying to contain the blush spreading across my cheeks. "Not to—"

"Exactly." He pressed his lips against mine, quick and soft, before he pulled away. He sauntered over to his closet giving me a full view of the tattoo on his back, it was huge and covered his whole back.

"Erm... so..." I worried my lip with my teeth and shoved my other leg into my jeans.

"What's that?" Ty gritted out.

This was it, this was when he'd tell me that it was all a huge mistake and he didn't want me. I felt him come closer and met his gaze but he wasn't looking at me: he was looking at my leg.

Specifically, the scar that Max had left me with. Luke had taken the stitches out weeks ago, but I was left with an angry looking scar.

It wasn't the first one he'd given me, if you looked closely you could see them all over my body, but I didn't want to tell Ty that.

"It looks worse than it is." I swallowed and pulled my jeans over it.

"I didn't realize..." He brought his gaze up to mine, anger flared in their depths. "I forgot." He shook his head and frowned.

"It doesn't matter." I pulled my zipper up and stepped toward him, raising my hand. I wanted to touch him but was so unsure that my hand just stayed suspended in the air between us.

I dropped it. "I need to—" I walked toward to the door.

"Sweetheart?"

"Hmm?" I turned back to face him, my hand on the door handle.

"We good?"

"Yep," I said, way too bright to even remotely come across as normal. "I'm going to..."

I met his eyes as I pulled the door open: I could get so lost in them. Movement had my eyes dipping low; his hand gripped the towel and pulled it open. I squeaked, rushing through the door and slammed it shut behind me.

After what we had done last night, I didn't know why I couldn't look at him. I seriously needed to get it together before tonight.

I spent a couple of hours with Eli and Miss

Maggie, watching cartoons and sitting on the front porch. She even brought Henry with her, who was currently off having a good look around the house.

Eli was beyond pleased when he saw Henry. He hadn't seen that cat for so long.

Kitty dragged me off to get ready a whole three hours before we were meant to leave. I managed to hold her off for half an hour but she was so persistent that in the end I gave up, said my good nights, and followed her to her cottage.

She'd been shopping for a gown that was "appropriate" as she put it. It had lots more material than the last one but that didn't make it any less revealing. The dip that displayed part of my cleavage made me want to sew the gap up. The soft green material swooped in an A-line all the way to the floor. It did make me feel like a princess but I refused to wear pumps so the new chucks that she'd bejeweled made it perfect.

We all met up in the warehouse half an hour before leaving to go over the plan again. Ty and I were going to the event, Evan would be in the warehouse listening and watching, and Luke and Kitty would be on the main road as back up.

I didn't feel as apprehensive going into the country club this time even though it was packed with people as soon as we got there. I hadn't expected there to be so many people but that worked in our favor as we could fly under the radar.

Ty placed his hand on the small of my back,

shivers ran up my spine as his hand made contact with the bit of skin on show at the back of the dress. By the grin that spread on his face, he knew what it was doing to me.

"You look stunning," he whispered, his lips grazing my ear.

"Ty," I admonished and shook my head, but I couldn't get the smile off my face.

We stopped next to the bar, Ty's front against my back, fully aware of every inch of his body that touched mine and every inch that didn't.

"I want you so bad." He peppered kisses down my neck, a moan escaped from my throat just as the barman handed us two glasses of champagne. He gave us a knowing look and walked away.

I spun around in his arms, bringing my eyes to him. I chewed on my bottom lip. "Ty?"

"Hmm?" He stepped closer.

"What is this between us?"

"I told you before, sweetheart. You were mine from the moment you stepped into my warehouse."

"So, does that mean—"

"Yeah." He dipped his head to mine "You and me. Together."

He slammed his lips down on mine, showing me how much he meant it. I got lost in the kiss. This wasn't the sweet, gentle, loving kisses that we had last night. This was raw and passionate, showing me just how much he meant it.

A throat clearing had us pulling apart.

"Hey." Daley winked and raised his brows up and down.

"Hey." Ty nodded back and picked up his drink, taking a small sip. "How's it going?" Ty tilted his head to the crowd of people.

"Yeah, good." Daley leaned against the bar. "Got loads of donations, not that these rich fuckers can't afford it." He laughed.

We laughed awkwardly with him, Ty nodded his head subtly to me, signaling that this was the time to start my mission.

"So..." I cleared my throat. "What is it the charity does?"

Daley stood straight and pulled the sleeves of his suit jacket down.

"We help children who have been abused, whether that be mentally or physically," he said as if reading it off an advertisement.

"Uh-huh." I picked up the glass, not intending to drink it but to give my hands something to do.

"We have centers in several states but we want to expand and reach more people." He shrugged. I would have thought for someone who ran a charity like this that he'd be more interested in it but he acted like he was talking about the weather.

"Wow, that's a really worthy cause." I nodded.

We'd come up with this plan. I was to find out what I could about the charity and Ty would jump in if it got too much. I saw it as my first real test and was happy that they had trusted me to find out something so integral to the case.

I didn't want to ruin any chances we had of getting those girls back.

"Did you set the charity up?" I asked and placed the glass back down, the smell was making me want to heave.

"Me and another benefactor." He laughed. "It's actually a funny story."

Ty lifted a brow, not amused while I smiled to show him that I was interested in what he had to say.

"This chick came up to me one day and out of the blue told me that she'd been watching me and wanted me to join her on a business venture."

"Yeah?" Ty wrapped his arm around my waist. I narrowed my eyes at Daley, trying my hardest to pay attention to what he was saying.

"Yeah, and she was fucking hot." His eyes widened at me. "Oh shit, sorry."

"No that's fine." I waved him off and smiled.

He shrugged. "Yeah, so I ask her what her proposal is and she says that she wants to set up a charity."

"Really?"

"Yeah, that was what? Six months ago?" He frowned at something in the distance. "She said she's coming tonight. Something about a surprise." He shrugged and downed his champagne.

"It would be lovely to meet her," I said.

Maybe this was the key that we were looking for. If this charity was set up by two people, then maybe she was the other person that we'd been searching for.

I coughed twice so that Evan would know I was signaling him. "I got it," Evan said in my ear. I was so excited that we may have a breakthrough.

"Looks like you'll get to meet her sooner rather than later." Daley smiled.

"That's great."

"Well, hey there," a sultry voice said from behind us.

I turned.

She was perfection, her light-blue eyes shone when the lights hit them and her blond hair hung in waves over one shoulder. She was wearing a beautiful black velvet dress with a slit all the way to the top of her leg, not leaving anything to the imagination.

"Hi." I held my hand out "I'm Kaylee and this is—"

"Tyson." She smirked.

I frowned and looked at Ty, his face pale and jaw clenched.

"I'm sorry." I laughed nervously, my hand still suspended in the air between us. "Do you know each other?"

Ty's hand slackened on my waist.

"Oh dear, did you not tell her?" She cackled.

"Tell me what?" I frowned.

She smirked, leaned closer, and sang, "I'm his wife."

ABOUT THE AUTHOR

Abigail Davies grew up with a passion for words, story-telling, maths, and anything pink. Dreaming up characters—quite literally—and talking to them out loud is a daily occurrence for her. She finds it fascinating how a whole world can be built with words alone, and how everyone reads and interprets a story differently. Now following her dreams of writing, Abigail has found the passion that she always knew was there. When she's not writing: she's a mother to two daughters who she encourages to use their imagination as she believes that it's a magical thing, or getting lost in a good book. If she's doing neither of those things, you can be sure she's surfing the web buying new makeup, clothes, or binge watching another show as she becomes one with her sofa.

Connect with Abigail

Reader group—Abi's Aces
Newsletter

Instagram
Goodreads
Amazon Author Page

www.abigaildaviesauthor.com
authorabigaildavies@gmail.com

ALSO BY ABIGAIL DAVIES

MAC Security Series

Fractured Lies (MAC Security Book 1)

Exposed (MAC Security Book 2)

The Distance Between Us (MAC Security Book 3)

ReBoot (MAC Security Book 4)

Flying Free (Standalone MAC Security Spin-off)

Broken Tracks Series, co-authored with Danielle Dickson

Etching Our Way

Destroyed Series, co-authored with L. Grubb

Destroying the Game

Destroying the Soul

Printed in Poland
by Amazon Fulfillment
Poland Sp. z o.o., Wrocław